IMPLICATIONS ®RETS

A. K. RAMIREZ

IMPLICATIONS & REGRETS

MARISSA AMBROSE WITNESS SERIES BOOK 3

4 Horsemen
Publications, Inc.

Table of Contents

Dedication

So much thanks is owed to the dogs for whom I sat while I worked hard on this book, who kept me company and provided the perfect distractions when I needed a break.

So thank you Myles, Glacier, Chia, Gus (and Hank the cat), Bismark, Savannah, Bindi, Annie, Bam, Marshall, Rikko, Rosie, and Kira!

There will be pictures of all the wonderful pups on my blog for sure.

Prologue

"We need to talk," Agent Nick Walker said, his eyes flitting from Mac to Marissa. Mac moved aside so Agent Walker could step into the entryway, and he held up a photograph.

Marissa's jaw fell open at the sight of her and Mac embracing, locked in a kiss on her front porch. Then Agent Walker held up another one of them outside the Seattle precinct from a couple of months earlier, again in an embrace.

She pulled her eyes away from the photograph and took in each man standing in her entryway. Agent Walker stood tall with straightened shoulders, intentionally taking up plenty of space while he glared at Mac. Agent Clyde Bennet's expression was unreadable, but his body language oozed irritation. Sheriff Herbert Jackson didn't look happy to be there but worse were *the sympathetic looks he kept giving her. Mac had stared back, straightening his own shoulders.*

It was a standoff.

Once she found her words again, Marissa shook her head. "Can we please move into the house?" she hissed at them, ushering the men in. As they all walked toward the kitchen, Marissa turned to close her door, locked it, and glanced down at Ellie, who stood at her side staring up at her.

"Here we go," she muttered under her breath to the dog before joining the men in the kitchen.

"Please, both of you have a seat."

Marissa didn't appreciate that Agent Walker was telling her to have a seat in her own kitchen. She didn't move while everyone around her found somewhere to sit.

On the counter beside her lay the flower and letter she had opened before they arrived. Casually, she covered it with a plate as though just moving it out of the way. When she caught Jackson watching her, she reluctantly took a seat at the table.

"Now, I don't have to tell you that while there isn't a law against personal relationships, having a sexual relationship with a victim of a case is not only a conflict of interest but extremely unethical. There are rules in place to keep these things from happening. And at the very least, you are required to report these kinds of relations so we aren't surprised when photos end up on our desks from anonymous sources." Agent Walker had taken in a breath, looking between her and Mac

before continuing, "*You can't ignore photographic evidence.*" *He almost mumbled that last part to himself.*

Marissa had been certain he already knew about her relationship with Mac after her interview with Daniel Fryer. She had been, to the best of her ability, vague—but even still.

"*Your actions not only question your own integrity but the integrity of the position you hold and this office. This is your third strike, Agent Mackenzie, and as such, I hereby suspend you until further notice.*"

Mac opened his mouth to speak, but Agent Walker threw up his hand to stop him.

"*I have handed the matter over to Internal Affairs, and they will start with the O'Rourke case. The integrity of the entire case is now being questioned, seeing as Detective Ambrose was given the collar under your supervision.*"

"*Wait—*" *Mac started, already back on his feet.*

Marissa rose as well but wobbled in place, the onset of dizziness like a slap in the face. Thankfully, Ellie appeared right beside her and stood perfectly still as Marissa held her balance between the kitchen island and the large shepherd.

Mac and Agent Walker were both yelling now, but Marissa had heard none of their words. Instead, the phrases "third strike" and "suspend you until further notice" and "Internal Affairs" whirled through her mind.

She hadn't meant to, but she turned a helpless look to Jackson, who studied her for a moment, expressionless, then got to his feet with a huff.

"Alright, let's all just take a breath." He spoke over the shouting in the room in his best authoritative-dad voice, which caught everyone's attention. "Some poor choices were made here regarding your relationship, but I'm sure neither of you has anything to hide, so everything will be just fine. Let's all just relax."

Hearing Jackson tell everyone to relax was the definition of irony since he was always on the verge of stroking out from stress and agitation.

"I will expect you to cooperate with the investigation." Agent Walker turned back to Mac as though Marissa didn't exist. "I will need your gun and your badge."

He held out his hand expectantly while Max forcefully extracted his badge from his back pocket and his gun from its holster.

"You can't do this," Marissa insisted, taking a few steps to stand beside Mac, glaring at the man who was scolding them like children.

"Unfortunately," Walker sighed heavily, handing Mac's things off to Clyde Bennet, who stood silently behind him, eyes cast to the floor. Walker turned to fully face her and ran his hand through his slick hair, his eyes shifting just away from hers. "Because of this investigation, my superiors have taken another look at your case and decided it does not fall under our jurisdiction—"

"You still have the full support of the police department," Jackson jumped in, shooting Walker a look of disdain.

She felt her shoulders slump forward. "You have to be fucking kidding me," she hissed through her teeth. Thick strands of her dark hair had fallen in front of her eyes, and she huffed, shoving them back and out of her way.

"However, if there is any escalation, please contact me. But without it, my hands are tied." Walker spoke to her gently, ignoring her outburst.

She knew he was probably being sincere, but it just made her angrier. She could feel the heat in her cheeks and the lobes of her ears as she buried her fist into Ellie's fur.

"All that being said..." His voice shifted back to his normal pitch as he glanced back from her to Mac before looking at her again. "Daniel Fryer is still our case, and we would still be very grateful for your help on the matter."

He turned back to Mac. "We will be on a plane back to D.C. in ten hours."

"Seriously?" Marissa snapped, disbelief thick in her tone.

Agent Walker opened his mouth to speak, but Mac shook his head. "No."

He had the attention of the entire room.

"No?" Walker looked like someone had slapped him.

"No, sir." Mac didn't budge, looking straight ahead and standing at attention.

"Dude, don't do this." Clyde elbowed Mac, a look of disbelief crossing his face. "Get on the plane. Just stay out of trouble while there's an investigation. No one is worth your job."

Marissa couldn't even take offense as she did her best to process everything that was happening.

"Agent Mackenzie. Your job is on the line here," Nick growled at him.

Mac glared hard at his superior before his shoulders dropped and he seemed to relent.

Agent Walker, however, did not appear to sympathize. "Outside. Now."

All three FBI agents left the kitchen, and Marissa heard the front door open and close behind them. She stood there for a moment before she took a step, intent on following them, but Jackson's voice filled her ears.

"Marissa." His voice was a command. She turned to look at him, feeling like a child who had been caught stealing snacks. "Don't. You'll only make it worse."

Marissa found her words. "But I should be able to defend myself. You know this is bullshit. And they are just using it as an excuse to shut down the investigation."

Jackson let out a loud huff. "Sit down, Marissa."

She frowned but did as she was told. This had always been their relationship—since that time she was fourteen and been caught shoplifting with her cousin, and he'd given her a speech about right and wrong.

"*Why must you always complicate things?*" he asked, almost joking but definitely still serious. When she didn't answer, he rose and crossed the kitchen to stand before the plate she had put over the note. "*What are you hiding under there?*"

Marissa twitched her nose before releasing a defeated sigh and lifting the plate to show him the letter and the flower clipping. He leaned over and let out a soft whistle, shaking his head.

"*Now didn't feel like the time to bring it up,*" she said.

Jackson nodded in agreement. "*Maybe. How about I come by tomorrow and we can go over everything? I imagine you two will have a lot to talk about tonight.*" He nodded his chin toward her front porch where the rest of the men had disappeared.

The rest of the night was mostly a blur. Agents Walker and Bennett came back inside, and Walker reiterated she was to call in the event of any escalation and that they appreciated all her work on the Fryer case. Mac trailed behind them, looking like a dog with his tail between his legs.

When the two FBI agents left, Jackson remained quiet, but when he was ready to leave, he gave Marissa's shoulders a squeeze. "*We'll talk tomorrow.*"

And then it was just her and Mac.

Chapter 1

Three Weeks Later

Marissa lowered herself into the chair, the familiar feeling of unease settling in her gut. Daniel Fryer sat across from her with an unreadable expression. He was looking down at his wrist, or rather, at the handcuffs that held his wrists to the table. The usual cheerful banter and amusement when she entered was missing, and the silence in its place sent a cold chill through her.

A moment passed and then another. She couldn't bring herself to break the silence, her fear growing of what was to come once it'd been shattered.

Finally, Daniel Fryer looked up and locked his gray eyes with hers. "Do you ever wake up in the morning and just don't want to do this anymore?"

"Do what?"

"This. Any of this. Wake up. Go about your day." He shrugged his shoulders before leaning back in his chair. "In my case, my days aren't exciting. I'm taken care of. I get three meals a day, a warm bed to sleep in. But this will be my routine until the day I die. I get the privilege of talking with you every few weeks, but only because they want something. Either when they get it or tire of trying, I'll be thrown back to the wolves to live the same day every day until the end."

Marissa listened, not having to feign interest. This was a switch in his demeanor for sure. The man had always commanded the room, confident he had the upper hand and reveling in that. Today, he was depressed. His sandy hair was messy, longer than it had been during their first interview. He let his wild bangs hide his eyes, and what had been just stubble the last time she'd spoken with him had grown significantly, now the beginnings of a mountain man's beard. He was older than her, somewhere in his late forties, but today the way he sat hunched over the table, and with the chains that held his hands, he looked so much older. He looked frail. Weight loss played a part. His cheeks had sunken since the beginning of his incarceration. Even his hands look thin and boney.

"I wasn't meant to live in a cage, Marissa."

The use of her name sent an involuntary shudder through her, which brought an unsettling smile to his lips.

"I don't think taking lives on a whim was a good way to live either," she said finally, unsure where this conversation was going.

He watched her, searching her face with an intensity she did not appreciate. She suddenly wished she hadn't convinced the agents to let her have the room to herself today.

"Don't get me wrong: I don't expect to taste freedom again. But I don't want to do *this* either."

She stared at him, realizing how much of a natural opening he had given her. "Mr. Fryer..."

"Please, *detective*, I think we are past trying to be formal."

"Daniel." She hated the way his name felt coming off her tongue. "By your own admission, you've been killing for decades. What was so different about Ohio that they caught you?"

This had been one of the ground rules in the beginning—Ohio was off topic. Probably because he could easily be extradited back there to face punishment for that murder. She no longer cared.

A slow, strange smile appeared on his lips, and he glanced over at the one-way mirror before raising an eyebrow at her.

"I was wondering how long it would take you to get there. You're a smart girl. I would have thought it would have been sooner. But I suppose you've had a lot going on."

"You're dodging the question."

"I'm not. I'm simply making an observation first." He sat forward, resting his elbows on the table. He watched her for a long minute, glancing at the door every few moments before he licked his lips and spoke. "You know the rules: a question for a question. Answer for an answer."

Marissa sighed in frustration but nodded her head. He looked pleased with himself.

"After that experience in the warehouse, Ben and I split up. You had gotten way too close. So we agreed to go our separate ways. I chose the Midwest to lie low. Because let's be honest—who spends time in the Midwest? It had been almost two years since I heard from him when he showed up on my doorstep one night. We went out, had a few drinks. I am ashamed to say I let my guard down. The next morning, police were banging on my door, and there was a dead woman in my apartment."

Marissa felt like someone pulled the rug from under her feet. "He set you up?"

"Interesting question, isn't it?" he mused, bringing his fist to rest under his chin, the motion pulling at the chains attached to his cuffs. "I definitely did it. No question about that. The strangulation marks on her neck matched my prints, and the torture she endured beforehand was everything I enjoy about what I do."

Bile was threatening to climb up her throat as she listened, the feeling of discomfort growing. With a determined sigh, she pushed it back down, adjusting in her seat and absently petting Ellie.

"I've just never been so sloppy. And someone had called the police. They knew exactly where I was."

"If he turned on you, why haven't you just given him up?" It seemed like the natural progression that things should have taken.

Daniel Fryer's eyes locked on hers, a cold light of amusement that hadn't been there moments ago suddenly appearing. "An answer for an answer, Marissa."

"Fine. Ask," she said in frustration, pushing back in the chair. She shoved a loose strand of hair from her face.

"What are you most afraid of?"

"What?" The question took Marissa by surprise. This wasn't the typical game she had gotten used to playing with him. Blinking, she leaned forward in the chair again, her knee bouncing anxiously.

"You heard me. As of this moment, what are you most afraid of?" He paused. "And don't lie to me. You have a tell, and I can always tell when you're lying."

Marissa's eyes fell past him as she thought carefully about her answer. There were plenty of things she was afraid of. Some that he had caused.

"That this will never be over," she said finally, looking back at him.

"Not of what was done or what could still happen to you. But that it just won't end?" He looked amused again. "It's a funny thing, isn't it? Your life is essentially on hold, stuck, and unable to move forward while you wait for answers."

He shook his head.

"Those psychological scars are so much deeper than the physical ones." He paused before letting out a long, heavy sigh. "To answer your question, that is the very reason."

Marissa frowned in confusion, but he continued, "Two years had gone by. You weren't any closer to answers. We had all but gotten away with it. And yet, he set me up? A show of his power. Because he simply could or because there was an agenda behind it?"

"But why not give him up? Why not give us a sketch, a description? A full name? Something tangible."

"Because Marissa, even here—" He motioned around to the room, pulling on the chain that held the cuffs. The clanking sound caused her to jump. "He is still in control. He is still on the outside, playing games."

The way his eyes stared into hers made her want to run from the room. But she held her ground and his gaze, raising her chin to hide any sense of fear.

"One wrong move, I could end up dead. And no, I don't want to live my life in a cage, but if I'm going to die, it's going to be on my own terms. Not his." He emphasized every word with conviction, as though he were talking to Ben and not to her.

Silence stretched on as they stared at each other before he leaned back in the chair once more, relaxing his body.

"My turn."

Marissa braced herself and waited... and was once again surprised by what followed.

"How many murders do you need to me to confess to for them to give me the death penalty? Which states?"

Marissa blinked. "What?"

"You and I have the same fear, detective. I am afraid he's going to be pulling my strings forever. So I'm serious," he said with resolve. His expression told her he had thought this through. "If I give you every single name of every single victim, I want to be tried in a state that still offers the death penalty."

"I-I don't have the kind of power to give you an offer." She shook her head.

"Find someone who can."

"You wouldn't rather just give us Ben? We could make a deal—"

"I don't want a deal. I want the death penalty. I will not live my life in a cage." He shook his head and lowered his voice. "I cannot give you what you keep asking for. I can tell you things, and I can help, but I cannot give you outright answers. And I cannot tell you why." He swiveled his head to meet her eyes and held her there, as though trying to convey a message to her without words.

Before she could answer, a quick rap at the door sounded before Clyde Bennet pushed through. "We're calling it for the day."

"No. Please." Marissa turned to him desperately. She needed more information.

"Let's go, detective."

Marissa groaned, turning back to Daniel Fryer with frustration. The expression the killer wore on his face was once again unreadable. Even if she had gotten her way, she had lost him.

"I'll see what I can do," she said softly before getting to her feet.

Once she was on the other side of the door, she whirled around on Clyde Bennet angrily. "Why would you do that? I was getting somewhere! He's offering something to bargain. We could have gotten our answers!"

"Detective Ambrose." ADA Gorden approached from the other side of the room, shoving his hands in his pockets. "When you started these interviews, you were told Ohio was off the table as a topic. We are here to make him answer for crimes in the state of Washington. There are at least a dozen. Including his crimes against you."

"Were you guys listening to that in there? I feel like we have bigger things to focus on than jurisdiction."

"Maybe we could put him on a twenty-four-hour psych watch?" Clyde Bennet shrugged a shoulder, looking between Marissa and the assistant district attorney.

"That's probably a good idea." Gorden nodded his head before looking at Marissa again. "I understand your frustration—"

"Do you?" She cut him off before she could think better of it. "Do you *understand my frustration*? Because this office didn't take me seriously when I told them we were looking for partners. Because I'm still receiving pictures and letters that no one has been able to catch in person, on camera, or by surveillance. The only reason I'm here is because he won't talk to any of you. You *need* me. A hell of a lot more than I need you," she hissed with very little care for the consequences. "So either let me do my job and get you what you need my way or get someone else. But good luck finding someone else he's willing to talk to."

She didn't bother waiting for a response, turning on her heels and exiting the building.

Once she was outside, she walked a few feet, leaned against the wall, and took several deep breaths. She was both anxious and irritated, which was a terrible combination. Rubbing her face, she tried to shake off the entire morning and all of the feelings it'd produced. It was only after she yelled into her hands that she noticed Captain John Cooper standing off to the side of her, smoking a cigarette. Ellie whined against Marissa's side, nose punching into her thigh.

"Things going well?" he asked, eyebrow raised as he took a pull of his cigarette.

Marissa turned to look at him before leaning her head against the wall and looking forward. "Oh. Just great," she huffed.

"You wanna talk about it?"

She looked over at him and let out a heavy sigh as she tried to release the tension from her chest. "I mean, what's there really to say?"

"I know they are looking into the O'Rourke case. That he's out while the appeal process goes through." He must have seen her expression drop. "Look. We both know you did your job and you worked your ass off. It'll be fine."

Getting compliments from Captain Cooper was no small feat.

"I never congratulated you on your promotion." She gave him a slight smile. He had been her lieutenant, but several months ago, he had been promoted to captain.

"I appreciate that." He nodded at her. "So seriously, how are you?"

She straightened and folded her arms across her chest. "Not great." She shrugged her shoulder. "Things could be better."

"Can't believe you're dating an FBI agent. Didn't you once tell me he was the absolute worst? An egomaniac, if I recall."

A genuine smile crossed her lips. "I may have used those words, yes."

"Things will work out. They always do," he said reassuringly, taking the final puff of his cigarette before shoving it in the ashtray. "See you later, Ambrose. And get inside—it's gonna start raining soon."

"Yes, sir."

She watched him go back inside and let out another heavy breath. Looking down at Ellie, she gave the shepherd a scratch behind the ear. It was overcast and the wind had started to pick up. Since it was nearly June in Seattle, rain was all but a guarantee.

"Now we get to go to therapy," she told the shepherd before she pushed off the wall, wishing she could just go home.

Marissa tapped her foot, leaned forward, and rested her elbows on her knees. She glanced out the window, overlooking the Seattle skyline, before she turned her attention back to Dr. Bailey, who was watching with piqued curiosity.

"I'm sorry. Did you say something?"

She realized Dr. Bailey had been talking and was waiting for a response. Her mind was still back at the station in the interview room with Daniel Fryer.

"I was asking if you knew when Mac was coming back," Dr. Bailey said gently.

Marissa appreciated her patience. She leaned back on the couch, and Ellie nestled her head into Marissa's lap, trying to bring her some comfort. Scratching the dog's ear, she shook her head with uncertainty.

"I don't."

Mac was still at the center of an Internal Affairs investigation. Those pictures, their relationship—this was apparently his strike three. Marissa still didn't know what strikes one and two were.

"How long has it been since he flew out to D.C.?"

Marissa didn't hesitate with her answer, looking down at her shoes. It had been a very long, agonizing three weeks.

"How are you feeling about the whole situation?" Dr. Bailey was frowning and taking notes, frequently trying to meet Marissa's gaze.

"Stressed. Upset. Anxious." She shifted once again, the discomfort rising in her chest. "Johnny O'Rourke is out on house arrest from prison while the investigation is going on. His lawyers are trying to appeal, claiming it wasn't a fair investigation."

The Johnny O'Rourke case had been a tough one, complete with murder, kidnapping, and human trafficking charges. It had been her first big media case. Marissa had gotten the collar not because of favoritism, as IA was suggesting, but because of hard, solid police work. Because her integrity and Mac's were being questioned, O'Rourke was back out on the streets, which left her with a mix of emotions that mostly made her nauseous.

Dr. Bailey nodded. "I saw something about that in the paper."

Marissa shuddered. "I don't want to talk about that right now."

She still couldn't believe the avalanche that had been hurling toward her in slow motion the past few weeks.

Dr. Bailey didn't miss a beat. "Have you spoken to Mac about the night he was suspended?"

Marissa shook her head, digging into the cuticles of her thumbs. "We've talked but not very much. And not at all about that night."

He had been wrapped up in interviews and meetings. Marissa rocked herself in place on the couch, unease bubbling in the pit of her stomach.

Dr. Bailey adjusted in her seat, her expression shifting slightly. For a moment, it was unreadable. "How has it been, being alone these last few weeks?"

Marissa straightened her neck and breathed deep through her nose. "It's been … different." She began rubbing her right arm, running her nails over her skin, the sharp sensation keeping her there in that moment. "I've been alone before. Before Mac came into my life, I was living in the same house alone. But … I got used to the noise, I guess?" She shrugged at her therapist, who nodded and jotted down more notes. "Noise and the comfort. We had fallen into a routine. And we had just put a label on our relationship."

She let out a small laugh, although the words were anything but funny. Marissa found it ironic that she had spent so much time pushing against making their relationship official, and when she finally did, all hell broke loose.

"It wasn't just Mac, either. I got used to having Kate around, too," she added after a moment. "It all just got so quiet, so fast."

"That's understandable. It was a lot of change to adjust to. And then it changed again."

Marissa nodded in agreement.

"How are you feeling about it? Like, when you think about that empty house, how does it physically make you feel?"

Marissa hated questions like this. "Empty. Just like the house." Her shoulders slumped back.

Dr. Bailey was writing again and nodding her head. A moment passed before looked back up at Marissa. "Are you currently working on any cases?"

She shook her head. Like everything else in her life, this was complicated, too. "No. I'm kind of just sitting in limbo."

"I'm sorry. That must feel frustrating." Dr. Bailey offered a sympathetic smile before returning to her notes.

"Extremely." She ran her tongue over her bottom lip, which felt dry.

"You just came from the station from an interview, correct?"

Marissa just nodded, her mouth suddenly dry, too.

"And how is that going? I know you can't give any details on an open case, but do you feel like you are making progress there?"

Again, Marissa shook her head. "No. We mostly talk in circles. He controls the room, has all the leverage. And he knows it. It's his show." She let out a heavy sigh. "He was weird today, though. Shut down. Suicidal, even?" Marissa twitched her nose. "I don't know. It was just off. More off than usual."

"Let's switch gears just a little bit." The older woman pushed the hair from her face behind her ear. "How do you feel you're handling sitting across the table from the man who tortured you blindly for three days and left you for dead?"

Marissa felt a sharp jolt rush through her, hearing the words aloud filling her with a cold dread. "I'm handling it to the best of my ability."

"I have no doubts that you are. But how do you *feel* about it?" Dr. Bailey gently pushed.

"I feel sick just thinking about it." Her voice was much quieter than she had intended it to be. "Every time he looks at me, my skin crawls and I just want to tear it off."

"That's not an unreasonable response," Dr. Bailey said gently. "What are you doing for you to take care of yourself?"

Marissa sat there quietly for a long moment, thinking about her answer. "I mean, I'm sleeping. I'm eating." *Sort of.* "I'm … showering?"

Dr. Bailey shook her head. "I'm glad you're doing those things, but those are basic needs. That's not exactly what I'm talking about."

When Marissa didn't say anything, Dr. Bailey continued, "Are you doing any kind of self-care? Anything to help you relax or put your mind at ease? It could be as simple as going for walks, coloring, reading, meditating … anything like that."

Marissa just shook her head.

"You used to run, right? Have you been able to do that at all?"

Again, she shook her head. "Not in a minute. My body won't work like it's supposed to."

Dr. Bailey nodded, giving her a look of sympathy before jotting down more notes. "Why don't we talk about some things you can do that are a form of self-care…"

Marissa knew caring for herself was solely up to her, and she appreciated the ideas, but getting out of bed every morning took up most of her energy. Not even bed, actually, but getting off the couch because she hadn't been able to bring herself to sleep in her bed since Mac left. She just didn't want to sleep in the large empty bed alone. But she nodded, trying to listen and take in Dr. Bailey's suggestions. It was hard to imagine that soaking in a bathtub would relax her the way her therapist seemed to think it would.

Chapter 2

Marissa stared at the whiteboard. She had come home from Seattle the day before and simply passed out. She had been so overwhelmed, she'd tried to sleep some of that stress away. The next day, she found some motivation. For the first time, she had a marker in her hand and things to add. Under Daniel Fryer's name were all the murders he had confessed to, which were up to six. Including Tom Disher. She added the words: *Ohio—setup?*

The idea that Ben, whomever he may be, had a hold over someone like Daniel Fryer even while he was behind bars was terrifying. Fryer didn't seem afraid of him exactly, but he was not keen to keep playing whatever game Ben had set up. This was one of the many questions she added to the board: *What game?*

It wasn't a game of chess. There were at least three players: Ben, Fryer, and her.

Who else was he controlling? How? What kind of leverage could he have had over Daniel Fryer to keep him from giving him up? The man was already confessing to murders.

Something didn't make sense.

Beneath Ben's name, she added the question: *Mastermind?*

Everything she had thought she knew was now in question. Because when the two men were murdering couples, it had been her understanding that Daniel Fryer was in charge and calling the shots. Under Ben's name were the names of the Couple Killer victims: *Miranda Harris and John Bolton. Christine and Anthony Cochren. Amy Teagan and Robert Turner.*

To the side, she grabbed a red marker and added: *Mac.*

If it hadn't been for "Ben," their relationship would have still been in the shadows. Mac would be there and not currently suspended. Marissa felt a tightness grip her chest.

Beside Ben's name was a large question mark for his new accomplice. The one that was last in Chicago, torturing a woman named Brenna they had yet to find. Or was Ben with Brenna and the accomplice was the one who'd remained local, leaving letters and flower clippings? One of these men had kept Brenna for several weeks now, which was not part of the Couple Killer's original MO. Part of Marissa wondered if she was already dead.

Toward the bottom of the board were other names: *Jack Carson, Clyde Bennet, Mac again, Samuel Trotter, Jacob Starr.* Even officers who had joined the Port Townsend PD in the last two and a half years. She noted all the people who had come into her life in the last couple of years since the warehouse.

She sat down on the floor and stared up at the board since her chair was covered in folders and paperwork that she still hadn't sorted from this case. Closing her eyes, she thought back to what she always worked so hard to forget: those three days she had spent in hell, blindfolded and disoriented.

Daniel Fryer had admitted to her own attempted murder. Starting from that point, she knew he was the pair of rough hands, always shoving her around, throwing her around like a ragdoll. That made Ben the one who treated her with gentle hands, despite the unspeakable things he did to her.

She nearly jumped out of her skin as she heard the Ring camera chime on her phone. Swiping to open the Ring app, her shoulders relaxed when she saw Herbert Jackson standing on her front porch.

"Come on in. It's unlocked. I'm upstairs," she said into the phone and watched him shake his head as her words came through the doorbell device.

Ellie didn't bark but went out on the landing of the stairs, wagging her tail in excitement. She heard

Jackson making his way up the stairs, grumbling under his breath.

"What are you muttering about?" Marissa said loudly enough for him to hear without taking her eyes off the board.

"Seriously, what is wrong with you?" The older man appeared in the doorway, looking annoyed and bewildered. "You have an active stalker taunting you, and you just leave the door unlocked?" He looked down as he gave Ellie pets on the head. "And this is a sad excuse for a guard dog."

Marissa huffed, shrugging her shoulder. "I knew you were coming. If it had been a stranger, I wouldn't have announced the door was unlocked."

Herbert Jackson shook his head before turning his eyes to the board. "Looks like you've added a bit."

He examined the notes on the board, looking at all the new information she had added in purple marker.

"How did it go today?"

"I don't even know," she admitted as she got to her feet. "It felt like maybe we were getting somewhere and then Clyde burst in and Gorden gave me a lecture." She shook her head, narrowing her eyes at the board. "I hate them," she mumbled under breath.

Jackson raised his eyebrow, waiting for her to finish.

"Fryer implied Ben set him up and that he's still pulling the strings even with him in jail. Fryer asked to be extradited for a death penalty sentence."

Jackson let out a whistle, his eyes washing over the board again. "Sounds like it was quite the visit."

"You could say that," Marissa said softly. "Anything on your end?"

He shook his head. "No. But you knew it was a long shot."

Marissa had asked him to try and run backgrounds on everyone she had placed on the lower half of the board. Anyone who had come into her world within the last two years. Jackson had come back with a lot in the first week or so. All that was left were the FBI agents. Asking him to look into them had been a tall order. She had really hoped he could have found something. Especially on Mac.

Words from that night still rang through her ears: *This is your third strike, Agent Mackenzie.*

Herbert Jackson turned his eyes to her and shook his head. "Just getting something on the board is a win, remember? You can't just will it to give you the answers."

He huffed and rubbed the back of his neck. "Why don't you let me take you to lunch?"

Marissa turned to her superior and gave him a halfhearted smile.

"No," she said softly. "Thanks, boss. But if there isn't anything to add, you should probably get back to work."

He nodded, looking down at Ellie uncomfortably. "Yeah. Okay." He hesitated. "I was thinking maybe we should go through those photos of yours this weekend. Maybe see if we can narrow down the differences in photographer."

Marissa nodded. They had discussed this before. But the idea of pulling out all the photos again made her head hurt. "Yeah. Alright."

Herbert Jackson gave her a sympathetic smile from the doorway. "Please eat something."

"Of course." She gave him her best confident smile, hoping he wouldn't see through it.

"Pain in my ass. Making me go up all these stairs just to tell me to go back to work," he grumbled but gave her a small smile before adding: "At least lock your damn door."

It was only when she heard the door close behind him that she let out a breath. In the last few weeks since Mac had been gone, Jackson had been making regular visits to her

house under the guise of helping her solve some of the mysteries that haunted her. She knew the old man meant well, but he could have very easily made a phone call to tell her he had nothing new.

Herbert Jackson had always been there for her; he was the reason she wanted to become a cop. He had arrested her when she was fourteen for shoplifting with her cousin, and from that point on, he had taken a special interest in making sure she and her family were okay. He was just a cop then, but his influence had stuck with her. There was a moment she thought maybe he was seeing her mom, but that was never confirmed. Herbert Jackson was the closest thing to a present father figure that she had until she reached out to her biological dad when she turned eighteen. Jackson had even shown up at the hospital after her kidnapping. He had always been there for her, and she was eternally grateful, especially now that the FBI were no longer in town. At least not officially. Clyde had moved from across the street from Marissa's house to the Mansera, which was at least somewhere she wasn't likely to run into him with Madilyn. She still couldn't bring herself to go inside the Mansera.

Not without Allison.

She had run into Clyde and her sister Madi a few times around town. She was not a fan of their relationship. Although they made a stunning couple, the whole thought made her cringe. Her sister, on the other hand, was glowing with happiness. Clyde had told Madilyn that he was sticking around in town for her, but Marissa knew he had promised Mac that he would stick around to keep an eye on Marissa. Mac had insisted, making it clear he was unlikely to board a plane if Clyde didn't agree. Marissa had no intention of popping her younger sister's bubble. They had been dating for almost two months now. It was good to see her happy. Someone deserved to be.

With some effort, Marissa managed to get to her feet from the floor, having to rock herself for the momentum. "Come, El." She smiled at the dog, who was already on her feet, watching Marissa closely with a slow wag of her tail. Marissa patted her thigh and motioned for the shepherd to follow her down the stairs.

By the time she headed down, it was already getting dark. She let Ellie out into the yard and stepped outside, feeling the warm air on her face. The days had grown longer, and the warm weather had begun making an appearance. Being Washington state, however, it could rain, snow, or hail at any moment. The tease of warm weather was something to look forward to.

Ellie did her business before making her rounds along the fence and then returning back to Marissa, looking pleased with herself.

Marissa couldn't stop herself from smiling. "Come on." She motioned for the sliding door, letting the shepherd run in before following behind her.

She made the effort and opened the refrigerator door, looking for something to eat before quickly closing it again. Food didn't sound appetizing. She turned the kitchen light off behind her as she walked through the entryway and glanced at the living room. It all felt so empty and quiet, just as she'd described to Dr. Bailey. Glancing toward the stairs, Marissa quickly decided it wasn't worth the walk back up. The lights were off. Being upstairs reminded her more than anything just how alone she was.

Instead, she plopped herself on the couch, and Ellie jumped up beside her. She clicked the TV on. This had become normal since Mac left. Even Wicket was curled up on the chair.

Just as she turned the TV on, her phone rang. Looking at her cell, she was surprised to see Lydia's name pop up.

"Hey Lydia, what's up?"

It'd been weeks since she had heard from them since Lydia had given back to the keys to the condo. She had texted to say she had made it to Ellensburg and that they were settling in, but that had been it.

"Hey, Marissa."

There was a sadness in her voice that brought tears immediately to Marissa's eyes. This was about Tom. She could feel it in her bones.

"Are you okay?" Marissa asked, breaking the silence Lydia probably would've let stretch on.

Lydia cleared her throat on the other end of the line. "I'm sorry. I was—I was going through Tom's things."

Marissa looked down at her feet, a chill coming over her. She had to resist the urge to apologize, again. Even though she knew the events that led to Tom's death weren't her fault, it never took away that feeling of guilt.

"I was looking through his things, and I came across a box full of case files, and they all seem to be from the same case." She paused for what Marissa could only assume, based on the unsteadiness of her voice, to regain her composure again. "Tom never brought work home, as you know, so I'm not sure what this is or what to do with it."

Marissa shook her head for no one. "No, he didn't bring work home." She frowned. "Can you take a picture of the front page and send it to me?"

Marissa hoped Lydia hadn't dug through its contents. As homicide detectives, cases weren't usually pretty.

"Of course." She sounded relieved. "Give me a second."

Marissa waited, and a moment later, her phone let off a notification *ding*. Pulling her phone away from her ear, she put Lydia on speaker and opened the text she had received.

It had a case number over the front as well as a date: *June 8, 2005. Jane Doe, Schmitz Preserve Park.* It was before Marissa had joined the police force, but it sounded familiar. Tom had mentioned this case a number of times. It had gone cold early on.

"I don't know the case personally, but I vaguely remember hearing about it."

"I just don't know what to do with it." Lydia sounded frustrated. "I thought about bringing it back to the department, but I wanted to reach out to you first, and see if maybe you wanted to take a look at it? I'm not sure he can get in trouble now for having brought it home but..."

"I'll definitely take a look at it." Marissa thought maybe she answered a little too quickly, but as a general rule, files weren't supposed to leave the office.

"I'm coming back for a couple of appointments with my mom in a few days. Would you be able to meet up with me? I can bring all of it to you."

"Of course. Just tell me when and where." Marissa paused. "How is your mom doing?"

"You know, good days and bad days."

They talked for another half hour about Ellensburg, Lydia's mom, and Tom and Lydia's daughter, Evelyn. They made plans to meet for lunch in Seattle in a week.

Once Marissa hung up the phone, she felt a wave of exhaustion flow through her. She considered taking a shower, but instead, she adjusted herself on the couch, pulling the blanket up and letting out a heavy sigh. She closed her eyes, and instead of sleeping, Marissa thought back to the first time she'd met Lydia.

It had taken Marissa a minimum of one hundred excuses before she finally accepted Tom's offer to come over for dinner. The truth was, she was tired of spending her nights alone. And Tom had been a breath of fresh air as a partner after her work in vice. She had hated vice. They had been working together for almost two months now, and he had been inviting her to his home for dinner since the beginning.

Tom was older than Marissa but not by too much. He was already in his late thirties when she was just closing out her twenties. She was almost certain her promotion to homicide had been part of a publicity stunt. Alongside her promotion, three other promotions had happened throughout the precinct: a black woman, a Hispanic man, and a much older gentleman who had only recently joined the force. They had hit all token points. But Tom had been very supportive of her transition and of becoming her partner.

Their most recent case had been the murder of a construction worker. He had been found in a parking lot of a warehouse ten miles from the construction site he had last been seen at. They had spent the week following leads and talking to witnesses, friends, and family. The break had finally come that morning when Marissa found inconsistencies in a couple of stories they had been told. By the afternoon, they'd had an arrest and a confession. She had been working on her paperwork when Tom came over and perched on the end of her desk.

"You did good work today."

Marissa dropped her head, the praise making her uncomfortable. "Thanks."

"Seriously. You did good work. I think that we deserve to celebrate." He smiled, clasping his hands together and resting them on his lap. "Come to dinner. My wife is really excited to meet you. Please. She's going to blame me if you don't come."

Marissa flipped her pen back and forth and glanced at the clock, unable to stop a small smile. "Yeah. Okay." They did deserve to celebrate. "I'm in."

Tom clapped his hands and grinned. "Perfect! I'll go call her and let her know." He got to his feet, and Marissa leaned back in her chair.

She had gone home to her empty condo and changed her clothes. She also grabbed a bottle of unopened wine to bring. She had almost talked herself out of going. She was still reeling from her second divorce, and the empty condo was a sad reminder of failures. She spent as little time there as she could. But she had also stopped going out and stopped socializing, choosing to work longer hours instead. She barely spoke to her family or Allison. She focused on work, determined to prove she deserved her promotion. But maybe a little socialization wouldn't be bad.

Lydia had met Marissa at the door and pulled her into a hug before ushering her inside. Marissa was surprised to be met by someone closer to her own age than Tom's. Lydia was young and vibrant, the sunshine to Tom's normal gloom and serious attitude.

The dinner had been amazing. They drank the red wine that Marissa had brought, and they ate a fancy pasta dish that tasted like heaven. When dinner was over, Tom took their plates and disappeared.

Lydia smiled. "Tom tells me you've really settled in?"

Marissa smiled shyly, playing with her wine glass. "It feels like I'm getting there," she said honestly. "Tom's been really great."

"I'm glad to hear it. Tom's last partner transferred. They didn't really get along." Lydia made a face that told Marissa she hadn't liked his previous partner either.

Marissa didn't know much about him, but she knew he had transferred or had been transferred to a different precinct.

"I think we're going to be great friends." The redhead grinned. "Which is great, because if I'm being honest, I don't have a lot of friends out here."

Marissa opened her eyes, feeling Ellie stretch across her legs, resting her head against Marissa's chest. Marissa wrapped her arms around the big black shepherd, closed her eyes, and let sleep take over.

Chapter 3

Marissa plopped down in the grass and breathed in a heavy sigh. The sky was overcast and gray, the warmth of spring nearly gone and the typical wet of the Pacific Northwest in its place. It felt appropriate since she was sitting in the middle of Laurel Grove Cemetery. She was sitting directly in front of Allison's tombstone, next to Allie's parents. Ellie sprawled out beside her, making herself comfortable.

"I know your birthday was yesterday, but I figured I'd give everyone a chance to come down here and be together. You know how I am with crowds." She studied the stone, running her fingers along her name. "Fuck, Allie," she whispered. "You should be turning thirty-eight."

Marissa shook her head, anger swelling through her. "This is such bullshit."

She unscrewed the top of her flask and took a big swig of the store-bought margarita mix she had from Allie's last birthday mixed with tequila.

"So much has happened. Mel finally had a boy. Preston Wayne Shaw. Not a B name. He's absolutely perfect." She shook her head, letting out a small laugh. "But I only know because Madi sent pictures. And mom called about a hundred times, but I haven't been to see them. I still don't think Mel wants me there. I sent a congratulations text to all of them. Brian texted me back: *Thank you.* It's the longest exchange we've had since last Thanksgiving."

There was a physical ache as she said the words out loud.

"I really fucked things up there. But I achieved the distance I wanted to keep everyone safe, so it's a win? I guess?"

Marissa looked down at the ground and shrugged her shoulders.

"I had a fourteen-year-old girl living in my house for a few months. A victim of a case I was working. She has a permanent foster home now. But I miss her."

She took another sip and paused. "*We* miss her. Mac and I are *all in.* Still figuring out what that means."

Marissa blinked back tears, regrets and guilt surfacing. "You would have loved Mac. I wish I had introduced you guys back when we first dated. He's so sweet and thoughtful. You would say his flaw is that he's too nice. Never boring though. He makes me feel safe."

She let out a heavy sigh and pushed the hair from her face.

"There was a moment when I thought he was done and leaving, and I was so afraid that it was over. Whatever this thing was. I didn't want to put labels on it."

"He came back with 'I can't do casual with you. It's all or nothing.'"

She took another long sip from the flask, exhaling before she continued.

"And if I wasn't ready, he would wait for me. But I told him I was all in, too. And here we are." Her voice had fallen to a whisper as she spoke. "I hate that you're not here, Allie."

She wiped the tear that had fallen down her cheek, doing her best to keep her voice steady.

"I'm so sorry I missed all the signs. I was not a very good best friend. Fuck, I wasn't even a good detective. I missed everything. I'm so sorry. I'm sorry I wasn't there for you."

Marissa's hand shot up to her eyes as though to keep the tears from falling. Sensing the shift in Marissa's emotions, Ellie nudged her arm and forced her way into her lap.

This was why she hadn't made the trip out here since the funeral. There was so much she had wanted to say, so much she *needed* to say. But putting it into words, actually speaking them, just left the guilt and anger burning a hole in her. So instead, she choked back the sobs and sat there quietly, wiping the tears from her face and holding Ellie close.

After what felt like an eternity, Marissa got to her feet and wiped off the loose grass clinging to her pants. After sliding the half-empty flask into her back pocket, she inhaled a shaky breath and patted her leg for Ellie to come to her side before she headed back to the car.

She had just started down the long stretch of road when her phone rang. The name that ran across her screen made her pause. Clearing her throat, Marissa clicked the green button to answer through the car's Bluetooth system.

"Hey, Meredith. What's up?" She didn't really need her to say the words, but she knew they were coming. There would be only one reason Meredith Parker was calling.

"Hey Marissa. It's Kate. She ran away from the Olsen's again. I was hoping maybe you had heard from her?" The case worker sounded exhausted and frazzled.

"Shit. I haven't." Marissa looked at her dashboard, trying to remember the last time she had spoken to Kate. It had only been a few days ago, and everything had sounded okay. "How long has she been gone?"

"They called me this morning, but she disappeared yesterday." There was a pause on the other end of the phone. "And Marissa, they don't want her back."

"Okay," Marissa muttered mostly to herself. "We'll figure it out," she offered, feeling for the exhausted woman. She was trying her best, but Kate wasn't making it easy.

"Okay. Let me know if you hear from her, please?"

"Of course."

As she pulled into her driveway, Marissa hung up the phone and let out a heavy sigh.

Kate hadn't been with the Olsen's very long, maybe coming up on two months, but it had been pretty turbulent from the start. She hadn't adjusted to the change well, and Mrs. Olsen was not a fan from day one. From what Marissa understood, Mrs. Olsen had a lot of house rules and a lot of opinions on how Kate dressed, spoke to others, and behaved. Her shirts were too tight; her shorts were too short. If she put on her hoodie, she looked too ratty. Mrs. Olsen had told Kate that everything she said was condescending and that she was far too friendly with the boys—and even men.

Meredith had spoken a couple of times about trying to find a different situation for her. She and Marissa had talked almost weekly since Kate left—mostly about Kate but almost like friends.

With the car in park, Marissa tried to call Kate, but the feedback she received was that the phone number was already out of service.

"Damnit," she muttered. She rubbed her eyes and shook her head before opening the car door. "Come on, Ellie," she directed the dog to follow her up to the porch.

Marissa did a quick check of her porch to make sure nothing had been delivered before she unlocked her door and pushed her way in. The cloudy skies made it appear so much later than it was.

Now that she was back home, Marissa wasn't sure what to do with herself. She wanted to go find Kate. But Tumwater, where the Olsens lived, was not exactly right around the corner. It was two hours away. The last time Kate had run away, they found her at a bus stop the next day. There was no reason to panic yet.

Marissa picked at her fingernails and looked around the empty house. Other than her own stalker case, which was an obsession in itself, she wasn't actively working on anything. She would be meeting with Lydia in a few days and could take a look into Tom's cold case, but for the moment, there was nothing to do but kill time. She walked into the kitchen, opened the pantry door before closing it, then opened the fridge and then the freezer. Nothing sounded good. She gave Ellie some food and headed into the living room.

"Hey," she answered, trying to keep her anxiety to herself.

"Hey... Are you okay?"

"Kate's gone again. The Olsen's called Meredith this morning." She paused. "They don't want her back."

"Shit," Mac mumbled.

"Yeah."

He paused on the other end of the line. "Have you heard from her?"

"No, and her phone is already saying the number is no longer connected." Marissa looked over at Ellie, who stretched out alongside her. "I was thinking of heading down south to try and find her."

Mac sighed softly. "Honestly, Riss, I would stay put. There's a chance she's coming right back to you."

"You think?" It had already crossed her mind, and it was part of the reason she hadn't left looking for her just yet, but it felt good to hear him confirm it was a possibility.

"Yeah. I think she's probably already on her way."

Marissa found that comforting. "Maybe."

God, she missed him. Closing her eyes, she leaned into her phone. "How are things going?"

Mac sighed. "They're ... going. Taking forever. I feel like they're dragging their feet."

"Any word on when you can come ho—back?" She'd almost said *home.*

If Mac noticed, he didn't make it obvious. "No. I have an interview next Wednesday, so at least another week." The disappointment was heavy in his voice. "I miss you."

"I miss you, too."

She peered around her, taking in her empty, still house, and felt a pain in her chest.

As though he could hear her thoughts, he sighed on the other end of the line. "Listen. Everything is going to be okay. I'll be back before you know it."

"I know," she lied.

She nearly told him about the letter she'd received from Ben the night of his suspension, but she stopped herself.

"It's getting late, so I'll let you go. Make sure you eat something, okay?" he said.

"I will and you, too. I'll call you tomorrow?"

"Definitely."

There was a short pause on both ends of the phone. "Goodnight, Marissa."

"Goodnight, Mac."

Chapter 4

Stepping off the ferry, Marissa looked down at her phone to check the time. She still had a few hours before she needed to meet Lydia, but she figured she and Ellie could kill time walking through the market. This was probably one of the biggest things she missed about living in Seattle—coming out once or twice a week and walking the market: getting fresh food and flowers, looking through the artwork, and meeting talented people. It was unique and always exciting—the smells, all the delicious food.

Marissa entered on the end by the park, approaching a booth that was selling handmade jewelry. She eyed a beautiful necklace with a blue stone in the middle when the sound of laughter caught her attention.

Marissa blinked. It was her mom's laughter.

Confused, she looked around the crowd for several moments before her eyes landed on what she immediately recognized as her mother's figure. She was standing in front of a flower booth a few stalls down, holding a beautiful bouquet of pink and purple flowers, while a man standing beside her held her hand and paid the shopkeeper for the flowers. In that moment, her mom looked years younger, laughing with a bright smile.

Marissa didn't recognize the man beside her. He couldn't have been much older than Marissa with light strawberry-colored hair and tall with sturdy shoulders. He leaned over and gave Marilyn a kiss on the cheek and she responded by pulling him in for a longer, less appropriate kiss. She knew her mom dated—more than thirty years had passed since her divorce—but Marissa had never seen her mom *with* anyone. Let alone kissing them in the middle of a public market.

Marissa felt ... frozen. Blinking again, she watched them for what ended up being too long of a moment, trying to decide whether to go up to them or run in the other direction and pretend she hadn't seen anything.

It didn't matter, though.

Her mom must have felt her watching because she turned and looked directly at her. She waved, but Marissa could make out the mixed emotion on her expression. Before she could do anything, Marilyn and her mystery man were heading her way.

"Hey, honey, what are you doing here?" Marilyn pulled Marissa in for a hug, her voice a few pitches higher than normal.

"I'm meeting Lydia later." Her eyes shifted from her mom to the man standing beside her as she pulled back from the hug. "What about you?"

Marilyn gave Marissa a sheepish smile before motioning to the quiet man beside her. "I guess the cat is out of the bag. Marissa, this is Greg Hargrove." His name sounded vaguely familiar ... but not familiar enough to be kissing her mother.

"It's nice to finally meet you. I've heard so much about you. I feel like I already know you," Greg said.

Marissa blinked. She didn't even know how to respond. "It's nice to meet you too." She looked between them. "How long have you been together?"

Greg hesitated, nervously running his hand through his hair and glancing down at Marilyn.

Marilyn ignored the question. "Have you had lunch yet? Why don't we all go sit down and get some food? We can talk a bit."

"I'm meeting Lydia for lunch." A drink sounded good, though. Depending on the answer to the question, Marissa might need one. Shifting her footing, she looked between the two of them when someone's phone erupted with "I'm Blue" by Eiffel 65 as a ringtone.

"Hey, I've got to take this." Greg gave Marissa a polite smile and kissed Marilyn on the cheek. "Sorry, ladies. I'll be right back."

Both women watched him leave before Marilyn turned to Marissa. "Why don't we grab a coffee and talk?" Her voice was softer than it had been a minute ago. "He'll probably be a minute. He's a lawyer."

Marissa just nodded and followed her mom's lead. They didn't say a word to one another standing in the line at Starbucks. It wasn't until they both had their drinks and had taken seats on the patio that Marilyn broke the awkward silence.

"I always worked really hard to keep my dating life separate from you girls growing up. I never wanted to disrupt our lives. And it was just easier to keep it that way even as you grew up."

Marissa let her shoulders relax. She understood, despite the surprise. "So, how long have you been seeing each other?"

"On and off for about nine years."

Marissa felt her eyes bulge. "Nine years?" She didn't bother hiding her disbelief. "How—Wh—"

Marilyn put her hand up, bringing Marissa to a stop. She took a sip of her coffee before she started talking again. "We met at a bookstore. He's a defense lawyer. He is thirty-nine years old, never been married. No kids. Has an amazing sense of humor. We ran into each other after I moved and sort of picked up where we left off."

That was two years ago. "And you were just going to keep him a secret forever?" Marissa raised her voice a little bit more than she meant to. "Didn't you just say conversations were being had? That it was nothing serious?" Marissa thought back to the lunch she had had a month ago with her mom, sister, and her nieces.

Marilyn shook her head. "The timing just never seemed to be right. Something was always going on."

"Mom—" Marissa started but Marilyn held her hand up again.

"Marissa." Her mother's tone made her sit back. "I'm happy. That's what matters, right?"

She couldn't argue with that. "It is," she said slowly. Her head was spinning, but she understood where her mom was coming from. "I'm sorry. I'm just surprised."

Marilyn nodded and gave Marissa what almost looked like a sympathetic smile. "I know, and that is my fault. I really did mean to tell you about him a while ago." She took another sip of her coffee, hesitating. "It is nice though, to have something be just yours, you know."

Again, Marissa couldn't argue. Something about the way Marilyn was smiling at her made her feel small, like she was eight years old again. She slumped down in her chair.

"We've all got secrets, right?" her mom said.

"Something like that," Marissa agreed, staring at her own coffee, which she hadn't even tried yet.

After a moment, she looked back up at her mom, who was silent and watching her.

"You look so tired, honey." The concern was written all over her face. "You've looked tired for a long time."

"I am tired," Marissa admitted.

"I know you keep a lot of things to yourself and that you probably have to keep it that way. But I'm always here, for whatever you need."

Marissa bit her lip as emotions swelled through her. She'd spent a lot of time avoiding her mom's calls and suddenly couldn't remember why. She hadn't been as close to her mom as Mel had, but Marilyn hadn't been a bad mom. When they were kids, Marilyn had always tried to make sure that the girls were happy. As Marissa grew up, she often felt like a source of disappointment for her—eloping in Vegas, two divorces. After nearly dying, Marissa had had a hard time connecting with anyone. When the pictures began arriving, she shut everyone out. Pushing down the urge to just splurge and confess everything right there, she simply nodded.

"I know, Mom."

"How is Mac?"

Marissa dropped her eyes back to her coffee and shrugged a shoulder. "He's in D.C. at the moment. Work troubles."

"Relationship troubles?" her mom asked, raising her eyebrow.

Marissa just shook her head. "No. We're doing good." She paused. "Better than good. We are both officially all in, whatever that means." She couldn't stop the smile from forming on her lips.

"I like him a lot, for what it's worth."

"That means a lot, actually."

"Good." Marilyn looked proud of herself. "Have you spoken to your sister recently?"

"I spoke to Madi yesterday—"

"I mean Melanie, Marissa," she said, her tone matter of fact.

Marissa sighed and shook her head. "Nope. She made it clear she doesn't want to talk to me."

"I'm sure you two can work out whatever the issue is." Now it was Marilyn's turn to sigh. "You two have never gone more than a day without talking to each other until all this. It's breaking my heart to see you both without each other."

"It is what it is, Mom. I've tried. I've reached out. She doesn't want anything to do with me. And neither does Brian. Or Jared." Her ex-husband's name caused her to shudder involuntarily.

Marilyn's lips twisted into a frown. "I can't speak for Jared, but Brian is just trying to appease Mel and keep her happy. She isn't making it easy for him." She shook her head. "She's struggling, Marissa. And maybe it's pride, maybe it's hormones, but she needs you. Don't give up on her."

Marissa was quiet for a long time. She had never given up on her sister; she was just offering her the space she asked for. "I'm not giving up on her, Mom. And I have tried. I'm just the person she's directing all her anger at. Which I guess she needed, too." She let out a long sigh. "I'm glad she's got Madi. And even Kirstie."

Jared's pregnant girlfriend and Melanie had become fast friends, bonding over what Marissa could only assume were pregnancy cravings and hating Marissa.

"I won't pretend to know what went on behind the scenes, but for what it's worth, she seems like a very nice girl."

Girl felt like the key word. She was a child compared to Jared. Marissa's nose twitched as she tried to hold back a frown. "Did you say Greg is thirty-nine years old?"

Marilyn gave her a shy smile. "I did."

"He's two years older than me." Her mom was fifty-seven years old.

"Yes, he is." Marilyn wiggled ever so slightly in her chair. "But he's got the stamina of a twenty-nine-year-old."

"MOM!" Marissa shuddered. "Too much information. TOO MUCH."

Marilyn laughed just as Greg came back into view, smiling at the two women as he slipped his hand around Marilyn's shoulder. "Sorry about that, ladies."

"You're good," Marilyn assured him, leaning up to give him a quick kiss and motioning for him to sit beside her.

They sat in Starbucks for a little over an hour, and Marissa got to know a little bit about the man her mom had been secretly seeing for nine years. He seemed nice enough—friendly, polite, funny, although he was wearing his nerves on his sleeve.

When Marilyn got up to go to the restroom, he stood and pulled out her chair. Once she was out of sight, he sat back down and smiled anxiously at Marissa.

"I am sorry it's taken so long for us to meet. If it had been up to me, we would have met years ago." He sighed. "Your mom is an amazing woman, and I love her very much. I only wanted to respect her wishes."

Marissa watched him for a long moment. He certainly seemed sincere. "You know, I'm probably the easiest of my sisters to meet."

"That's interesting. Your mom gave me the impression you would be the hardest."

"Only because I'm the detective. Because you know I'm going to go home and run a background check on you."

"I would expect nothing less." He smiled.

"So nine years?" Her disbelief resurfaced.

Maybe she really needed to turn in her badge; she'd missed so much. Before everything had even happened. But like Allison had pointed out before her death, when she had been living in Seattle, Marissa might as well have been on the other side of the world.

He nodded his head. "Nine years."

"Wow." The idea that her mom could even keep a secret that huge for so long was absolutely mind blowing. She needed to change the subject. "Mom said you're a defense attorney?"

Again, he nodded. "I started in the district attorney's office years ago, but it was too much politics for me."

"Ah." She couldn't stop her face from reacting, remembering her last conversation with ADA Gorden.

"Based on that look, I assume you have some experience."

"I've been working with the ADA on a case for the last couple of months, and he's … not my favorite."

"Luke Gorden?"

Marissa nodded.

"I don't personally know him, but I've seen him around. He's got lofty goals for himself. He's the perfect example of why I didn't fit into the district attorney's office."

Marissa nodded. "Yeah, that sounds about right."

Her mom returned, and they continued to visit for almost another hour before Marissa realized it was time to go.

"I've got to go meet Lydia." She got to her feet, Ellie emerging from under the table and stretching, her tail slowly wagging. "It was really good to meet you." She smiled at Greg and gave her mom a hug. "It was good to see you, Mom."

"You know, I only live, like, fifteen minutes away. We could visit more often," her mom said with a raised eyebrow as she pulled back. "Also, I know this is probably awful of me to ask, but can you not say anything to your sisters? I want to get you all in the same room so I can tell them about Greg. You can absolutely pretend to be shocked."

She smiled. "I can do that."

"Good. Call me soon." Her mom wrapped her arm up in Greg's, who took it with a smile.

"I can do that, too."

Marissa opened the door to the restaurant and looked around. Where she should have been on time or even early, she was now nearly ten minutes late. Thankfully, the redhead was easy to spot, right in front waving her down.

"Hey, Lydia." Marissa leaned in to hug her.

"Hey, Marissa, it's so good to see you!" She had a genuine smile on face.

"You look good!" Marissa meant it; Lydia did look good. She looked like she'd gotten some sun, and it had breathed a little bit of life back into her.

Marissa slid into the booth as Ellie went under the table and immediately lay down.

"Thanks. I'm feeling a lot better. Even with my mom, the change of scenery has been really good for us."

"Good." Marissa had to force down the lump in her throat, and with it, the urge to once again apologize. Not once had Lydia ever blamed her for what had happened, but it didn't stop the guilt from weighing her down.

"So, this bag is full of all the files that I found. It was two boxes' worth. I didn't really go digging through..."

"Good." Marissa was grateful to hear it. Lydia was tough—she had to be as an ER nurse—but nothing could prepare a person for homicide.

"Also, Evelyn may have put something for you in the bag as well."

"How is she doing with the move?"

"Better than me. She's adjusting really well." She paused and sighed, looking out into the crowded restaurant. "I almost wish we had made the move sooner." She looked at Marissa quickly. "Not that I'm not immensely grateful for you letting us stay in the condo. I just wonder if maybe I would have been closer to being in a better place sooner. Everything reminds me of him." She shrugged a shoulder. "We have history all over this city together. It just feels empty now."

Marissa swallowed. "Lydia... I wish—"

Lydia put a hand up, shaking her head. "Marissa, I'm not saying any of this to make you feel bad. Tom was a cop. We both knew what he signed up for when he left the house every day. Please, stop blaming yourself."

Tears ran down Marissa's cheeks despite her efforts to keep them from falling. She dropped her head a little as Lydia took her hands.

"Seriously. Look at me. The only thing you've done is take all the blame and guilt on your shoulders. Let it go."

The waitress came over and lingered over them awkwardly for a moment before scurrying off after muttering she'd be right back.

Marissa wiped her eyes and nodded her head, still not trusting herself enough for words.

The rest of the lunch was a lot lighter as Lydia told her all about Evelyn's adventures in daycare and all about the house.

Chapter 5

Seattle had been more than Marissa had been mentally or physically prepared for. There were far too many emotions that had run through her in what amounted to only half a day. As she walked off the ferry, she silently applauded her forethought to park the car in the shopping center so she didn't have to walk the hills back to the house.

Seeing Lydia also brought on a wave of guilt and grief. She still felt responsible, even though, logically, she knew it wasn't her fault. But now Lydia was a single mom, dealing with her sick mother and raising her toddler. They used to go out on double dates, Lydia and Tom with Marissa and Jared. They had game nights together. Tom had been the older brother figure she had grown to look up to. A good friend. If only she had stopped him from running in before their backup had arrived. If she had gone in first. Seeing Lydia always brought those thoughts to the forefront. She couldn't stop it.

She tossed the duffle bag with the files from Tom's box into the back seat and sighed at it before closing the door. She opened the passenger door, letting Ellie get in before she walked around to get into the driver's seat. The least she could do was take a look at a case he'd deemed important enough to bring home with him.

As she started the car, she shook, trying to shed off the feelings of guilt and sadness. In its place, Marissa thought about her mother and her secret boyfriend. That had her conflicted. On the one hand, she felt like she should call her sisters immediately and tell them everything. She wouldn't because she promised her mom. And she understood the feeling of having something that was just her own. That she didn't have to share with anyone else, closing herself off to judgement. If she was being really honest, she was proud of her mom for finding someone who made her happy.

The five-minute drive up the hill into the neighborhood felt like it took longer, getting stuck at both lights and behind slow drivers. As she finally pulled into her driveway, Marissa audibly gasped. There, sitting on the steps of her front porch, was Kate. She was leaning against the banister with her eyes closed, possibly asleep, with her backpack in her lap. Marissa grabbed the bag with the case files out of the seat behind her and stepped out of the car, waiting for Ellie to jump out before she closed the door.

The sound of the car door startled Kate awake, and she jumped to her feet. She swung her backpack over her shoulder and stood there nervously. As Marissa approached, she noted Kate's exhausted bloodshot eyes.

She stared at the tired teenager before letting out a heavy breath and opening her arms. Kate didn't hesitate, rushing in for the hug, embracing Marissa tighter than she had since the day they'd met. Marissa hugged her back, a sense of relief washing over her.

After a few moments passed, she pulled back and looked Kate over, brushing the hair from the teenager's face. "Are you okay?"

Kate swallowed, her blue eyes fighting back tears as she nodded. The feeling that there may have been something to Kate's running away was clawing from the back of Marissa's mind, but she gave her a smile. "Good. Let's get inside."

Marissa led the teenager to the front door, quickly glancing around her porch for any unwanted mail before unlocking the door and letting them in.

"I didn't touch anything in your room," Marissa admitted as she started turning on lights. "Why don't you go take a shower and get changed and I'll order some pizza? Then we can talk."

Kate swallowed what Marissa thought might be a sob but nodded her head. "Thank you, Marissa."

"Always, Kate." Marissa held her breath until Kate had made it up the stairs. Closing her eyes, she swallowed down her own worries and pulled out her phone.

A woman's voice answered on the fourth ring. "Hello?"

"Hey, Meredith. It's Marissa." She opened her back door and let the shepherd outside, leaning against the door frame. "She's here."

"Oh, thank god." Meredith sounded as relieved as Marissa felt. "Is she okay?'

"She says she is. As far as I can tell, she seems at least physically alright."

"Okay." Meredith breathed. "Can she just stay with you for now? Just while I get to the bottom of what happened and see if I can find placement somewhere else?"

"Of course." Marissa looked out over the yard before she spoke again. "Focus on figuring out what happened. She can just stay here." She had meant to add *for as long as she needs*, but the words didn't follow. She was still being stalked; this wasn't safe.

"Thank you, Marissa. I'll be in touch."

Marissa hung up the phone and paused before she pushed Mac's contact. He answered on the third ring.

"Hey, Riss." The sound of his voice made her heart beat a little faster.

"Hey. I wanted to let you know you were right. Kate came back today."

"Is she okay?"

"Honestly?" Marissa looked up the stairs where the teenager had disappeared. "I'm not sure." She paused. "But I told Meredith she can stay."

There was silence on the other end of the line for a long moment before she heard Mac sigh.

"Good. We'll figure it out." He paused again. "I need to go, but I will call you tomorrow, okay?"

"Yeah, okay." Marissa nodded her head to no one.

"I miss you, Marissa."

"I miss you, too."

Once she hung up the phone, she pulled up the pizza app on her phone and made an order for delivery. With dinner situated, she headed up the stairs, duffle bag in tow. She opened her office door and slid it in before closing the door again. The bathroom door was open, steam emerging from the room, signaling that Kate was done in the shower. Marissa made her way to the end of the hall and knocked gently on the door.

"Hey, can I come in?"

"Of course," she heard Kate say from inside the room.

Marissa pushed the door open to see Kate using the towel to dry her hair, already in pajama pants and a tank top.

Marissa walked into the room, leaving the door open so Ellie could follow her in, and sat on the bed.

"So, do you want to talk about it?" She looked the teenager over carefully. Kate looked tired but otherwise in one piece.

Kate stopped drying her hair and looking at Marissa with wide blue eyes before she let out a quiet sigh and shook her head. "Not really."

"But you're okay? You aren't hurt or anything?"

Marissa wanted to pry. She wanted to know what had prompted the abrupt departure and what made her travel just over a hundred miles without so much as calling for help. She so wanted to pry, but she also didn't want to push.

Kate looked grateful, understanding that Marissa was holding back.

"Yeah, I'm okay," she said finally, "but I can't go back there."

"Okay. That's fine. You're here until we figure something out."

Kate sat down beside her and set her head on Marissa's shoulder. "I left Pico, though."

"Do you want me to go get him tomorrow?"

Kate shook her head and Marissa let out a breath of relief. "He fell in love with the foster boy they have. He's like seven. They bonded so quickly."

"Okay." Marissa may not have been a fan of the beagle, but if Kate had asked her, she would have retrieved the stupid dog. He was Kate's mom's dog.

"Well, pizza is on the way." She paused. "I'll have to make a run to the store to get some food and drinks and stuff."

"Where's Mac?" Kate asked.

"He's in Washington D.C." Marissa twitched her nose. "He left a couple of weeks after you. Work troubles."

"So not relationship troubles."

Kate's concern brought a smile to Marissa's face. "No, not relationship troubles. Relationship adjacent but not problems between us."

"Well that's good." She hesitated. "I'm sorry he's been gone for so long, though."

Marissa nodded. "Yeah, me too."

Marissa let out a soft sigh as she looked at the closed door to the room where Kate safely rested. They had eaten pizza, watched a little trash TV, and now Kate was safe in bed with Wicket sprawled across her legs. The cat was obviously also happy Kate was back. Knowing Kate was safe and warm had brought on a sense of calm Marissa didn't know she had needed.

Glancing at her closed office door, she paused. The duffle bag with Tom's case was sitting behind that door. Marissa had planned on coming home and flipping through it, but the arrival of Kate had thrown off her plans for the evening. She pulled her phone from her pocket and checked the time. It was a quarter to ten. Not too late. And she honestly wasn't feeling very tired anymore. The day had been draining, but the sight of Kate on her porch had brought on a second wind.

She let Ellie follow her into the office before closing the door and flipping on the dim light over the desk. She cleared the piles of work off in an almost organized-slash-chaotic sort of way. She placed the duffle bag on the desk and started pulling out its contents.

The first file was the original report. The first page was from the patrol officer who took the call. He had been sent out shortly before 7:00 a.m. to investigate a call about a dead body on the trail at Schmitz Preserve Park on June 8, 2010. She was thrown right off the trail, about eight feet from the base of the tree with debris tossed over her. The body was of a woman somewhere in her twenties based on first looks. Her body was face up, her arms flung to the side, tied together at the wrists with what appeared to be shoestring. She had long dark hair that had fallen wildly behind her head. She was only partially dressed. Her shirt was completely missing, and her pants were around her ankles. She had visible bruising around her neck and on the right side of her face, close to her eye. On the side of the files were sticky notes with Tom's handwriting. There was a note that said, *Talk to the first officer who arrived on scene again.* There was another note that said, *Go through missing persons to find a match to the victim.*

It was overcast and about 50 degrees when the investigator arrived. He interviewed the patrol officer, Officer Miller, and had him isolate the scene and start to check the perimeter with the backup officers who arrived to help. Marissa raised an eyebrow seeing Tom Disher's name listed as one of those officers. Making a mental note, she read on. There were no witnesses, except the dog walker who stumbled upon the body. She had been walking her client's dog when he moved off the side of the trail to use the bathroom, and she saw the victim's hands and a chunk of her hair peeking out from beneath the debris that had been sloppily thrown across her. There was a sticky note that said, *Reach out to interview the dog walker again.*

Marissa flipped through a couple of pages and stopped on the autopsy page. She was only listed as a Jane Doe, as of now, still unidentified. The cause of death had ultimately been strangulation, but she had also had a stab wound in her abdomen. Toxicology came back with traces of opiates, but they never delved into that any further. There was a sticky note that said, *Heroin? Addict?*

Flipping through more of the reports, she sighed. She was glancing at the reports but reading all the sticky notes Tom had attached. Marissa sat back and just stared at the files on her desk, swaying in her computer chair just slightly. She knew this was the cold case Tom would go back to from time to time. It may have been too late in the night to go through this after all. It had been a long day with a lot of emotions: her mom and her boyfriend, seeing Lydia, Kate coming back. Now the realization that Tom had kept this case that he had been present for and tried to solve, but died before he had solved anything, broke her heart.

Chapter 6

Marissa felt like an outsider in what had been her own home away from home for so many years. She and Ellie sat in the waiting area at the precinct, waiting for someone to come get her for the interview with Internal Affairs. Kate was back in Port Townsend, spending time with Veronica, one of the Port Townsend officers. An interview with Internal Affairs was not something Kate needed to be present for. Marissa had nothing to hide; she had done nothing wrong. It had been her own hard work that had solved the case, not favors. And yet, her nerves were already shot. Despite Ellie's best efforts, resting her head and front paws in Marissa's lap, she couldn't stop her knee from shaking.

"Detective Ambrose?"

A woman Marissa had never seen before appeared, a thick file in her hand and a smile that felt plastic on her face. She was maybe just a little older than Marissa with light caramel skin and dark eyes. Her dark hair was pulled back in a loose pony-tail, and she was dressed in a gray two-piece that made her stand out and look more professional than anyone else there.

Marissa got to her feet and offered a weak smile. "That's me," she said lamely, wishing she could have been anywhere but there.

"Come on. I'll show you to the conference room."

Marissa knew where the conference room was. This had been *her* station for years. But she bit her tongue and followed the woman.

"Please have a seat." The dark-haired woman smiled at her. "My name is Miriam Rodriguez. This is my partner, Sean Boswell."

She pointed to the man sitting across the table from her, who sat back in his chair with a smug expression plastered to his face. It was clear who was playing bad cop. She hated him immediately.

"We are here today to discuss your relationship with Agent James Mackenzie and the O'Rourke case." Miriam was clearly going to do most of the talking. "Why don't you tell us about how you two met?"

Marissa sighed, feeling like it was going to be a very long interview.

Marissa huffed, plopping herself heavily into the chair and not bothering to hide the feelings on her face.

Tom shook his head, sitting down across from her, looking amused. He was long and lanky, making the office chair appear small.

"Don't take it so personally." He shrugged his shoulder. "It's procedure."

"Well, it's a stupid fucking procedure."

The captain had informed them that the FBI would be joining their current investigation and that they were to cooperate in any way they could.

"I don't disagree. But honestly…" He let out a heavy sigh, scratching his beard, which was only about a week old, before he leaned forward on his desk and lowered his voice. "We could use the help. We've got nothing but dead ends. And we are up to three kids."

The kids in question were teenagers, two who had been abducted from a mall and another who disappeared on the way home from school. The connection had been through a person that two of the three kids had been chatting with on the newer social media platform, Snapchat. Someone pretending to be a senior with a picture out of a catalog. They had found the backpack and cell phone of the boy who had been walking home. They hadn't found any trace of the girls who were taken from the mall, but after a little digging, they had made their way into one of the girls' socials. Cameras from the mall had caught a blue van with no license plates leaving the scene.

It had been two days since the last abduction. A week since the first. The FBI had been called in for assistance.

It made sense. Marissa knew it made sense. Time was of the essence. And she had already made detective. She had nothing to prove.

"I know. I know you're right. I just don't feel like we've been given a chance..."

Tom gave her a smile.

"Give it time. This is one of those times we should be grateful for the calvary," he offered gently.

Tom Disher may not have been much older than Marissa, but he was old enough that his black hair was peppered with gray. He had big round hazel eyes with deep circles beneath them, the exhaustion from the previous week catching up with him. He wasn't a big or intimidating man, but athletic enough to get by with a soft face that usually wore a stern frown.

"They'll be here in the morning. We should go home and rest while we can, start fresh tomorrow with a few extra sets of eyes. There isn't much we can do right this moment."

Neither of them had been home since the second abduction.

Marissa glanced down at her phone, tapping the screen with her finger. It was already after nine.

"I think I might stick around for a little bit longer, just go through it one more time." She ignored the look Tom was giving her and retrieved one of the folders from his desk. "Give Lydia my love, okay?"

Tom sighed but nodded as he got to his feet, grabbing his bag and throwing it over his shoulder. "I will."

He walked around to her desk and gave her shoulder a squeeze. "Go home soon, okay?"

"I will. I promise," she lied with a reassuring smile.

He hesitated but finally turned and headed out of the precinct and to his wife. Marissa turned back to the files on her desk and tried to pick a place to start. She wasn't particularly in a hurry; it wasn't like she had anyone to go home to. She'd been divorced almost a full year. She had already memorized most of everything they had in the file, but she was sure she had to be missing something.

Marissa was startled awake by the sound of a door closing loudly. Jolting upright, she wiped her face with her hand as she tried to gain her bearings, taking a minute to realize she was still at the station. She had fallen asleep on her last look-through of the case files.

The clock on the wall told her it was just past 4:30 a.m. Rubbing the sleep from her eyes, she glanced around to see where the noise had come from. She could make out three figures standing in the captain's office. She took note of a few faces she didn't recognize while they set themselves up at empty desks.

One of the men noticed her gaze and turned to face her. He was tall with broad shoulders, thick dark hair, and dark brown puppy dog eyes. He flashed her a small smile that made her momentarily forget he was FBI, and she didn't want him there. Without returning the gesture, she started gathering her papers and organizing the chaos that was all over her desk. She was so focused on the papers, she didn't notice when he walked up to her.

"Good morning. I'm Agent Mackenzie with the FBI." She didn't bother to look up as he stood there, waiting for her response. When it was clear she wasn't interested in pleasantries, he continued, "I'm going to need you to give me everything you have on the recent abductions."

As she put the last of the papers in its corresponding manila folder, she looked up at the man standing before her. He was staring at her expectantly, hand out, clearly waiting for her to hand over her case. Something about his expression made her cheeks grow hot with anger all over again.

"You mean hand over all the hard work that I've done over the last week so you can swoop in for the credit when we catch this son of a bitch?" She hadn't intended to be hostile, but her tone dripped with disdain.

A look of surprise flashed across the agent's face before it was replaced with something unreadable. "Look, Detective—" He glanced at her name plate. "Detective Ambrose. We are all on the same side here. We just want to bring those kids home." He paused, softening his tone. "It's not a turf war. And I'm certainly not here to step on your toes."

Marissa caught herself staring into those brown eyes and forced herself to turn away, shaking her shoulders out.

"Forgive me. I'm just tired," she mumbled under her breath. She hadn't meant to come across like a bitch, but she still didn't like the idea of giving up her case. She stood and placed her folders into the hands of Agent Mackenzie. "This is everything we have."

She brushed past him without as much as another word and stormed off to the bathroom to splash cold water on her face.

This was supposed to be her first big case since making detective, and it was simply being handed over to the FBI. After all the work they had already put in. It was infuriating. Of course, it wasn't about ego. It was about those kids.

Sighing, she stared at her reflection. The dark circles under her eyes stood out. Normally, Marissa would have worked hard to cover those up. Her makeup would still look perfect, and her hair would have been brushed and styled. Now, it was down and unnaturally curly after being up in a messy bun for two days. The only makeup that remained on her face was remnants of her eyeliner, which made the circles under her eyes appear even darker.

It didn't matter. She wasn't there to look her best. She was there to bring those kids home. Splashing her face once more, she shook off the bitterness and the tiredness and left the bathroom.

The agent was still standing at her desk, her files in his hands, flipping through.

"Is there anything else I can do for you, Agent..." His name had already slipped her mind.

"Mackenzie," he said without looking up from what he was reading. "And no, I just want to familiarize myself with what you've got. The goal is to deliver the profile by 8 this morning."

She expected him to move or go to his own space, but he continued to just ... stand there.

Resisting the urge to loudly huff at him, she moved around him to sit back down in her seat.

"If there is nothing else—" she started, but he closed the file he was reading and looked at her expectantly.

"This is a good start, detective. We'll take it from here."

Instantly, she felt annoyed again. "Thanks."

Summarizing their first meeting was easy enough. Talking about how they worked together on the case was a little less so.

"He was arrogant and frustrating to work with. We did fall into a groove eventually, and he did notice things that we missed the first time around."

However, she was the one who'd found the connection between the kids and the murders on Queen Anne. From there, they had been able to narrow things and caught on to the operation O'Rourke was running.

"And when did your relationship change from professional to personal?"

"After the case was over and O'Rourke was arrested. He asked me to dinner, and we dated for almost a year."

"And what caused the breakup? Who did the breaking up?"

Marissa couldn't stop herself before she glared at Sean Boswell. She wasn't sure that their breakup was relevant. "I broke up with him to give it another go with my ex-husband."

"How did he take it?"

Marissa sighed, leaning back in her chair and folding her arms. "He took it like a gentleman. We stayed friends after."

The meeting included more intrusive questions regarding what their dating life was like before they moved on to what her record as a detective looked like.

When they got around to asking questions about Mac's record as an agent, there was a lot she couldn't answer. Which was probably the right way to respond. But it was a good reminder, Marissa thought, that she really didn't know a lot about him, not in the way most knew their significant other.

By the end of the interview, Marissa was drained. The fact that she still had to ferry back to get home just made her feel more tired.

Marissa froze at the sight of the envelope, this time thrown over her welcome mat just outside her door. A lump formed in her throat as she stared. Instinctively, she went to pick it up but stopped herself. What if she just stopped playing his game? What if she left it there and stopped taking the bait? She wanted to scream into the void that she was just fucking done. She wouldn't keep playing his games.

And then Kate opened the door.

"You're back!" Her excitement was put on hold as she saw Marissa's expression. "Are you okay?"

Marissa took in a few slow breaths before nodding and giving Kate a smile. "Yeah, it was just a long morning." She bent down and grabbed the envelope before following the teenager inside.

This was why she would keep playing his games. Because if she didn't, there were too many people she cared about for him to target.

Marissa waited until she was sure that Kate was in bed before she pulled the envelope back out from its hiding spot. She stared at it for a long time, silently cursing it and the fear it brought on. How something inanimate and plain could cause so much trouble was strange and a little surreal. Locking the doors for the night and double-checking all the windows, Marissa headed upstairs into the office. Once Ellie followed in behind her, she turned on the light and closed the door, plopping down in her chair. With a sigh, she unsealed the envelope and dumped its contents on the table. She didn't bother with gloves anymore. There weren't going to be any prints. There never were.

There appeared to be no letter, just photographs. Marissa let her eyes scan them before she spread them out. She saw mostly photos of herself but noticed a few of Mac from a few weeks earlier in Port Townsend and a single photograph of the brunette she didn't think she recognized.

Pulling the photograph from the top, she studied the girl. It wasn't Brenna Thompson, who she had assumed it might have been. The woman had shoulder-length light brown hair that had a slight wave to its body. In the picture, she was in a line, looking down at her phone. It almost seemed to Marissa like this photo wasn't supposed to be there.

Chapter 7

She stopped at the door and braced herself for whatever this visit was going to bring. Thinking back to their last meeting, a chill ran up her spine and a gnawing began in the pit of her stomach. She didn't know which Daniel Fryer she was going to find: the cold, calculated serial killer or the broken shell of a man who was giving up. She wasn't sure which was worse.

Opening the door, she gave him her forced half smile. It was the best she could muster before she sat down at the table. Ellie sat down beside her, the shepherd keeping her eyes trained on Daniel Fryer.

"Good to see you again, detective." He was leaning forward, elbows on the table. His face was considerably thinner than the last time they had met, but he looked more alert this time.

"You look like you're feeling better." Marissa adjusted in the hard chair, clasping her hands together and resting them in front of her.

He shrugged. "I'm not feeling worse, so there's that." He glanced around the room, his eyes stopping on the one-way glass. "I have to say: I'm enjoying these visits with just you and me. I know they're over there, watching and listening, but the feeling of it just being us is nice."

Marissa visibly shuddered and he laughed. "So where is your special agent today? I noticed he wasn't here last time either."

Marissa shook her head but remembered that she was here to play his game. "He's busy," she said finally with a slight huff.

"You gotta give me more than that." He cocked his head to the side.

"No I don't." She snorted at him. "Why should I?"

"Because there is clearly more to tell." He gave her an unsettling grin and sat back, just waiting.

Marissa looked at the one-way glass before dropping her shoulders. "He's in Washington D.C." She stared him down for a minute, waiting to see if that was enough. Daniel Fryer's cold, unimpressed, and unmoved stare told her it wasn't. "He's suspended."

"Oh! Now that's juicy." He adjusted in his seat, almost looking like a dog wagging its tail in excitement. "We're definitely going to circle back to that. But first ... your turn."

Marissa held back a sigh. These games were getting old. "I need names. We agreed to names."

For a moment, she thought he actually looked disappointed. He studied her face long enough to make her shift in the hard chair and look away from his gaze.

"Okay," he said finally. "Anna Ross. She went missing just outside Ellensburg. She was hitchhiking out of a truck stop." He drummed his fingers on the table, looking at her thoughtfully. "My turn. Tell me more about your agent's suspension."

Marissa had finished taking down her notes and looked back up at him, keeping her expression less than excited.

"I'm not really sure what I can tell you. I don't have all the details. I just know he landed on strike three."

Whatever strike one and two were. She tried to keep her face as neutral as possible, but he grinned in a way that said he saw right through her.

"Tell me more," he taunted.

"You first. Tell me more about Anna Ross."

Fryer cracked his neck and let out a sigh. "Alright." He stretched in his chair before leaning forward again. "College student. She's still listed as a missing person. She had gotten into a fight with her boyfriend. She told me all about it. He took her car keys, so she was hitchhiking to her parents' house back in Seattle." He paused. "Do you want the details of how I killed her too?"

Marissa rolled her neck, bringing one hand up to rub her face. She didn't want to know, but as she glanced over at the one-way mirror, she knew this was part of the deal.

"Yup. Everything you can tell me."

"Well first… what does strike three in the FBI look like?"

Pushing her hair behind her ear, she took a deep breath, her eyes down at the table. "It looks like hiding a relationship where there may be a conflict of interest."

"There it is." He grinned at her. "I called that the first time we met. Well, face to face anyway." He mused at her. "Tell me, what gave you away to the suits?"

"Photographs."

That made Daniel Fryer raise an eyebrow. "Do tell, detective."

Marissa shifted. "Photographs were sent to his supervisor…"

"Marissa, you are leaving out some crucial details here. Tell me about the photos."

She had to stop herself from hissing at him. "Two photographs of us together."

"Holding hands? Having a conversation?"

"Kissing."

"So you ARE playing house."

Marissa sucked in a breath. "It's really no one's god damned business—"

"Except he is working on a case that involves you." Daniel Fryer looked exceptionally proud of himself. She wanted nothing more than to slap the smug smile off his face.

"Hence the suspension. Can we move on now?"

"Don't think we won't be circling back. This is an intriguing development." He snickered at her before shaking his head. "Anna Ross. Beat her to death with a hammer that was in the back of my car. Buried her near the border just outside of Spokane in the middle of the night."

Marissa shuddered and couldn't stop the question from coming out, dripping with horror and disgust. "But why?"

"Why not?" He grinned at her, and she found herself pushing the chair back slightly. "Honestly, there was no plan in place. When I picked her up from the truck stop, I didn't plan on killing her. But it had been a long time, and when she wanted to get out of the car, that was when I decided. The hammer was just in the back seat."

"When was this?"

"My turn first." He leaned forward with his elbows on the tables, suddenly making Marissa glad he was cuffed to the table.

"What Ben must think of this development." He looked like he was musing to himself before he turned his eyes back on her. "To think, you got rid of your ex-husband so he wouldn't be a target, and now you've put a target on poor Agent Mackenzie's back."

"Is there a question there somewhere?"

"I'm just curious... does the fact that he's FBI make him capable of being able to stay alive, or now that there are photos, do you plan on dumping him too?"

"I'm so fucking tired of this," Marissa said in a low voice. She knew they could still hear her outside the room, but they could work for it.

"For what it's worth, detective, I think you make a lovely match. And I'm sure you have Ben absolutely infuriated." He leaned back and drummed his fingers on the table, bringing his voice back up. "It was September 2002."

Marissa nodded and started jotting down her notes again. When she looked back up, she straightened, realizing how closely he was watching her.

"What's your plan, Marissa? If you aren't playing his game anymore, you can expect things to escalate. So what's your plan?"

She stared at him for a long moment before she answered, more honestly than she had planned on. "I don't know." Marissa leaned down and lowered her voice. "The last time I was here, you said you would try and help. So help."

"Finally."

Amusement suddenly glistened in his eyes. Daniel Fryer set his elbows on the table and leaned forward to meet her halfway, close enough to make the hair on the back of her neck stand on edge. "You need to be ready. He's not slowing down."

"No shit." Her voice was louder than she meant, and her eyes swept over to the glass. "Give me something to work with. That does not count as an answer."

She paused.

"He sent me a letter, the day he sent the photos to the FBI," she started slowly, lowering her voice further. "He said he was disappointed. That I should know better. What do I actually know about Mac in the first place."

As he stared at her, she could see the calculating going on behind his eyes. She wasn't sure she could trust anything that came out of his mouth. He rubbed his chin, frowning slightly.

"Let's break that down. The most honest thing he's probably ever said: he's disappointed. That is just him stating a fact. The rest of it though..." He glanced toward the door like he expected someone to come through any moment. "He's playing mind games with you, probably while he decides the next move. But you can bet it's not going to be good—"

"Time's up, detective." Agent Walker's voice came through the intercom.

Marissa straightened and huffed in exasperation. "I guess that's it," she said to the killer who sat across from her. Picking up her notepad, she waved it at him. "Thanks for this."

She turned to head out the door when Daniel Fryer's voice stopped her.

"Marissa. Be careful."

She blinked and stared at him for a long moment, the feeling of unease traveling through her as she made her way to the door.

Once she was on the other side, she exhaled. Ellie whined and pushed her nose into Marissa's thigh. Reaching down, she gave the dog a reassuring pat and turned to face the men who were clearly waiting for her.

All three of them were frowning, but ADA Gorden had a file in his hands, his expression grim. He handed it over, and Marissa saw it was Anna Ross's file. Missing since September 17, 2002. Her picture showed a happy young twenty-something blonde with a bright smile on her face, hugging a cat. Last seen in Ellensburg by her boyfriend of two years. Wearing blue jean shorts and a white short-sleeved shirt with a giant smiling sun on it.

"Jesus," Marissa mumbled before looking back up at them.

"It seems like the information he's giving you is legit." Agent Nick Walker was looking past her, at the door she had just come through. "However, you didn't exactly stay on task."

"You remember I'm actively being stalked, right? And none of you have been able to do anything to help me. If he can give me any insight, I don't understand why you keep blocking me."

She was out of patience. Clyde Bennet whistled softly under his breath and the ADA turned around and walked away, too busy or important to be bothered. Nick Walker, however, met Marissa's eyes.

He was quiet for a long moment before he nodded his head. "Technically, the case is out of our hands but—" He held his hand, stopping her as she was about to protest. "I won't stop you as long as you keep getting names and details. The more families we can bring closure to, the better." He sighed, looking past her, around the office. "Believe it or not, I'm on your side."

Marissa narrowed her eyes at him, but he continued.

"I know it probably doesn't feel like it, with everything going on with James right now, but there's a protocol and a way things have to be done. No matter what I think, rules are rules for a reason." He paused again before taking a step forward and meeting her eyes. "But like everything else, I think there is something to what he says. Be careful."

A little while later, while sitting in the car, she stared at her steering wheel and replayed the conversation over. The numerous *be carefuls* had left an uneasy feeling in the pit of her stomach.

The way Daniel Fryer talked so casually about ending someone's life made her nauseous. It was a good reminder of the cold-blooded killer he was. But it made their last encounter even more unsettling.

Chapter 8

Marissa couldn't sleep. She grumbled, stretching out her arm and fumbling around on the coffee table for her phone. When she finally found it, she turned the screen on to see the clock read 6:07 a.m. It was too early to be awake, but the chances of her going back to sleep were slim to none.

She couldn't stop thinking about Daniel Fryer. About the amusement in his eyes as he made her tell him things he already seemed to know. It had made for an uncomfortable night tossing and turning. Reluctantly, she swung her feet off the couch and slowly sat up, groaning as aches riddled her body. Ellie lifted her head and watched Marissa for a second before stretching her way off the couch, giving a slow wag of her tail as she came over and kissed Marissa's face.

Marissa rubbed behind the shepherd's ear and sighed. "You wanna go outside?"

Ellie gave her the typical shepherd head tilt before getting up and trotting into the kitchen.

"I'm coming," she told the dog, getting to her feet and stretching her arms out as best she could.

Everything hurt. Sleeping on the couch wasn't doing her a lot of good. And seeing Daniel Fryer's eyes every time she closed her eyes made it a lot worse.

She opened the back sliding door to let Ellie out, who took off at a sprint the second she passed the threshold. Marissa watched her run along the perimeter before she pulled the sliding door closed again and headed for her coffee pot. Today was going to require more than tea.

She scrolled through her phone and sighed. She needed something to focus on. Anything else to focus on other Daniel Fryer. She headed to the back door and let Ellie inside and grabbed her a scoop of food. Now that Kate was back in the house, Marissa had taken Wicket's bowls upstairs since the cat had essentially abandoned Marissa for the teenager.

Marissa stood in her doorway and stared at the state of her office. It was a fucking mess. Her white board, which had her own case scrawled all over it, was covered in different colored markers and situated directly in the middle of the room. She stepped in and moved it back against the wall, right next to her desk. All of her notes from the Hannah

Hennessy case were sprawled all over her desk. She gathered them and placed them in an empty folder and filed it away into a box. She always kept her own notes from all of her cases. She opened the closet to reveal boxes, most labeled by year, and put her new box on top of the smallest pile. She was going to need a better solution eventually for her cases. Marissa found herself wondering if she would continue adding to those cases or if she would call it quits when this was all over. If she lived through it. Allison's box caught her eye, sitting near the window. She left that one where it was.

Once the room was usable, she opened Lydia's duffle bag again, plopped herself on the floor, and started pulling files out. She may have cleared the desk, but she needed more room for this. She started making piles: A pile for the initial investigation, everything that came out of those couple of days. A pile for the autopsy and anything related to Jane Doe specifically. A pile for the first re-investigation. And a final pile for all of Tom's notes and observations. She sat in the middle of her floor, trying to find a starting place. Most people would start from the beginning. Instead, Marissa reached for the pile with Tom's notes and findings.

The first few pages were notes he had taken when he reinterviewed the dog walker in 2015. Her name was Kayla Wells. Ms. Wells was only twenty-three at the time she stumbled upon the body, working for a dog-walking company. Most of her story seemed to stay consistent with her first interview.

She was on her second walk of the hot August day. She was taking the same route she always took with one of her favorites. On the side of the paper in smaller writing, Tom had noted *Onion, brown mixed breed*. Marissa smiled. Tom had loved dogs. Unfortunately, his wife was less of a dog person. He would have loved Ellie.

Marissa stretched out her hand and gave Ellie a few pats on the head, and the shepherd placed her head between her front feet beside Marissa.

Schmitz Preserve Park didn't have trail signs, so Kayla, the witness, couldn't tell Tom the exact location of her memory, but Onion, who was normally well mannered on walks, had started tugging and pulling. It was unheard-of behavior for him, and he'd almost knocked her over. He had started whining and giving off mini howls at the body. She admitted she screamed when she saw it, gathered up the dog, and moved several yards back before she called the police. She wouldn't have noticed the body at all if Onion hadn't started losing his mind over it after a much-needed pee. The body was partially covered by leaves and underbrush from the park's floors, but Kayla saw most of the girl's face, shoulder, and hand sticking out. There was a note in bold red ink that said, *Does not match the original report. Says she only saw the girl's hand sticking out from the underbrush.*

It probably didn't make much of a difference, but she could hear Tom's voice in her head: *"Even the smallest details matter."*

The park had been empty that morning, and the witness had only seen one other person on the trails, a jogger, but she couldn't remember any details about him.

Marissa grumbled and audibly huffed, putting the interview on the bottom of the pile as she looked over the next set of notes.

She pushed Tom's pile a little bit farther away from her, needing the space to signify her desire to move to something else. She grabbed the autopsy pile and pulled the stack of papers close. She looked at the paper on the top of the pile from the medical examiner and read over it once again. Manner of death was ruled homicide. The cause of death was strangulation. Decomp had already begun, fluids leaking and bloating in full effect. Since it was summertime, it was likely the August heat had sped up the process. The medical examiner, based on the autopsy, said Jane Doe had been dead anywhere between two and five days. Marissa skimmed over most of the medical terminology. Going over autopsies always made Marissa's head hurt. It was part of why she appreciated Port Townsend's medical examiner, Kennedy Foster, who could dumb it down to her level. Marissa was smart and more than capable at her job, but there was a reason she hadn't gone into the medical field. The report may as well have been written in a foreign language.

What Marissa did understand were the sticky notes attached to the medical examiner's report, scribbled in Tom's handwriting. One note said: *Even if drugs played a part in her death, they didn't cause the bruising on her neck or fractures in her neck bones.* Another note toward the bottom of the page said: *Bruising around her mouth implies she was forcefully made quiet or mouth held closed to force pill down her throat.*

Tom had been really focused on the drugs in her system not being there voluntarily. She wasn't sure if he was just fighting against all the pushback or if he was following a hunch, but either way, he'd felt strongly about it.

Flipping to the next page, she read the description they had originally written up on their victim. Approximately between the ages of 22 and 28, she had been tall at 5'8". She had long black hair and blue eyes. She had a scar on her left knee from a broken bone that had received surgery and had completely healed, probably from her teenage years. She had a single tattoo on her right ankle of an anchor and a butterfly, intricate lines connecting the two. It was a unique and beautiful tattoo. She hadn't had it very long based on what Marissa was looking at in the up-close picture. The lines still looked fresh and dark, even after its exposure to the elements. Marissa put her stack of papers down in her lap and leaned forward, grabbing Tom's notes again. She scanned through it all, doublechecking that they hadn't mentioned anything about the tattoo. It was over a decade ago, so the chances of following that lead were slim to none. Back then, they could have reached out and tried to find anyone who had done that very same tattoo, but from what she could see, it either wasn't worth mentioning in the paperwork or it just didn't happen.

The clothes she had been found with had not been in the best shape: torn pants, ripped underwear. The shirt was never found. She hadn't had any forms of identification on her when they found her. No one reported anyone matching her description missing, and no one came forward recognizing her. Every page Marissa flipped through seemed to just lead to more dead ends.

There had been skin fragments underneath her fingernails, but the DNA searches hadn't come up with anything. It did signify that she fought her attacker as best she could, though.

Marissa flipped through the pages. The suspect had left nothing with the exception of particles under her fingernails. There was no semen, no blood. Nothing. Chances were the murder had taken place somewhere else, and he had used the park as his dumping ground. Picking herself off the ground, she took two large steps over the piles of paperwork and plopped into her computer chair, swaying from side to side as her monitor turned on. There was a soft knock at the door as the door creaked open a crack.

"Hey, Marissa?'

"Hey, Kate. I didn't wake you or anything, right?" She wasn't used to having people around the house anymore.

Kate shook her head with a smile. "No. I actually wanted to see if you were hungry or wanted anything?"

They had done a little bit of food shopping after Kate's arrival. Mostly easy things to make. She glanced over at her untouched coffee and shook her head. "No, but thank you." She glanced down at the piles that covered the floor. "I promise I won't be in here much longer. We can do whatever you'd like today."

"That sounds great."

Once Kate disappeared behind the closed door again, Marissa sighed, glancing at the clock. It was already 11 a.m. Frowning, she looked back at the piles on the floor.

She momentarily forgot what she had come to the computer to do and simply stared at the screen blankly for a few moments.

After several moments passed, it finally came to her. Going to Google, she typed in "Schmitz Preserve Park deaths." The first page was full of articles about bodies having been found after overdoses. Lots of overdoses. She didn't find anything about their Jane Doe until she clicked the second page, but even then it was just a blurb: *Girl found dead in Schmitz Preserve Park.* That was it.

This search wasn't getting her anywhere either. She huffed and twirled her chair to stare at the piles on the floor. She wished she could talk to Tom.

She made a face. Maybe she could talk to someone who worked with Tom. Maybe someone he had shared the case with. She leaned down and grabbed the top page again, looking to see who was working at the time. She didn't recognize many of the names, but it occurred to her that maybe Tom's old partner might know something—his first partner as a detective and the one he had been worked with the longest. If Tom was working on the case on his own time, his former partner might know.

Then again, if that had been the case, why hadn't Marissa ever heard of this one? He had never mentioned it or shown it to her. Since their first day on the job together, it was true that they had stayed busy, but she was certain he had looked over these files in the five years they had worked together. After a quick search in the system, she found Tom's partner's information and shot him a quick email.

Hello Mr. Wilkenson,

> *My name is Marissa Ambrose. We met once at Tom Disher's funeral. I was his partner. I am looking through an older case of Tom's, and I was*

wondering if you would be available and willing to meet with me. I have a couple of questions.

Thank you for your time.
Marissa Ambrose

She felt a stab of sadness, followed immediately by guilt. Something Dr. Bailey had told her recently ran across her mind. Even if she had gone into the warehouse first, if she had gotten ahead of him, she would have been the one killed instantly. But the likelihood that they would have kept him alive was nearly zero. Maybe they would have tortured him, but it wasn't very likely he would have made it out of there alive. If they had waited for backup, the men would have escaped, and they would probably have dozens of additional dead bodies to deal with. The truth was that no matter what anyone said, right or not, she was never not going to feel guilty about that day. Even if she took and reworked every scenario. She was here, and he wasn't. He had left behind a wife, a baby girl, and this case he'd never solved.

She looked at her piles and sighed. She wasn't getting anywhere right now. Staring at it wouldn't get her anywhere. Pushing herself up from the chair, she stepped over the carefully made piles and opened the door. Ellie got up from where she had been lying under the window and followed Marissa out of the room. Marissa closed the door behind them and glanced down the stairs, where she could hear the TV.

"Hey, Kate. I'm gonna hop in the shower and then we can go out. Maybe like brunch or something."

"Sounds good!"

She smiled at Kate's enthusiasm. It was good to have her back.

Marissa peeled off her clothes and tossed them on the floor, not bothering to turn on the light. The natural light from her bedroom was more than enough to shower in. She turned the water on and leaned against the glass door, waiting for the water temperature to rise, exhaling. She felt disconnected at that moment. Everything was so out of sorts. She focused on her breathing. She needed to get out of her own head. Lunch with Kate would help.

Chapter 9

Marissa shifted, adjusting the pillow under her head. She had fallen asleep on the couch before she had set up the pullout mattress again. Shifting again, she tried to find a comfortable position for her hips as she groggily opened her eyes to glance around. Kate had clearly thrown a blanket over her before heading up to bed. The TV was off, and there was a dim light coming in from the windows as morning was beginning to make its appearance. Ellie, situated on top of Marissa's legs, shifted with her. Closing her eyes again, Marissa convinced herself it was already too late to fix the couch into a bed, and it was certainly too far of a walk to go up the stairs.

Just as she drifted back off to sleep, Ellie raised her head and whined. Marissa opened one eye to look down at the shepherd, who was staring intently at the front door. Before Marissa could react to the odd behavior, Ellie jumped down and hurried over to the front door, beginning to whine. Marissa forced herself to sit up, a cold sensation dropping into the pit of her stomach. She started rocking to gather the momentum to get to her feet when the front door opened. Ellie's tail began to wag wildly as her whining grew louder.

Mac stepped into the entryway, placing his bag on the floor as he greeted the shepherd, trying to quiet her.

"Easy girl." Looking over, the smile that spread across his face when he saw her made her heart flutter. "I'm sorry. I didn't want to wake anyone up."

Marissa opened her mouth but no sound came out. She wasn't certain she wasn't dreaming. By the time she managed to push off from the couch to get to her feet, he was standing in front of her.

"God, I missed you," he whispered before cupping her cheek and pulling her into a kiss that left her breathless.

"You're back," she managed, hardly believing it.

"I'm back." He held her face in his hand, looking her over. "Are you okay? Why are you sleeping down here?"

Marissa swallowed. She had no plans to tell him she had been sleeping on the couch since he left.

"I'm better than okay now," she admitted with a smile, ignoring the question about the couch. "I missed you so much." Her voice was still soft.

"I missed you, too." He leaned back down to pull her into another kiss, this one just as breathtaking as the first.

"Mac! You're back!"

Kate suddenly appeared on the stairs, startling Marissa, who took a step away from Mac and bit back a laugh.

"Hey, kid. So are you," Mac said with a huge smile, breaking away from Marissa to give Kate a hug as she hurried into the living room. "What are you doing up? It's early."

"I heard Ellie." Kate was proving to be a very light sleeper. "I'm so glad you're back."

The sight of them both there in Marissa's living room brought a sense of ease. It was like the last month and a half hadn't happened, and it was back to the way it was supposed to be.

"Are you back for a while, or do you have to go back to D.C.?" What Marissa really wanted to ask was if he was back for good.

"I am back for the foreseeable future." He smiled at her before he took a look around the room. "Since we're all up, why don't I make us breakfast!"

Kate's face lit up. "That would be great."

"So... if you want to make breakfast, a trip to the store is gonna be necessary," Marissa added.

Mac paused, frowning at her but nodded with a quick smile. "We can do that."

The rest of the morning was as close to perfect as it could get. After breakfast, Kate settled down on the couch with her sketchpad. Marissa watched her for a minute, leaning against her stairs and thinking about the sense of relief she felt this morning. Kate had opened the curtains, letting in the little bit of sun that had risen.

Mac came around the corner from the kitchen and put his arm around her waist.

"Hey," he said softly in her ear.

She craned her neck to smile up at him. "Hey."

"I was going to call you last night before I got on the plane but decided to surprise you. I hope that's okay."

"Of course it's okay. I'm just glad you're back." She leaned into him. "You really don't have to go back?"

"No." He shook his head. "I've got a hearing set for the end of June, but that will take place here. I'm not going anywhere."

That was still four weeks away.

"How did you make that happen?"

He shrugged his shoulder. "This is where I'm supposed to be." He kissed the top of her head. "Are we going to talk about the empty fridge?"

She looked back up to see him raise an eyebrow at her. Marissa gave him a sheepish shrug and shook her head. "Nah, I don't think we need to."

He frowned but hugged her tighter. "Come on. I need to get out of these plane clothes."

Mac grabbed his bag with one hand and her hand with the other, and they headed up stairs. Mac stepped into the bedroom and paused, eyebrow once again raised.

"Have you been sleeping downstairs this whole time?" He was staring at the only slightly rumpled bed before looking back at her. He really had gotten to know her well.

"No. Maybe." She sighed. "It's empty when you're not here. Before you, it was fine. But it's not the same anymore. And I just feel alone."

Mac put his arms around her waist and pulled her close. "I'm not going anywhere."

She knew he meant well. Hell, he probably meant the words he spoke. But if the last several weeks had shown her anything, it was that things could change in an instant.

"I mean it, " he said gently, as though he could hear her thoughts. But rather than saying anything else, he pressed his lips against her. "I'm not going anywhere," he murmured as he pulled back.

Marissa stared up at him, wanting nothing more than to believe him, but she couldn't let herself. Mac shifted back on the bed with his back on the pillows and motioned for her to follow. He wrapped his arms around her as she moved next to him. "So. Talk to me. What's been going on the last few weeks?"

She shrugged her shoulder against him, looking forward. "Lydia brought me a case file from Tom's things. It's a Jane Doe homicide from 2010. No suspect. He was actually one of the first responding officers at the scene before he made detective." She sighed. "It looks like he kept going back to it."

Mac nodded his head against her. "Makes sense. Most of us have cases we can't let go."

"I reached out to his former partner to see if I can get more information. I'm hoping to meet with him to go over it a little bit. The files are pretty thorough; you can tell they've been gone through over and over."

She pushed the hair back from her face, as Ellie jumped up onto the foot of the bed.

"Tom never took work home, but he had two boxes' worth on this case. Lydia didn't know what to do with it. So I told her I would look into it. It's not like I'm doing anything else..." She trailed off.

"And you feel some sort of misguided responsibility to finish what he started," Mac finished for her.

She looked up at him grimly, but he just gave her an understanding smile. "I get it," he said gently. "I'm still on suspension, but I'd be happy to help in any way I can."

"What about you? What happened in D.C.?"

Now it was Mac's turn to sigh. "A lot of interviews. Paperwork. Doing an insane history run through. I also had to meet with a psychologist." He shrugged a shoulder. "I passed that. Now they're going through all my history and my interviews and are coming to a decision. At the hearing, I get to make a statement in defense of myself and then they decide."

"I'm so sorry," she said softly.

He looked down, and with his free hand, he lifted her chin to get her to look at him. "What are you sorry for?"

"It's my fault you're in trouble."

He turned his body slightly to face her, his hand still holding her chin in place. "No. Don't do that." He shook his head. "Should we have reported our relationship? Probably. But you have nothing, and I mean absolutely *nothing*, to apologize for."

"It's my fault we were photographed in the first place."

"This is nothing you had control over. The only thing we could have done differently was report the relationship. And chances are, we would still be in the same position." He ran his thumb over her cheek, searching her eyes. "I have no regrets."

Marissa had to close her eyes, the intensity of his gaze making her feel vulnerable. "I just don't want to be the reason you lose your job." She opened her eyes again, meeting his eyes. "I have no regrets about us," she reassured him, melting slightly under his gaze.

He leaned down to kiss her before adjusting with his back against the wall again, arm still around her shoulders. "So tell me more about your mom's secret boyfriend."

She had only been able to give him the CliffsNotes over the phone the night she had found out.

"Oh my gosh. Nine years... they've been dating on and off for *nine years*. He's a defense lawyer. He seems like a really nice guy. And I'm not sure I've ever seen my mom so happy before."

"Well, that's a good thing then," he said, with only a little hesitance in his voice.

"It is. I just wish she would tell my sisters already." She sighed heavily and leaned her head against his shoulder. "It still weirds me out; he's only thirty-nine. He's two years older than me. That's weird." She frowned and shook her head before resting it back on his shoulder. "He's got a pretty good record as a lawyer though. He worked for the DA's office for a hot minute before making the jump to defense. He's got a solid record of wins."

"Aside from the age difference, and the fact that it's been going on for nine years, it seems like a good thing."

Marissa nodded. "I think so, yeah." She closed her eyes for a moment, fatigue lingering over her. "I saw Daniel Fryer the other day. It was almost as unsettling as it was a couple of weeks ago. But in a different way."

"How so?"

"Well, I told you about him asking for the death penalty, right?" Mac nodded, so she continued. "He was so shut down. And then this time, he was back to his normal self. A question for a question, answer for an answer." She paused. "He got a lot of personal information I would have liked to keep to myself. But I did get another victim out of him." She swallowed. "He told me to be careful. So did Nick Walker."

"Obvious, but good advice."

Marissa shuddered. "I hate interviews with him."

"You know you don't have to do it, right? You are under zero obligation considering everything he put you through. I feel like, on a professional level, it's unethical. And on a personal level, it's just cruel."

He had been against her one-on-ones with Daniel Fryer since day one.

Marissa sighed again. She didn't necessarily disagree with him. She still couldn't speak about everything she had gone through out loud, not even with her therapist. And yet...

"He won't talk to anyone else. I feel like, if I'm ever going to get answers about everything that happened, about Ben, it's something I have to do. And I need answers."

Mac sighed reluctantly. "I get it. I do. I just worry about you."

Marissa couldn't argue that. She would be lying if she had said she wasn't anxious every time she stepped through that interrogation room door. Before she could stop herself, she yawned and relaxed into him.

"Here." Mac adjusted them both lower on the pillow and pulled her closer so that her head was resting on his chest.

"I've missed you so much," she breathed, closing her eyes. The feeling of safety and warmth was back, and she could feel herself relax, really relax, for the first time since he had left. She listened to the evenness of his breathing while he stroked her hair, and everything else that had been plaguing her, weighing her down, simply started to dissipate.

Chapter 10

William Hendrickson had agreed to meet with Marissa on a Sunday afternoon at a Starbucks in Seattle near the ferry. When she arrived, he was sitting outside, soaking in the bit of sun that slipped out from behind the clouds. Although both Mac and Kate had offered to go with her, she had insisted they stay home. Mac was exhausted, still jet-lagged and feeling the stress of his suspension and upcoming hearing, and she didn't see the point in subjecting Kate to case details.

"Thank you so much for meeting with me, Mr. Hendrickson."

"Please, call me Bill." The older man smiled at her. He was exactly what she pictured when she imagined Tom's old partner. He'd talked about Bill a lot. Bill was an older black man with a bushy mustache and lines around his amber eyes. He couldn't have been more than in his late fifties, maybe early sixties, with hair peppered with white and a tiredness in his eyes that Marissa was growing accustomed to seeing.

She had met him once at Tom's funeral. But they hadn't spoken much other than to exchange condolences.

He smiled at her and stood, pulling out her chair for her.

"Thank you, Bill." She smiled at him as Ellie sat at her feet, looking up at the man expectantly.

"And who is this pretty girl?"

The shepherd tilted her head, knowing she was being talked about. "Her name is Ellie."

"Well, Miss Ellie, you're beautiful." He smiled at her, respecting the working vest and resisting the obvious urge to pet her. "I'm a dog lover myself. I have a black lab named Raider at home."

He turned his eyes from Ellie to Marissa. "You said on the phone that there was a specific case you had questions about?"

"It's a Jane Doe case, found in Schmitz Preserve Park in 2010. Does that sound familiar?"

A look of recognition flashed over his eyes, and he nodded his head. "It does. We looked over that case together maybe a dozen times. His white whale case—the one he couldn't let go."

"His wife found two boxes' worth of files on this case in his things. She handed them over to me, and

I've been trying to make heads or tails of it." She paused. "I was wondering if you had any insight that might not be included in the notes?"

"Two boxes' worth?" He raised his eyebrow, looking her over as she confirmed. After a moment, he nodded his head. "Did you bring them with you?"

"I did. In my car."

"Let's get to it then. We should probably get some coffee."

Marissa smiled and nodded, getting back to her feet.

He shuffled through the files carefully, making sure to keep them exactly how they were before he put them down, placing them on the table instead of back in the bag. They were still separated the way Marissa had set them up in individual piles with her own sticky notes over the front of the folders. Marissa watched him quietly with great interest, seeing how his body language and his facial expression changed several times. She noted maybe three times when he found something among the files that caught him by surprise.

She waited patiently and quietly, trying not to just stare as he went through it, drinking her coffee. Ellie shifted below at her feet, looking up with her big dark eyes. Reaching down, Marissa scratched behind her ear, and the shepherd leaned in to get as much as she could.

"If nothing else, Tom was really thorough," Bill Hendrickson said finally. "Most of it is all the same." He sighed, taking his reading glasses off his face. "That being said, the second interview with the dog walker and the further look into her toxicology is new. It also looks like there were more possible matches to the Jane Doe. But it looks like that was just another dead end." He rubbed the bottom of his chin. "It never made sense to me, a pretty young white girl no one was looking for. The detective on the case chalked it up to her being an addict and had burned all her bridges."

Marissa shifted in her seat a bit. "Based on his notes, Tom didn't agree."

"He didn't. He was convinced that the drugs in her system were used to subdue her or to throw the scent off. Part of the murder." He sighed heavily. "Unfortunately, because we were running across so many overdoses in the city, there was a stigma that followed it. And as soon as drugs were found in her system, they pretty much put the brakes on."

Marissa had to bite her tongue and resist the bubbling anger. The prejudice toward addicts was still an issue, especially in Seattle. The rate of overdoses had only been climbing, and the attitudes of some police were lacking empathy.

"I'll never forget the day Tom got in an officer's face who asked why he was wasting his time on an addict. His whole face turned beet red, and he said, and I quote, 'No matter who she was, what she was, she deserves to have her name back.'" Bill grinned.

It sounded like Tom. Marissa blinked back the tears, thinking of her former partner, and nodded. "I can picture him saying that."

"Tom always said that if nothing else, it was about giving her her name back. But he believed that once he could ID her, that the pieces would just fall into place."

"It says the last time he ran DNA was 2016?"

"Yeah. The technology hadn't made it there yet. Her fingerprints didn't land a match, and she wasn't in the system."

"My plan is to try and reach out to the DNA Doe project."

Bill nodded. "I don't think they were in existence the last time we ran her DNA through the database."

Marissa nodded and they both sat in silence, sipping at their drinks. The DNA Doe Project focused on giving people their names back through DNA and genealogy. Technology had come a long way in the last few years. They had even caught the Golden State Killer. Marissa's eyes scanned the coffee shop. It was fairly well populated, strangers staggered around at tables, some by themselves, some on their phones, some groups or couples deep in conversation.

"So tell me. How are you doing since the whole ordeal? Are you back to work?"

Marissa shrugged. "I'm … surviving." That was the truth. Maybe not doing particularly well but definitely surviving. "I was back to work and now I'm back in limbo again. Not for any medical or personal reasons. Just on hold while an old case is being looked at."

He nodded. "The O'Rourke case. That was a huge bust." He paused, studying her face. "It'll be fine. This happens more often than you think." Another pause. "You're a good cop. You have good instincts. Don't let anyone tell you otherwise."

Marissa couldn't help but smile. "Tom used to say that all the time."

Bill laughed. "Because I said it to him almost daily when we worked together. He had this uncanny sixth sense, but then would doubt himself for a minute. Sometimes longer." He paused again, taking a sip of his tea. "I can see why you two were partnered up. You would have been a good match."

Silence hung around them, and then both took drinks from their cups before Bill spoke again. "I can't say I've ever experienced quite what you've gone through, but we've all gone through something during our time on the force. Don't let it weigh you down. Use it. Learn from it. Let it make you a better cop."

Marissa felt herself relax more than she had thought possible. She always had her guard up. She had to. But something about William Hendrickson reminded Marissa so much of Tom, she felt at ease.

Thankfully, the conversation fell back to Jane Doe. Unfortunately, Bill didn't have much more to offer that wasn't already done in writing. Tom had always been the note-taker of the two, with both Hendrickson and herself, and this case was no different. Bill couldn't tell her anything that wasn't already written up in the reports or on the sticky notes. It had been a dead end, though not necessarily a waste of time, because talking about Tom with someone who didn't immediately make her feel guilty was something she hadn't known she needed. Whenever Marissa heard Lydia's voice, all she could remember was the sound of her crying over her husband's casket as it was being lowered into the ground. Lydia may not have blamed Marissa, but that didn't make Marissa feel less guilty. Bill Hendrickson, on the other hand, simply reminded her that Tom knew the risks every time he went to work, and that no one could have talked him out of running into the warehouse without backup.

The whole drive back, Marissa couldn't stop thinking about what Bill had said. She decided, rather than waiting for the ferry, she would just make the long drive home. She needed time alone to think. There were things that were nagging her about this cold case and her own case that were constantly scratching at the back door of her mind.

Tom's case. His entire goal was to give the girl her name back. It wasn't about finding or catching a killer; it was changing her status from victim to someone. Because she had to have come from somewhere, from a family. And they deserved closure.

Since the files had landed in Marissa's hands, she had been looking at everything, trying to find all the answers. Narrowing it down made a lot of sense. Taking it one step at a time. And with all the time that had gone by, giving her back her name made sense as a priority. More than that, maybe Tom was right. Maybe once they had her identified, maybe the pieces would fall into place.

And all of that brought Marissa back to her own case. None of the pieces were falling into place. She felt like the answers were right there, but she couldn't make anything fit. There were so many names on her board, and she couldn't tell if she was any closer to narrowing it down.

What she did know was that, two years ago, she had lost complete control of her life. Control had been taken from her in that warehouse, and while she lived through the ordeal, she had only been surviving ever since. Treading water, barely holding her head over the currents that were trying to pull her down, getting nowhere. The person she was before that day had died in that warehouse. The person who was revived twice at the hospital, the one who went through rehab and intense therapy, the one whose body betrayed her on a daily basis—that was someone else. Someone who required so much just to get through the day, who should have been afraid but only found herself feeling numb to the always-present danger. Sometimes, she thought it would have been better if she had just died that day, although she would never say it out loud. It certainly would have been easier.

Now Bill Hendrickson's words echoed in her ears. *Let it make you a better cop.* She regretted not asking for more clarification. Because how did someone take a near-death experience and let it make them better? If anything, it had slowed her down. Before, she had been in peak physical shape. After? Her body sometimes gave up on her and literally kept her in bed for days at a time. Before, she was focused and driven. She had been one of the youngest in her unit to make detective in a nearly all boys club. There had been only one other female detective on her squad. Now, she spent most of her time on the bench, useful to no one. Sure, she was working a cold case, but statistically speaking, under fifty percent of cold cases were solved. And depending on where in the states, that percentage could be closer to thirty. It wasn't necessarily promising.

She knew Bill had meant well, that his intentions were good. But his advice reminded her of the look of sympathy people wore at a funeral: they could empathize and understand the basic concept of grief but could never understand the full connection between someone and their loss. Marissa shook her head, trying to be rid of this line of thought. She knew it wasn't helpful, and that there was wisdom in what Bill had said. But it was hard to reconcile.

Ellie grumbled from the back of the Mini and made her way to the passenger seat. Marissa cracked the window enough so the shepherd could stick her snout out and smell the fresh air as they made their way off the I-5 to the 16, toward the Narrows Bridge. Leaning her elbow out the window, she sighed. Maybe she should have just taken the ferry. She was tired. Not from lack of sleep, because since Mac had come back, she had been sleeping like a baby. Mentally, though, she was drained. Ellie pulled her attention from the outside to nudge Marissa's arm gently, offering reassurance she didn't know she needed.

By the time Marissa pulled into the driveway, she was exhausted in just about every way a person could be. Her body ached, pain from the heel of her foot shooting up to her lower back. She groaned as she put the car in park and put her feet on the concrete. The tiredness didn't help the pain in her back at all. She looked at the back seat where the duffle bag had been tossed and decided she could grab it in the morning. After Ellie jumped out, Marissa spotted Mac standing on the porch as she closed the door.

"Perfect timing!" He smiled at her, and she felt her shoulders instantly relax.

"Oh?" The smile spread across her face naturally.

"We made dinner." He met her at the bottom step of the porch and gave her a quick kiss.

"I like dinner." She perked herself up, partially for his sake but dinner also sounded nice. She hadn't realized how much she had missed what normalcy Mac had brought into her life.

Ellie ran inside ahead of her, excited to be home. Mac wrapped his arm around Marissa's shoulder as they headed inside. The smell of something delicious filled her senses. Kate was standing in the kitchen, a look of pride taking over her expression.

"I made spaghetti sauce from scratch." She paused. "With help, but I made it!"

Mac grinned. "She's a natural in the kitchen." He had a look of pride, too. "So we've got spaghetti and meatballs and garlic bread." He leaned down to whisper in her ear. "And some red wine."

"That sounds amazing."

She gave both of them a genuine smile, watching as Kate grabbed plates and Mac grabbed wine glasses. Leaning against the kitchen island, she felt conflict brewing in her chest. She couldn't imagine coming home to anything better. This was *normal*. This was *perfect*. This warmed her from the inside and brought out a happiness she hadn't thought possible anymore.

And that made it dangerous.

Just by being there with her, Mac and Kate were in danger. Mac understood that, and he made the choice anyway. Kate didn't. And that was why she couldn't stay. This could not be long term. Kate needed safety and security. Glancing at Mac, she couldn't help but think he should have stayed in D.C. He wasn't in danger if he wasn't with Marissa.

And yet, as they sat down at the table, she couldn't stop the smile that spread across her lips. She wished the moment could last forever. She knew it couldn't, but just for a moment, she let herself imagine what that would feel like.

Chapter 11

Marissa opened the door to see a woman standing on her front porch. She recognized her immediately from the pictures she had seen. Her long golden hair pulled back off her face into a high, tight ponytail, highlighting big brown eyes with perfect cheekbones. She already stood taller than Marissa, but the heels she was sporting made the woman simply tower over her.

"You must be Kim." Marissa suddenly felt very small and not just because of the height difference.

The tall blonde woman met her gaze with a cool smile, giving a half nod. "And you must be Marissa."

She held out her hand, which Marissa accepted, responding with a friendly smile of her own.

"And this." Kim turned to her side where a boy stood, though his attention was elsewhere as he looked over everything except Marissa. "This is Ethan."

Marissa's chest felt a weight hit it as she took a moment to look at Mac's ex-wife and their child standing on her porch. Stepping to the side, she opened the door further. "Come on in."

As though on cue, Mac appeared at the bottom of the stairs.

"Kim." He sounded as surprised as Marissa felt. That was at least a little comforting. "What are you doing here?"

"I told you I wasn't going to leave you without representation," she said plainly.

Ellie, who was still at Marissa's side, sat down but reached out with her nose, trying to meet Ethan, who was already smiling at the dog.

"And I told you I have it handled."

Mac gave his ex-wife a look that made Marissa feel cold. But his expression softened as Ethan suddenly pulled him into a big hug, throwing his arms around his dad.

"Hey, kiddo. I'm glad you're here," he said softly, looking up at Marissa. "Kim, Ethan—this is Marissa. Marissa, this is my son, Ethan, and Kim."

"We met at the door," Marissa said. She felt like an intruder in the moment, despite the fact that they were all standing in her entryway. "Here, why don't we get out of here and we can all go sit down? Did you want anything to drink?"

Marissa blinked, realizing she was falling into hostess mode. That had always been Mel's thing, not hers.

"No, but thank you," Kim said with sincerity before giving Mac a practiced irritated look. "But if you could, I'll take a recommendation for a good hotel we can use for the time being. That way we can get settled."

Marissa's first instinct was to invite them to stay. Thankfully, she thought better of it.

"There is the Mansera Hotel. It's like two minutes away." A somewhat unexpected ache blossomed in her chest as she thought about Allie. "It's a castle. And really cool."

She glanced at Ethan and decided to keep the haunting lore to herself.

"I can make a call and get you a room? They usually keep a few rooms blacked out for family and friends."

"That sounds perfect." Kim looked relieved.

Marissa knew it was tourist season, so finding anything with vacancies wouldn't be easy. "You're welcome to hang out here, though. As much as you need."

She glanced at Mac, who raised his eyebrow, and then back at Kim, and noticed the former couple was having a conversation with their eyes. Marissa suddenly felt out of place standing in her own living room.

"I'm ... going to check on Kate."

The teenager didn't need checking, but Marissa needed to escape the room. She didn't wait for anyone to respond before darting past Mac and up the stairs. She reached the top of the stairs and headed down the hallway toward Kate's room before gently knocking on the door.

"Come in."

Kate was sitting at the desk, pencil in hand, focused on the drawing she was working on. She only briefly glanced at Marissa before turning back to her sketchpad.

"Hey. What's up?"

Marissa leaned in the doorway and couldn't help but smile a little. Kate had made herself at home. Legitimately at home. Her backpack was hanging off the back of the chair she was sitting in, and it was empty. She had put clothes in drawers and settled in.

"Nothing. Just thought I would come and check on you."

Kate turned to Marissa with a raised eyebrow.

Marissa shrugged. "It got really crowded downstairs. Mac's ex-wife and son are down there." She paused. "I almost offered to let them stay here." She shook her head. The fact of the matter was Kate shouldn't be there either.

"Oh." Kate put the pencil down to turn her attention to Marissa before nodding. "That's ... interesting."

"That's a word for it." Marissa shook her head, laughing herself off. "What are you working on?" She nodded to Kate's desk.

"Just doodling." She held up the drawing. It was a beautiful sketch of Wicket, sleeping in the window just off to the side of Kate's desk.

"Kate, this is amazing. If this is doodling, I'd love to see what actual sketching looks like."

Kate laughed. "Thank you. Drawing calms me." She looked at Marissa, pausing for a moment. "What calms you?"

Marissa was taken aback by the question.

"Well. Running, if my body will let me. Naps are also definitely a big one." She didn't need to speak of the more unhealthy habits she had. "Okay, I should probably go back down there." Marissa made a face and shook her head. "Carry on."

She gave Kate a smile before closing the door behind her and heading back downstairs. Marissa grabbed her cell phone and stepped into the hallway, and then into her office, dialing the number for the hotel.

The standoff seemed to be over when Marissa returned, and they were now all sitting in the living room. Mac got back to his feet when he saw her.

"I made a call to the Mansera. You're all set with a room," she said, giving Kim a nod before turning to Mac.

"I'm going to run to the store to get something for dinner." He leaned down and kissed her cheek.

"Can I go?" Ethan was ready before Mac could even respond.

"Sure," Mac said, smiling at the thirteen-year-old who hurried to be alongside his dad without waiting for his mom's permission.

Marissa was sure Mac hadn't left her sitting in the living room with his ex-wife on purpose, but here they were. They sat across from each other silently for a long moment before Marissa got to her feet.

"Would you like some wine? Unfortunately, I don't have anything stronger."

Kim let out what Marissa thought was a breath of relief. "That would be great."

"Follow me to the kitchen. I can give you a quick tour of the downstairs."

After the tour, Marissa and Kim sat at the kitchen counter, glasses full of red wine.

"I wish we were meeting under better circum-stances," Kim said after several sips, looking Marissa over. "I've wanted to meet you for a long time."

Marissa couldn't say she was surprised. She had been curious about Kim as well. "Oh?"

Kim looked her over, searching her face, con-sidering her for a moment. "You made quite the impression on him when you first met. He was an absolute wreck when you broke up with him." Marissa winced, but Kim shook her head. "It was good for him. Don't feel bad."

Kim took the final sip of wine from her glass before she continued. Marissa passed her the bottle for a refill, taking a sip of her own. "I'm pretty sure he wasn't that devastated when our marriage ended."

Marissa took a gulp.

"He's a different person with you," Kim said after a long moment of silence. "He is willing to put his job on the line, to walk away from it—for you."

She shook her head, her hair staying perfectly in place. "I'm not sure how much he has shared about us…" She paused, waiting for some kind of response.

Marissa was honest. "Not very much, if I'm being honest."

Kim nodded, not looking surprised. "One of the biggest problems we had was that he always put his work first. Always."

She drummed her fingers on the counter, dropping her gaze, lost in memory.

"Don't get me wrong—he is the best dad he can be—but when it came to *us,* we always came last, if we made the list at all." Her gaze fell back on Marissa, her big brown eyes soft. "But he was literally willing to walk away from his job for you. Willing to just give it all up if that's what it took to be able to come back to you."

Marissa had to turn her own eyes away, confident she could keep the smile from her lips but not her eyes. A rush of warmth came with Kim's words. But also, a feeling of guilt.

Kim must have seen the guilt because she put her hand over Marissa's. "Please don't think I'm telling you this in bitterness or jealousy. I'm so grateful to see my best friend happy and in love."

Marissa stared and Kim grinned.

"He may not have said it yet, but I promise you, he will."

She let go of Marissa's hand and took another swig of her wine. At the rate they were going, they were going to need more wine.

"So, tell me about yourself. I know you were the youngest officer to make detective in your division. And that you've been through a lot." She paused before quickly continuing: "We don't have to talk about that. I know you were also married once?"

"Twice. To the same man. He was my childhood sweetheart."

It was Marissa's turn to finish her glass and give herself a refill.

"We are not on good terms. Or speaking terms. Or even friends anymore. It's fine." She met Kim's eyes and realized the line of questioning had been a trap. "He's out of the picture," she reassured the blonde, who studied her for a minute before nodding.

"For Mac's sake, I hope so." She ran her finger across the top of her wine glass, looking Marissa over once more before changing the subject. "So who is Kate?"

Marissa frowned before she remembered she had used the teenager as a momentary escape.

"She's ... complicated. The simple version is she's temporarily my foster daughter." Marissa hadn't used the phrase before. She didn't hate it. She did hate the reasons it could only be temporary, though.

When Kim raised an eyebrow, she took a sip of her own wine before continuing.

"The longer version is she is the collateral damage of a case I worked on recently. And she kept running away from her foster parents and came back here."

"That must be hard," Kim said after a moment.

"If I'm being honest, so far it really hasn't been bad. I love having her here. I just feel terrible for the situation that put her here. She's a really good kid."

"You don't have any kids of your own?" Kim already knew the answer, but Marissa provided it anyway.

"No. My ex and I tried for a while, but it wasn't in the cards."

"Well. I believe everything happens for a reason." She smiled. "I'm glad to have finally met you."

"I'm glad to finally meet you too."

The rest of the evening had been uneventful. When Mac returned, he kicked the two women, who had broken into a second bottle of wine, out of the kitchen. Kate came down and helped him with dinner, as did Ethan. Dinner was unsurprisingly perfect. Mac had made a roast with potatoes and green beans. Marissa had not only missed him and his presence but also his cooking. She had barely eaten while he had been gone.

Looking around the table, Marissa felt strange. She was comfortable despite the fact that Mac's ex was sitting on the other side of him. Ethan and Kate, only a year apart, were getting along really well, having quiet conversations that erupted every so often in laughter. Kim and Ethan may be staying at a hotel, but as she listened to Mac and Kim talk about going over strategy, it sounded like they would be around quite a bit.

The whole scene felt normal. Marissa hadn't realized how much she missed feeling normal. Of course, on the flip side of this, Marissa had to remind herself that she had chosen to isolate herself from everyone. She had pushed them all away so that they could stay safe. So far, it seemed to be working, but at a higher cost than she had imagined.

Chapter 12

The next couple of days felt crowded. Only a couple of weeks ago, Marissa had been trying to function within the silence and emptiness of the older craftsman house. Now it was filled to the brim during the day. Even when Kim and Mac weren't talking about his case, Kim and Ethan always found their way back to the house.

Ethan and Kate became fast friends. They spent time watching the same teen dramas in the living room or just occupying the same space quietly. He was a reader, quiet with his nose almost always in a book. And Kate, who always had her sketchbook and pencils, would draw. Kim seemed to be always moving, always busy. She was either on the phone, sorting through documents, or writing on legal pads. She was a contained sort of chaos.

Mac's ex-wife was a force. Between Kim's sharp brown eyes and quick wit, Marissa couldn't stop herself from liking her. At the end of the first week in town, Kim tried to make everyone dinner at Marissa's house. While it was better than anything Marissa would have managed, it was clear why Mac had always been the cook.

The second week they were there, Kim offered to take Ethan and Kate out for ice cream and a walk down the beach, giving Marissa and Mac the morning to themselves. He made them breakfast—bacon and eggs on a bagel—and they relaxed in the backyard. It was a sunny day without being too hot—perfect weather for the middle of June. Marissa closed her eyes, felt the wind blowing across her face, and smelled the salty air.

When she opened her eyes again, she looked over at Mac, who was sitting beside her on the swinging bench, watching Ellie patrol the back fence.

"I need to tell you something."

Mac turned to look at her, concern already all over his expression. "Okay."

Marissa stood, shifting her weight from one side to the other, picking at the cuticles of her thumbs. "I started looking into everyone who came into my life recently, including you. Or I tried to."

She avoided his eyes, looking at her feet. There was no shame in what she was saying—she knew it made sense, and she knew he would understand—but it felt like an invasion of privacy and a lack of trust. "I needed to account for timelines."

Mac was watching her, nodding as he listened. "I'm actually surprised you waited so long. What made you decide to do it now?"

Marissa hesitated. "Hold on."

She scurried inside and up the stairs, into her office, digging underneath the files on her desk. With the letter in hand, she made her way back down the stairs, slower than she had gone up, and out the back door.

"This came. The night you got suspended. I was waiting for the right moment, but there hasn't really been one." Marissa inhaled deeply as she passed the letter over to him, and his brow furrowed with concern.

The quiet that followed hung in the air like a thick cloud of smoke that would not disperse. She stared at the pavement, as though to give him privacy to read the letter she had been holding on to for months. Finally, he released a soft sigh and put the letter down on the glass table beside him.

She met his dark brown eyes, which were full of worry. "Why didn't you tell me?"

"I don't know. Like I said, when it arrived, it didn't feel like the right time. And then I just kept putting off. There was already so much going on..."

"You trust me, though, right?"

In that moment, she realized the look on his face was a mixture of hurt and confusion.

"Of course I do." She shook her head. "It's not about that. I just didn't want to add to the pile of everything going on."

"Have you shown it to anyone else?" His expression hadn't changed, and he didn't look convinced.

"Jackson saw it the night you were suspended. And again the next day when he came back. But that's it." As she spoke, she saw his expression fall even further.

"I hear what you're saying," he said after a moment, shaking his head. "But it feels like you didn't show it to me because maybe you weren't sure if you should trust me." His eyes fell back down to the letter. "This implies that I'm keeping secrets, and that you didn't come to me right away makes me feel like maybe you weren't sure."

She processed his words as he spoke. It had made her wonder if there were things he had been keeping from her, but in the same breath, it never diminished the trust she had in him.

"I never doubted you, Mac. Everyone has secrets."

He raised his eyebrow at the statement.

"Don't look at me like that. You know what I mean."

The implication that she was keeping secrets from him remained an unspoken question, but she moved on.

"So, what do you want to know?" he asked, turning his whole body to face her on the swinging bench.

"Mac—we don't need to—"

"Marissa, I don't want any secrets between us." He sighed gently. "So, I'm an open book. What do you want to know?"

Marissa stared at him and hesitated.

"It's okay," he coaxed her. "Just ask."

"What do I not know about you?" she said finally. Marissa had wanted nothing more than to ask about the strikes Agent Walker had mentioned when he was giving him his formal suspension, but they hadn't talked about it at all. "Just tell me everything."

Mac kept his gaze on her eyes and seemed to understand what she wanted to ask.

"When I joined the FBI, I was part of the organized crime unit. I had personal insight, and my first collar was a huge faction in New York, a faction my uncle all but ran. That was my first strike. I kept my relationship with my uncle to myself until after he was arrested. Had I disclosed anything, they would have pulled me from the case. I changed my name to put distance between us, and I switched to violent crimes to stay with the FBI. It was well over a decade and a half ago. My mother still hasn't spoken to me, and neither has my brother since. It's been fourteen years. I am no longer welcome there."

He paused, as though it was something he hadn't thought about in almost as long.

"Kim and Ethan became my whole family. And now you've met them."

He sighed and ran his fingers through his hair, clearing his throat to continue.

"My second strike was just after my partner, Derek Chapman, died. I wasn't in a very good place. The very next case I worked was a serial rapist. We had an eyewitness who backed out of her testimony, and he was going to walk. They accused me of using force in the interrogation room to coerce a confession out of him."

He sighed heavily, shaking his head as he ran his hand along his jaw.

"The confession was tossed, and I had to enroll in mandatory therapy for six months. He did end up going to jail because our eyewitness was convinced to go through with her testimony. There isn't much more than that. I have had four different partners in all my time at the FBI. The first was in the organized crime unit, where he still is to this day. The second and longest was Derek until his death. Then it was Chris Holdstern, but he retired. And now Clyde Bennet, who I met and became friends with back when we were in the academy but hadn't seen until I came back to Seattle."

His gaze fell down to his hands that were resting in his lap.

"As you already know, I married my high school sweetheart. We tried really hard to make it work." He paused for a moment, looking lost in thought. "But she accused me of loving the job more and harboring a temper that the job had just fueled. It took a minute, but we did finally learn to effectively co-parent, and we are still good friends."

He looked up and met her eyes again.

"I haven't been with anyone else since we broke up five years ago. When I heard about Daniel Fryer's arrest and transport back to Seattle, I threw my name in. Just hoping to see you again. And that was before I knew about your involvement."

Marissa's mouth opened and closed again, words failing her. Mac looked rather proud of himself when she didn't know how to respond.

"I don't really think there is much more to tell," he said, still smiling at her dumbfounded expression. "What about you, Riss? Any secrets I don't already know?"

Marissa studied his expression. He was smiling, but his eyes were searching hers, a concern that hadn't been there suddenly staring back at her. Slowly, she shook her head, slightly unsure of herself.

"I don't think so," she admitted honestly. She had secrets from literally everyone else. He knew everything there was to know. Even her worst secrets. Trying to lighten the moment, she put on a big smile. "You already know all my secrets."

Mac let out a breath. "I wish you would have told me sooner."

"I know. I just..." She was shaking her head and the words just trailed off.

After a moment, she shrugged her shoulder, turning her eyes to avoid his gaze, which was still holding her.

"I couldn't actually find any information on you or Clyde Bennet. Because of FBI security."

"Yeah, that makes sense." He nodded. "I can't speak for Clyde, but I've been working in D.C. since the O'Rourke case to stay close to home for Ethan."

Marissa nodded, glancing at the letter. "I know he's just playing mind games with me. The timing just ... really got stuck in my own head. I'm sorry."

Mac leaned forward and took her by the hand. "You have absolutely nothing to apologize for. It's your life that's been turned upside down, and I'm glad you are being vigilant. You're resourceful and smart. And you're going to get this guy."

Putting his arms around her, he pulled her into a hug.

She shifted to lean into him, burying her head into his chest, breathing him in and letting the feeling of calm wash over her. But as reassuring as he was, a tiny voice in the back of her mind told her otherwise. Despite the surveillance, not much had really changed. She knew the statistics: twelve percent of stalking cases result in criminal prosecution.

They stayed like that long enough for Marissa to drift off into a dreamless, calm sleep. She wasn't sure how long she had been sleeping, but as she shifted, she felt Mac's arms hold her just a little tighter.

"Sorry," she mumbled without making any effort to sit up. "I didn't mean to fall asleep."

"Stop apologizing." He laughed softly. "You need to rest more anyway." He tried to sound stern but mostly he just sounded sleepy.

"I should be working on the Jane Doe case." She sighed, still making no effort to move. Ellie huffed softly, lying beneath the swing they were resting on.

"You can't work a case if you aren't getting any rest, Marissa. You're running yourself into the ground."

She shook her head against his chest but didn't say anything.

"You aren't going to be able to make heads or tails of either case without a clear mind, and you can't have a clear mind if you're overworking yourself." He kissed the top of her head. "Just stay here with me. Let's enjoy the rare quiet moment. Because you know this never happens."

He wasn't wrong. Something was always urgent, always needing their attention.

"Yeah. Okay." She nodded her head against his chest. "But just for a little bit longer." Her eyes were already closed again.

She felt him nod. "Just a little while," he murmured.

Chapter 13

"Marissa?" She didn't recognize the voice on the other end of the line.

"Yes?"

"This is Greg. I'm calling because—"

Marissa didn't let him finish. "What's wrong?"

"We are at Jefferson Medical Hospital. Your mom is stable, but she collapsed."

Marissa's breath caught in her throat. "I'm on my way."

She glanced at Mac, who understood the severity of the situation and started getting Ellie geared up.

Marissa winced at the next thought as it entered his mind: "You know I have to call my sisters."

"Yeah, I know." Greg almost sounded sad in his response.

"I'll be there in less than ten."

"Drive carefully," he added before she hung up the phone.

"My mom is in the hospital," she said in a neutral tone, giving herself exactly a second to acknowledge the absolute panic that was coursing through her before she hit the 4 on her speed dial. Mac nodded and immediately grabbed Ellie's harness. Kate, who had been sitting on the couch watching TV with Ethan, looked on.

"Hey, Riss, what's up?" Madi asked cheerfully.

Marissa didn't waste any time. "Mom is at Jefferson Medical Hospital. I'm on my way there now."

"Oh fuck. What happened?"

"I'm not sure. I just know she collapsed."

"But how—"

"Madi, just meet me there. And call Mel."

She didn't wait for a response. She just hung up the phone and shoved it in her pocket. As she did, Kate walked up to Marissa and Mac.

"I'll come too."

Marissa just nodded. "Okay, let's go."

Marissa made impressive time—under five minutes. She let Mac park the car and hurried into the emergency room.

"Hi, I'm here for Marilyn Ambrose?"

The nurse had only begun to look through the names on the computer when Greg came up alongside her.

"She's in an exam room," he said anxiously. "They kicked me out. They want to take her up for an MRI."

"Okay." Marissa looked around nervously before looking at him. "What happened?"

"We were having dinner at her place, and I got up to take care of the dishes, and she was going to the living room, and I heard a crash, came out, and she was just on the floor."

Before Marissa could respond, Mel and Kirstie appeared, Mel carrying the baby Marissa still hadn't met, and Kirstie pregnant and huge as ever.

"What happened?" Mel's eyes were red, and she looked like she had been crying.

"Mom collapsed. They're taking her up for an MRI."

"Have you seen her yet?"

"No, I haven't."

Mel frowned before turning her attention to Greg, who was standing beside her in low conversation with the nurse.

"Over here." Marissa motioned for the group to follow her away from the nurse's desk. The waiting room was empty, probably because it was already after 6 p.m. on a Sunday. Marissa noticed in that moment that Mel was actually wearing pajamas.

"So what the hell happened?" Mel was clearly losing patience, swaying with the baby, who had already fallen asleep.

"Your mom—"

Mel whirled around on Greg so fast, Marissa felt bad for the guy. "Who the hell are you?"

"I'm Greg. I'm your mom's boyfriend—"

"BOYFRIEND?"

"Mel, lower your voice." Marissa glanced over at the nurse, whose irritation was all over her face.

"I'm sorry. Did you know Mom had a boyfriend?" Melanie snapped at her as Madilyn approached them and pulled her jacket off.

"Boyfriend?"

Marissa resisted the urge to roll her eyes but didn't respond. Her silence was enough. Melanie's face turned a new shade of red. Thankfully, Mac and Kate were coming down the hall. Marissa took the opportunity to grab Greg by the arm and led him over to Mac.

"Why don't you guys go get snacks or something? We're going to be here for a while. And it's going to be a long night."

Mac nodded without asking any questions and smiled at Greg. Then he looked past Greg at Kirstie, standing just to the side of the sisters, who were wrapped up in a private but intense conversation.

"Kirstie, why don't you come with us for a minute?"

Kirstie looked between Mac, Greg, and Marissa before looking over at Melanie. When Mel didn't say anything, Kirstie nodded. "Okay."

"Thank you," Marissa said softly, leaning up to kiss his cheek. He gave her hand a squeeze before turning and leading the group away from the empty waiting room. Before Marissa turned back to her sisters, Kate broke away from the group and ran over to Marissa, gave her a hug, and ran running back over to Mac.

Letting out a heavy breath, Marissa headed back over to her sisters. Madi had taken the baby and gave Marissa a look of disbelief. "Mom has a boyfriend? And you *knew*?"

"Lower your voice," Marissa hissed. She was already so tired.

"Of course she fucking did. The queen of secrets," Mel snapped.

"Okay, that's a little fucking dramatic," Marissa snapped back. "I ran into them just a couple of weeks ago in Seattle. She was planning on getting us all together and telling you soon."

"How long have they been dating? I didn't even know Mom went on dates." Melanie had one hand on her hip, her eyes looking everywhere but at Marissa.

This was a question Marissa had not wanted to answer. Thankfully, someone walked in behind her, grabbing Madi's attention: Clyde Bennet. He walked over to Madi and wrapped his arm around her waist, looking between the women. "So what's going on?"

"I'm not sure yet," Madi said, glaring over at Marissa.

Marissa ignored her sister and sighed. "Mac just took Kirstie, Greg, and Kate to look for snacks toward the cafeteria."

Thankfully, the FBI agent caught on to the tension in the room and nodded. He leaned down and gave Madi a kiss on the top of her head before letting her go. "I'll be back," he promised softly.

Marissa may not have been his biggest fan, but she couldn't deny that they looked good together. Once he vanished from sight, her younger sisters turned on her.

"Seriously, you knew Mom had a boyfriend?"

"Now really isn't the time. Mom was going to tell you both. She asked me not to say anything until she had the chance to talk to you." Marissa tried to keep her tone as calm as possible. "I'm more concerned about the whole collapsing and being rushed to the hospital thing."

Mel grumbled, but Madi's expression softened, and she nodded.

"Now. I'm going to go talk to the nurse and see if I can get any information, if you could stop attacking me for five minutes." Marissa didn't bother to wait for them to respond before turning and walking the few feet back to the desk.

The nurse offered her a sympathetic look. "Your mom is stable, but the doctors want to run a few more tests. They should be out soon." The nurse looked around and glanced at Marissa's sisters before leaning down and lowering her voice. "If you want to stay up here for a few while no one else is waiting, you are welcome to."

"Thank you so much," Marissa said, giving the nurse a grateful smile. She glanced back over at her sisters, who were clearly in deep conversation. Mel looked like she had been woken from a dead sleep to rush over whereas Madi was dressed as though she'd been on a date. Clearly Clyde had driven in with her. Marissa realized then that Mel had come in with Kirstie, not her husband. He probably had the rest of the kids.

With a heavy sigh, she turned and made her way back to her sisters.

Marissa wasn't sure how long they had been sitting in the waiting room, but it had been long enough for Jared and Brian to make it to the hospital. Brian's parents had already had the girls for the night; he had been spending the evening in Seattle with Jared.

No one was talking. Marissa looked around the room. Mel was deep in quiet conversation with

Kirstie, Brian cooing at the perfect baby boy in his arms. A baby that Marissa tried to ignore, one she hadn't held or even been introduced to. Her sister's anger was a force to be reckoned with. Jared stood beside Kirstie's chair, leaning against the wall with his arms folded in front of him, a baseball cap covering most of his face. Madilyn was on the other side of him, bouncing her knee and leaning back in her chair with her head resting on Clyde's shoulder. Marissa was across from them with Mac and Kate on one side of her and Greg on the other.

Trying really hard to keep herself calm, Marissa was digging her nails into her cuticles and studying the room. She was grateful that the arguing had come to a stop, but the silence was leaving her unsettled. Ellie forcefully nudged Marissa's leg before resting her head on Marissa's knee. Maybe it was out of old habit, but her eyes landed on Jared. He must have felt it because he met her gaze.

Her ex-husband couldn't even manage a look of sympathy in her direction. As their eyes met, she could feel the anger that he held just for her. It was enough to make her audibly wince and shift several times in her chair before she got to her feet, Ellie jumping up with her.

Mac reached out and took her hand, giving it a gentle squeeze, and looked up at her. "Do you want me to come with you?" He didn't ask what was wrong. He didn't ask if she was okay. He knew those answers.

Marissa shook her head. "No. I just need to go get some air."

She fucking hated hospitals. She had never liked hospitals, and then she had died twice in one, so being in one now felt unbearable. She walked down the long hallways until she had reached a door leading out to a small courtyard. She wanted to scream. The fear of not knowing and that something could be seriously wrong with their mom was overwhelming enough. The anger that was coming at her from so many different directions made it feel like she couldn't breathe.

She took one deep breath after another, trying to reign in her own emotions, but hot tears had begun streaming down her face. Refusing to let the sobs escape her throat, she let her eyes wander over the courtyard. It wasn't empty, but like the waiting room, she only spotted a few individuals. There was a child sitting with his parents at a table who looked like they were engrossed in a deep, serious conversation. The little boy looked over and caught sight of Ellie, letting out a squeal of excitement. The child's excitement brought a small smile to Marissa's lips.

"Hey, stranger," a familiar voice broke through, causing Marissa to turn on her heels. Brian no longer had the baby, and his hands were stuffed into his jean pockets as he walked up alongside her.

"Hey," Marissa said softly, trying to wipe the tears from her eyes. More came pouring out when he pulled her in for a hug.

"It's gonna be okay," he said with feeling. "Your mom is going to be fine. She's a tough lady."

Marissa nodded as she pulled back from the hug.

He motioned to a nearby bench. "Want to sit?"

"Sure," she said after a moment, nodding and sitting beside him on the bench.

"I guess now is as good a time as any to say I'm sorry."

"Sorry for what?" Marissa frowned at him, confused.

"For telling Jared everything—"

Marissa threw up her hand. "If anyone should be apologizing, it should be me. It wasn't fair of me to put all of that on you."

"But I understand why you did. And I wouldn't have said anything at all, but Jared told me Mel thought I was cheating on her…"

Marissa shook her head. "You don't have to explain. It's okay. I'm just sorry for putting all of that on you. And then for going radio silent. I just wanted to stay out of the way." She paused before smiling at him. "Congratulations, by the way. Your son is perfect."

Brian couldn't help but grin. "Thank you, isn't he?" He paused, running his hand through his hair. "You haven't gotten to even hold him yet, have you?'

Marissa shook her head. "No." Sighing, she gave Ellie a few scratches behind the ear.

Brian let out a sigh. "I was kind of hoping she'd have the baby and forget why she was mad. Instead, I think it had the opposite effect." He paused. "Which—thank you for sending Madilyn. I don't know how we would have made it through the last couple of months without her."

"Good, I'm glad she's helping. And it's good to have her home," Marissa admitted but quickly looked up at him. "But don't tell her I said so."

Brian laughed, shaking his head before a more serious expression crossed his face. "How have you been?"

Marissa shrugged, looking out into the courtyard. "I've been—okay."

"Convincing." Brian raised an eyebrow at her. "Are you still receiving photos?"

Marissa looked down at her feet and nodded. "Yep."

"I see the FBI is still hanging around." He bumped her shoulder with his as she let a small smirk appear.

"Sort of. But Mac is still in the picture."

Brian went to say something but stopped before starting again. "Is he here in an official capacity or a personal one?"

Ironically, this was now a complicated question. "A little bit of column A, a little bit of column B."

"Does he make you happy?"

Marissa was surprised by his forwardness but nodded. "He does."

"Well good then." He let out a long sigh and shaking his head. "He doesn't hate you, you know."

Marissa looked at Brian and raised an eyebrow. "Could have fooled me." She knew the conversation had shifted to Jared. She started picking at her cuticles again absentmindedly.

"He's angry. But if he didn't care, he would be indifferent. Anger means he still cares."

"Maybe." His words made sense, but she was certain that her ex-husband would never speak to her again. "He's never going to forgive me though."

"I don't think you're giving him enough credit."

Marissa paused. "Is he happy?"

Brian made a face before trying to force an impartial look. "It's not really my place to say."

Marissa sighed, looking back out to the courtyard. "I get it—"

"He's excited about the baby, but mostly I think he's just going through the motions." Brian sighed. "I'm not even sure he likes her half the time. I'm not sure what they have in common other than this baby." He shrugged his shoulder. "But I can't say anything because my wife adores her, and she makes *her* happy."

Marissa took the opportunity to shift the conversation. "How is Mel doing? Since she had the baby?"

"We're having good days and bad days." Brian sighed heavily. "Preston is an easy and happy baby, so it makes it that much easier. She's still pretty angry at me eighty percent of the time." He shook his head. "I can't believe she actually thought I was cheating on her."

Marissa watched the people eating their lunches in the courtyard before she turned to Brian, brushing the hair out of her face. "If you need to tell her the truth, tell her the truth. I never should have put that on you."

Brian looked at her, surprised as he thought over what she was saying. After a moment, he shook her head. "I think the person she really needs to hear it from is you."

Marissa's nose twitched, but she nodded, leaning forward on the bench with her hands grasping the edges. "Maybe."

Of course, in order to tell her anything, Melanie would have to talk to her first.

There was a long pause before Brian once again shifted the conversation. "Who is the girl with Mac?"

"That's Kate. It's … complicated. But it's like a temporary foster situation."

"Interesting," Brian said slowly, nodding his head. "But you're still being stalked?"

"Like I said, complicated."

There was a small sound behind them, and both Marissa and Brian turned to see Kirstie standing there, her petite frame hidden behind a very large, round belly. "They're looking for you," she said quietly before retreating.

Brian suddenly looked panicked. "Do you think she heard what I said?"

Marissa winced and watched the tiny pregnant woman disappear inside. "It's possible."

"Fuck."

Marissa and Brian came back into the waiting room to see Mel and Madi already on their feet.

"They want to talk to us," Madi announced, rubbing her hands nervously.

"Can you take him?" Mel asked, already handing off Preston to Brian. He nodded and instantly beamed as he cradled his son.

Marissa glanced around the room. Kirstie was sitting back down already, her eyes forward and face expressionless. Jared was watching them, though avoiding her gaze. Kate was leaning on Mac's shoulders with headphones in, and both Mac and Greg were staring back at Marissa, full of concern.

"Okay. Where?" As she asked, the nurse came up behind her and gently tapped her shoulder.

"Follow me."

She led them to a small room off the nurse's station. There were chairs and a bench, and the walls were bare and white. Marissa let her sisters sit before she grabbed a chair just off to the side of them. Rather than tucking under Marissa's chair or legs, Ellie rested her head on Marissa's knee, feeling the waves of anxiety and worry coming off her.

"Someone will be right in with you," the nurse said gently before closing the door behind her.

Mel said what they were all thinking: "I don't like this."

Madi leaned over and pulled Melanie in close by the shoulder. "It's going to be okay."

Marissa looked between her two sisters but said nothing. It didn't feel like it was going to be okay.

A moment later, there was a knock on the door before an older woman came into view and stepped into the room. "Hello. I'm Dr. Malone, and I've been taking care of your mom."

Mel barely let the doctor finish talking. "What's the matter with her?"

She gave them all an empathetic smile that made Marissa's blood run cold. "So, we found a mass," she spoke slowly. "We're going to run some more tests…"

Marissa didn't hear anything after that. She sat there numbly nodding her head while Melanie broke down in tears and Madi rubbed her back, trying to hold her own tears back. As the doctor finished talking, Marissa found her voice.

"Thank you."

It was all she could muster as Mel and Madi spouted question after question.

Mom had gotten pretty banged up from the fall and had arrived in quite a bit of pain, so she was currently sedated. The mass was in her chest, and the CT scan would show more about where it was, its size, and whether it had spread. They were doing blood work. They were admitting her until they knew more. Their mother was currently resting comfortably until they needed her for more tests. Blood tests had already been sent out. They could, and should, go home for the night and come back in the morning. It was a lot of information.

Marissa didn't remember returning to the waiting room but found herself standing there, leaning against Ellie to keep steady while she listened to Madi relay the basic information back to everyone waiting. Melanie was too upset to make words work. As Madi spoke, Marissa kept her gaze down, unable to meet anyone's eyes. At some point while she was talking, Mac stood and stepped up alongside Marissa, rubbing her back. She never looked up.

Then everyone was talking, but all Marissa could hear were sounds, unable to focus long enough to make out any of the words. Jared and Brian were staying out of the way, exchanging looks that summed up the severity of the situation. Her sisters huddled together with Kirstie, who, to her credit, appeared to be supportive. There was no room for Marissa there.

"Greg, do you need a ride?" Marissa asked suddenly, breaking through the conversations happening all around her.

Greg gave her a grateful smile but shook his head. "No, but thank you."

Marissa nodded and looked over at Kate, who was still sitting with her headphones on and watching them all quietly. "I think we're going to go." She looked at her sisters, who both looked at her as though they had forgotten she was even there. "We'll talk in the morning."

The walk back to the car was a quiet one. Mac and Kate were both a little bit behind her, encouraging her family to also go home and trying to reassure them everything would be okay—doing what she should have done but didn't have the capacity for right then. Marissa got to the car before they even exited the hospital, and as soon as she sat down, she couldn't stop herself from sobbing at the wheel.

Chapter 14

"Marissa." Mac's voice broke through the loud ringing that whistled through Marissa's ears. Her hands were frozen on her knees, staring down at the floor. They were parked in her driveway, and Mac was kneeling beside the open passenger door. Marissa didn't even remember the drive. She couldn't stop thinking about the bare walls in the room where they told her that her mom might not be okay. It had taken a few solid minutes back at the hospital for Mac to convince Marissa to let him drive, but it was definitely the right call.

"Hey." Again, Mac's voice broke through the haze. Slowly, she turned to look at him, trying to force herself to focus. "Let's go inside." His voice was soft.

Slowly, she nodded, but it took more effort than it should have to let go of her knees. Mac took her by the hand, placing his other hand behind her back, and led her toward the house. Ellie and Kate were right behind them.

"Kate, you want to get Ellie's harness off? I'm gonna get Marissa upstairs."

Kate nodded and started following his instructions. Mac, with his hand still behind her back, led her to the second floor.

"Come on." He helped her sit on her bed. "Can I do anything?"

Marissa just shook her head. Words were still difficult.

"Okay. I'll be right back, okay?"

She nodded this time and watched him walk out of the room before gripping the comforter with both fists. Her whole body was rapidly growing hot. Her clothes were suddenly smothering her. She inhaled sharply and again. She needed to get out of her clothes. Getting to her feet shakily, she wandered into her bathroom, all but clawing her clothes off. She didn't bother turning on the light. She headed toward the shower and turned on the hot water.

Marissa crumpled on the shower floor, pulling her knees close to her chest and gripping her knees as tightly as she had held her legs in the car. She tried over and over again to catch her breath, but it just kept getting away from her as she choked on her sobs, which had finally come pouring out.

"Hey, I'm here." Mac got down on the floor beside her and pulled her into him. He had managed to pull his shirt off but was otherwise fully clothed as the shower rained down on them. "I'm here. But you have to breathe."

She locked her eyes on him. *You have to breathe.* Shuddering, she tried to follow his instruction but couldn't get past choking on the inhale. The panic attack was overtaking her.

"Baby. It's going to be okay. Just breathe. You have to breathe."

He was trying so hard to coax her, stroking her wet hair. Marissa did her best to listen to his voice and follow his directions, but she suddenly felt so heavy.

When Marissa came to, it was dark outside. She was lying in bed, and she wasn't sure how she had gotten there. The last thing she remembered was being in the shower. She sat up slowly, using the wall to brace her. Her head was pounding. For a second, she didn't remember why. But it all came rushing back as the events of the day ran through her mind.

"Hey."

Mac suddenly appeared, a glass of water in his hand. His hair was wet, and he wore only his gray sweatpants. She remembered the breakdown in the shower, remembered that he had sat there with her and tried to help her calm down.

"Here. This is for you." He offered her the glass of water.

She met his brown eyes and stared for a long moment before she reluctantly nodded and took the water.

"And these will help." In his free hand were all the pills that were just right for the moment.

"You're too good to me," she mumbled after she swallowed the pills.

He got into bed right next to her and shook his head. "No such thing." He put his arm around her, and she curled right into his chest.

"I'm sorry," she said softly. "I'll be fine tomorrow."

She just needed one night to let herself feel it all at once, so she could put it in a box and continue functioning as she needed to.

"You don't need to be fine, Marissa." He spoke softly. "It's okay to not be okay."

She just shook her head. "I'll be fine," she repeated, closing her eyes and trying to convince herself to relax. She saw the off-white plain walls where the doctor had met with them. She shuddered involuntarily, and Mac held her closer.

The next morning came too soon after a dreamless sleep. Mac slipped out of bed, trying not to wake her, but she heard him. She knew he was probably going for his morning run. Grumbling to herself, she rolled back over on to her side and huffed. Ellie snorted in response and crawled off of her legs and right alongside Marissa, close enough to lick her face. Throwing her arm over the shepherd, she hugged Ellie before leaning over to grab her phone from the nightstand.

She stared at it for a moment, not sure who to call. She had decided to start with her mom's cell. It rang twice before Greg's voice came on the line. "Hey, Marissa." His voice was hoarse.

"Hey, Greg." Her heart dropped a little, although she hadn't really expected her mom to answer. "I just wanted to call to check in."

"Honestly, I was going to call soon anyway." He sighed. "She's resting right now, but she's doing okay. No one is really telling me much, but the plan is to send her home today."

"Do you know what they are looking for?"

She heard Greg draw in another deep breath. "Not really, but it shouldn't take long to get results."

"Okay." Marissa paused, staring at Ellie who was watching her. "I'll call again in a little bit. But call me if anything changes?"

"Of course."

Marissa hung up the phone and put it back on the nightstand. Pulling her knees up to her chest, she sighed when there was a gentle knock at the door.

"Marissa?" She heard Kate's muffled voice.

"Come on in," she managed. She considered for a moment getting up, but the pounding in her head dictated that would not be a thing. Instead, she shifted back down, pulled the blankets close to her face, and gave the dog another squeeze.

Kate made her way into the room, closing the door behind her. "Are you okay?" she asked softly, seemingly aware of Marissa's headache.

Marissa looked at the girl standing at the side of the bed and shook her head. "Not really." She had wanted so badly to wake up and just have it be a bad dream. She had also hoped that somehow over the course of the night, she might have been able to force herself to be okay. Just like she had insisted to Mac she would be. Neither of these things were true, and the pounding headache from all the crying lingered.

"I really like your mom." Kate sat down next to her, pulling her knees up to her chest. "I hope she'll be okay."

"Me too." Marissa felt the tears pushing against her eyes and shook her head, trying to shake them back. They both sat there in silence for a moment as Wicket pushed her way into the room and jumped on the bed, curling up in Kate's lap.

"You have a good relationship with your mom, right?" Kate suddenly asked.

Marissa paused but nodded. "Yeah. Mostly. We were close when I was growing up. Less so since I've come back to Port Townsend." She glanced over at the teenager whose expression was conflicted.

"I've never had a good relationship with my mom," Kate said finally, shaking her head while she looked down at Wicket. "I think she tried sometimes, but she never really acted like a mom. She gave most of her attention to Hannah, and it was always yelling. I was okay with being invisible."

Marissa sighed. Marlene was a lot of things, but Mom of the Year definitely was not it. "Have you spoken to your mom recently?"

Kate shook her head. "No. She called while I was at the Olsens', but I didn't take it." She shrugged a shoulder, stroking the cat in her lap. "I don't want to talk to her. I don't know what I would say."

Marissa just nodded. "That's fair." She meant it. She couldn't blame Kate in the least. Marlene hadn't been much of a mom to either of her girls.

"You think she's okay in there?" Kate asked weakly after a long moment, looking at Marissa with big blue eyes.

The truth was Marissa wasn't sure. She hadn't spoken to Marlene in a couple of weeks. Not since her hearing. She did know that Marlene wanted nothing more than to talk with Kate.

"I hope so," Marissa said honestly. "But I'm sure she will be. She's a tough lady." She was something alright. Marlene was looking at twenty-five to life for the murders of her husband and her son-in-law.

Kate snorted. "That's a word for it," she muttered, shaking her head. Turning to Marissa, she got herself comfortable and leaned against the back wall, stretching her legs out alongside Marissa. Wicket remained on Kate's lap, just along for the ride as she continued to stroke his gray fur. "What was your mom like growing up?"

Marissa smiled, still lying down but letting the blanket go. "She was pretty big on rules when we were growing up. Moreso after my sisters were born, though. But even though she had big rules, we also did things like movie nights, living room campouts. She would wake us up in the middle of the night to go stargazing." She smiled at the memory.

"Stargazing?" Kate looked at Marissa.

She nodded. "She would wake us up, and we would all pile into my mom's station wagon and drive out to a field or an empty beach. Once, we just parked on an empty road in the middle of nowhere and sat on top of the car. And we would just watch the stars on nights that it was clear."

"That sounds amazing."

"Next time we have a clear night, without headaches, I can take you out and show you."

"That would be great!" Kate said with a smile, slouching down beside Marissa. She was quiet for a moment before she turned to look at Marissa. "What about your dad?"

Marissa met Kate's eyes and sighed softly. "My dad left after Mel was born. He had a whole other family on the east coast, which was a whole scandal."

Kate's eyes widened. "Wow. I'm so sorry."

"Don't be. My dad and I actually have a good relationship now. He reached out to me when I turned eighteen. We talk on the phone every couple of weeks. He even came to visit me shortly after I was in the hospital." She shrugged. "My parents weren't good together. It was better."

"Do your sisters have a good relationship with him?"

"Oh god no." She shook her head vehemently. "I don't think either of them ever speak to my dad. He sends them Christmas cards and birthday cards, but they don't talk to him." She paused. "What about your dad?"

Kate's dad was an unanswered question. Marlene hadn't put anyone on the birth certificate and had refused any kind of answer when asked about it. The only thing that Marissa knew for sure was that Paul hadn't been her biological father.

Kate just shrugged. "I don't know. He left when I was three or so. Hannah used to talk about leaving to go live with him. I'm not sure if there was any weight to it, though. She threatened to go live with just about everyone when she would fight with Mom and Paul. I don't really know what her relationship was with him."

Marissa just nodded, pinning the thought in her mind to ask Marlene again. Something about that whole situation felt off, and she wasn't really sure why. Taking a deep breath, Marissa adjusted again.

"Do you need anything?"

"No, but thank you," she said softly. "I think I might just stay in bed for a bit."

As far as Marissa was concerned, when she finally got up and out of bed, she needed to be okay. She just wasn't quite there yet. She knew Mel was going to be emotional enough for everybody. She couldn't add to it.

"Can I stay here with you for a bit?" Kate's voice was soft as she looked down at the cat purring on her lap.

"Of course, hon." She smiled at Kate before resting her head back. "I might close my eyes, though."

When Kate didn't protest, Marissa shut her eyes and let the exhaustion take over.

Chapter 15

Marissa was sitting in her office. Her mom was still in the hospital, waiting on her discharge papers. They had been told she could go home the day after she'd been admitted, but the next morning, they had come back with more tests. Now they were sitting at a week later, and she was still there. Marissa had gone to visit her a few times, but Mel had practically moved into their mom's hospital room. It made visiting uncomfortable.

The flare that came out of that first night at the hospital was still lingering, making all of Marissa's movements significantly slower than they should have been. Every move made her whole body ache.

She twirled her chair back and forth slowly, trying to get herself back into the zone, looking at the piles of files at her feet. She couldn't think about her mother anymore. They needed to meet with the doctor and talk about what they found and next steps, and if Marissa was being honest, she didn't want to. The second they talked to the doctor and had a diagnosis, there would be no going back. She wasn't really ready for that. Besides, she had a case to work on. She typed in her password to sign on to her computer and waited.

After the visit with Bill Hendrickson, she had gotten in touch with the Doe Project and sent them what she could in hopes that maybe something would come out of it. She had also sent the funds out of pocket, which time-lost pay and Washington State L&I made possible. Not to mention the extra she was making from the condo as an Airbnb.

She waited as the computer came to life and then opened her email. She frowned at an email that had come in the day before. The subject line read "Attention." Marissa clicked the email open.

Hello, my name is Detective Carmen Vega, of the Vancouver PD. I heard through the grapevine that you have a cold case with a Jane Doe, homicide with opioids in her system. I'm reaching out because I've been working on a case with similarities, and I think we should talk. I'm in Seattle for a couple of days and I'm hoping we can get together. If you can

*give me a call back or email me, that
would be great. My number is—*

Marissa reread the email two more times before she grabbed her phone and dialed the number. It rang four times before it went to voicemail.

"Hi Carmen, this is Marissa Ambrose. I just read your email and would love to get together while you're in town. I hope to hear from you soon!"

She felt a jolt of excitement at the possibilities. Considering there hadn't been any movement since her visit with Bill Hendrickson, which had truly been nothing but good company and a much-needed talk about her late partner, any kind of lead was an exciting one.

Now she just had to wait. Marissa stared around her office and let out a sigh. Nothing was going to happen just sitting here. She pushed herself out of her chair. Focusing was going to be difficult.

She headed down the stairs. It was still early; Mac had only left for a run within the last half hour. The house was still quiet. With Ellie following behind her, she went through the kitchen and let the shepherd out into the yard. Her phone buzzed from her back pocket as her Ring camera alert went off. In the app's video feed, she saw Kim at the front door, Ethan beside her. She placed her teapot on the stove and headed to the front door.

"Good morning," she said with a small smile, opening the door. "Mac is still on his run, but he should be back soon."

Kim nodded, smiling back. Ethan almost smiled and stepped inside, glancing around.

"I think Kate might still be asleep."

Ethan nodded in acknowledgment and headed into the living room, opening up the book he was carrying.

Marissa closed the door behind Kim as she walked in, shaking her head. "I bet he's a great student."

"Most of the time. He just loves to read. Sometimes, he'd rather do that over schoolwork."

"I'm heating up some water for tea. Do you want any?" Marissa asked, heading back to the back door and letting Ellie inside. The shepherd greeted Kim as she entered the kitchen.

"Thank you, but I've got coffee." She held her coffee cup.

Marissa nodded, grabbing herself a mug. Dropping a tea bag into the mug, she leaned against the counter and smiled. She actually liked Kim.

"How's all that—" She motioned to the files in Kim's hands. "—going?"

Kim frowned and let out a sigh. "Honestly, taking longer than it should."

Marissa poured her boiling water into her teacup and added some milk before she headed over to the table where Kim had made herself comfortable.

Marissa paused, taking a sip of her tea. "Most of the legalities are over my head, but just knowing he has you in his corner helps."

"Too bad he doesn't see it that way." Kim laughed softly. "His pride is probably his biggest flaw."

Marissa looked down at her tea as she held the cup with both hands, letting the heat soothe the aches in her fingers and wrist. She hadn't experienced too much pridefulness with Mac this go around, but thinking back to the first time they met, she could see it.

"Sorry. That was probably inappropriate." Kim suddenly looked very uncomfortable.

Marissa laughed. "Not at all. The first time we met, I thought he was an egotistical asshole."

Kim laughed and openly relaxed. "Okay, good. Because I don't want to talk shit about him, but I could tell you stories. He's a good man at heart though. He tries."

She wouldn't argue that he was good man. He had proven that time and time again. Marissa shifted in her seat and took another sip of her tea. "'I'd be interested in some stories."

"Oh, where to start." Kim pushed around the files in front of her before glancing up at Marissa. She looked at Marissa as though trying to size up what she could safely share.

"He's seen me at my literal worst. Which includes physically trying to tear myself apart." She motioned to the scar running down her chest. The new damage she had done to it wasn't healing as smoothly as it had the first time, and it still looked rough. "Maybe knowing he isn't perfect will make me feel less undeserving or inadequate."

"Okay, first of all, you are in no way undeserving or inadequate. And James Mackenzie is in no way perfect." Kim made a face. "So, sure—he is an amazing cook. But do you ever notice that dirty dishes literally never hit the sink?"

Marissa glanced over and saw her sink was completely empty.

Kim continued. "Like, it's one thing to clean as you go, but it's another to grab things before you're even done with them. Like taking your cup when you're still drinking from it."

"The OCD is real," Marissa commented. She recognized it, though she didn't think about it often.

"Oh my gosh, so real." Kim made a face. "I think he's getting a little better the older he gets. It used to be a lot worse, if you can believe it." She took a sip of coffee. "OH! And speaking of his amazing cooking skills! Taking him anywhere for dinner is nearly impossible because he will tell you all the things that the cooks did wrong or what they could improve on."

Marissa laughed. At least he was an amazing cook. It made pretty much any flaws in the kitchen worth dealing with. She glanced around her very clean kitchen and raised an eyebrow.

"I'm pretty sure he's rearranged the kitchen twice now. But I can't really tell because I literally never cook."

"Yeah, that sounds about right." Kim laughed slightly, a strand of her perfect hair falling in front of her eyes. As she brushed it behind her ear, she paused, hesitating slightly. "On a bit of a larger scale, he's got some anger issues. Tried anger management a couple of times. Was repeatedly kicked out." She sighed, looking into her own mug. "I remember when Derek, his partner, died at the courthouse. He tried so hard to internalize all that anger, but it was rough. It's the only thing I think Internal Affairs actually has any potential grounds on." She huffed in frustration. "It was a bad time. I don't think I've ever seen so much anger in a single person. I think that that was when he closed himself off from everything, including us."

She met Marissa's gaze and smiled.

"Honestly. Seeing him with you has been so different. And refreshing."

Marissa could feel her cheeks grow warm.

Kim hesitated again. "Another thing about Mac is, even though he hides it well, he can be pretty insecure." She paused. "Like, when he came back to D.C. after your argument with your ex-husband."

Marissa sighed and nodded. She had figured Mac had probably talked to Kim about the whole thing. "After the way I broke it off before, I don't blame him."

"He was devastated the first time. When he thought it was happening again, he sort of went into a spiral. He'd probably stop speaking to me if he knew I was telling you this, but it is a real struggle for him."

"I have no intentions of hurting him."

"I didn't think you did." Kim paused, her demeanor having shifted. "It's the unintentional things that make me nervous."

"If I'm being honest, this relationship we have now was unintentional. My goal was to keep everyone at a solid distance. I'm not sure what exactly happened." This was the truth. This was something she hadn't said out loud. "When I broke it off with him five years ago, I was never sure I had made the right choice. Since he came back into my life, I'm certain I made the wrong choice then. I have no plans or desire to jeopardize that." Marissa made a face, bringing her tea up to her lips as she realized how easily the words came out.

"Good." Kim straightened in her chair, the uncertainty she had been displaying a moment earlier having dissipated.

Marissa's phone rang in her pocket. She recognized the number but couldn't remember why for a moment.

"I'll be right back." She smiled at Kim before heading to the back door and stepping outside to answer.

"Hi, this is Detective Carmen Vega calling for Marissa Ambrose?"

"Hi! Thank you for calling me back!"

"Not at all. Thank you for your response." She sounded as breathless over the line as Marissa felt. "Getting right to it—your Jane Doe case has some similarities to a case I've been building that are too similar to be a coincidence." She paused on the other end of the line momentarily. "Cause of death and your toxicology report. Opioids in her system, strangulation. Found just off the side of a walking path. I have six individual cold cases with the same MO, mostly down here in Vancouver, one just outside of Portland and another in Ridgefield. Mostly minorities. All ranging from 1997 to 2013. I was hoping that maybe we could get together and compare?"

Marissa was nodding on her end, despite the fact that there was no one to see it. "Yeah, that would be great. When are you in town?"

"I will be in Seattle at the beginning of July, about a week and a half from now. I'm in town for four days."

"I can make that work."

Detective Vega answered quickly. "Can I text you the details of my schedule and you tell me what works for you?"

"Absolutely!" Suddenly Marissa felt excited, despite her best effort not to allow herself to get her hopes up.

"Great! I'll send that info your way before the end of the day."

Marissa got off the phone and took a deep breath. She was more optimistic than she wanted to be. Sitting again at the kitchen table, she took a long drink of her tea. "Where were we?"

"I believe we were talking shit about my ex-husband, your current boyfriend."

The term *boyfriend* felt strange to her ears. It reminded her of high school.

"Yes. I do believe we were."

Kim and Marissa spent the next hour talking, mostly about Mac but a little about themselves. It was almost like they were becoming friends. When Mac returned from his run, they shared a laugh after having discussed his obsessive need to run every single day. And then Kim headed back to the living room with all of her notes, getting comfortable in the recliner chair while Kate and Ethan controlled the TV.

Marissa stayed at the table, staring out the back door, looking into her backyard. She felt Mac's eyes on her a few minutes later and turned to smile at him.

"Hey there," she said softly.

He leaned against the entryway in a fresh set of clothes, crossing his arms, and smiled back at her. "Hey, beautiful." He watched her for a long moment before walking into the kitchen and sitting in the chair across from her. "Can I just say: it's both wonderful and unsettling that you two are becoming friends?"

"You've got good taste. What can I say?" Marissa shrugged playfully and smiled. "I like her a lot."

"She likes you too. And that's rare because, honestly, she doesn't like many people."

"I can hear you!" Kim announced from the living room.

Mac laughed and Marissa snorted, shaking her head and letting out a sigh.

"What's on your mind?" Mac asked.

Marissa shrugged her shoulders. "I was contacted by a detective in Vancouver working a cold case. She thinks there are enough similarities between her case and mine that we should meet."

"Oh?"

"Yeah, so we are meeting next week. She's going to send me over the details."

"That's exciting!" Mac sounded relieved. Even though he hadn't voiced his opinion much, she knew he wasn't a fan of cold cases. There wasn't much to be a fan of. They were usually cold for a reason.

"I'm ... cautiously optimistic." She sighed. "I know the chances of getting answers are slim. But

I have to at least try." Marissa's voice caught in her throat. "For Tom."

Mac nodded his head in understanding. "Let me know what I can do," he said gently.

"How was your run?"

As Marissa asked, her phone buzzed on the table with a text from Carmen Vega. She had given Marissa a choice between three days and the location of a hall in Seattle. "And there it is. I'll meet with her in just over a week."

"Nice!" Mac smiled. "And it was a good run. The weather here makes it so much nicer to keep up the running habit." Now it was Mac's turn to shrug.

"I wish my legs would let me join you." She hadn't been able to run in a minute. Her legs, which now regularly spasmed, were no longer good for runs. She genuinely missed the ability to run.

Before she could say anything else, her phone rang, Jackson's name flashing across her screen.

"I need you to come down to the station right now."

Chapter 16

Jackson had been vague on the phone when he said he needed her down at the station. A knot was growing and twisting in the pit of her stomach on the way there. She had gone through a dozen scenarios, but none of them included Sean Boswell from Internal Affairs.

Marissa blinked at the sheriff while he explained why he had called her.

"He came in here, showed us his credentials, and asked to speak with you. He hasn't said anything more than 'it's classified.'" Jackson looked irritated. He didn't like people who weren't supposed to be in his precinct.

"Okay, where is he?"

"Interview room two."

Marissa nodded and let out a heavy breath. She took a couple of steps but then paused, turning back to Jackson. "Is it just him?"

Jackson nodded. Marissa frowned. "Okay."

She headed over to the room and pushed the heavy door open.

Agent Sean Boswell stared at Marissa from across the table as though waiting for her to confess something. It made her nervous. Mac's hearing was rapidly approaching, and she assumed that was what this was about.

"Was there something we didn't cover in our last meeting?" Marissa finally asked, tired of the man's silent stare.

Sean Boswell's naturally red, round face seemed to twitch at the sound of her voice. "Actually, I asked you here today to talk about your own case, if you would be willing."

Marissa had to actively tell herself not to narrow her eyes at the agent sitting across from her. She was certain she wasn't in any trouble; she hadn't done anything wrong. So she shrugged her shoulder. "Sure."

"Two serial killer cases in five years? You know what the odds of that are?" He paused for effect but then continued without bothering for a response. "Serial killers make up right around one percent of murders." He shook his head. "Although, O'Rourke was less of a serial killer and more of a mob boss with all the fixings under his belt." He leaned back in his chair, resting his arm on the back of it, still watching her thoughtfully.

"Is there a question in there?" Marissa asked. This line of questioning was confusing.

"I've just taken a bit of interest in your case is all." He drummed his fingers on the table between them. "Daniel Fryer. You are certain he was one part of team that held you in that warehouse."

Marissa frowned. It was true that she had mostly taken the FBI at their word when they brought him in, but from the first conversation, Marissa hadn't had any doubts. "Yeah. I'm sure," she said slowly.

"Were there only two or were there were more? It almost seems like a bigger operation, you know? Someone tracking you here, following you around and taking pictures, someone out in Chicago, taking women and sending pictures. The fact that these envelopes keep making it to you despite cameras, police, and feds all watching your house. It's just real curious."

Something about the way Sean Boswell summarized her case made it sound even worse than it already was, sending a shiver down her spine.

"It sounds ridiculous." She stared at the table, knowing that was what he was getting at.

"Don't get me wrong: I'm not questioning you." He held a hand up and shook his head. "But I do feel like there are some questions that should be asked."

"I don't disagree," she said cautiously. It certainly sounded like he was questioning her, though.

"I know you've gone over it hundreds of times now, but can you just run me through what led you to that warehouse and what you remember?"

Marissa hesitated. In that first year, she had repeated the story more times than she could count. Reluctantly, she nodded. "Of course."

She adjusted her body in her seat. Ellie, noticing the change in Marissa, sat up and rested her head in her lap.

"We were at the point in the case where the same vehicle had been seen leaving the last two crime scenes, and we had put out an APB. We were scrambling. And obviously, we had opened up a tip line, but like all tip lines, there were a lot of bogus allegations and dead ends and things that might have been valid were getting buried. I received a letter addressed directly to me. In the letter, it said that they had tried to go through the tip line but hadn't heard back, and they were sure that the car we were looking for was located outside a warehouse in the industrial district. We took it to Lieutenant Cooper, who gave us the go ahead to check it out. When we got there, we found the car. There wasn't a lot inside of it, but we were able to narrow down which warehouse they were likely in."

Marissa sighed, shaking her head.

"We argued inside the car. I wanted to wait for backup. We had already radioed it in. Tom didn't want to wait. He said I could wait if I wanted and got out of the car. I followed right behind him."

She could still remember everything about that afternoon.

"And when you walked inside?" Boswell asked, his gruff voice a little softer than it had been before.

She took a deep breath and continued, "Tom got to the door. I was maybe three steps behind him. When I crossed the threshold of the doorway, I heard the gunshot and I saw him drop to the ground in front of me. Before I had a chance to do anything, I was hit on the head from behind and knocked unconscious." Ellie adjusted her head in Marissa's lap, nudging at her hands to stop digging into her nails.

"When I woke up, I was blindfolded, handcuffed to a pole or a post. I had headphones on that were blaring metal music in my ears. They always put those on me when they were in the room, talking. It was disorienting, which was the point. When the headphones were off, my head was always pounding, and I couldn't focus on any sounds. And the blindfold never came off. Not once."

Boswell nodded his head. He had started taking notes while she was talking. Once he finished whatever he had been writing, he looked up at her.

"What about your other senses? Were there any distinguishing smells? Did you feel anything worth noting or taste anything?"

He was trying to be gentle but also trying to keep her focused.

The fact that it had been two and half years had not made any of the memories fade, as much as she wanted them to. Shaking her head, she shrugged her shoulder.

"Mostly just the metallic taste of my own blood in my mouth. Everything in the warehouse felt hard and cold. Even when they were dragging me around. The cement floor was always freezing. I was so disoriented by the end, I couldn't tell you which way was up and which way was down."

Sean Boswell nodded. "Understandable."

He flipped the page of the legal pad up to reveal what looked like a typed-up transcript and read through it, still nodding his head. Finally, he huffed and let the page fall to cover the typed-up page.

"When they were moving you around specifically, do you remember any distinguishing features or anything about them that is worth noting?"

Marissa thought for a long, hard minute before she spoke.

"One set of hands was rough. Like, not just rough with me but was actually rough with callouses. He had long fingers, and his hands were always cold. The other set of hands were different. They were softer. They were gentler with me, although the bar was very low. Shorter fingers, warm hands."

"Okay." He wrote down everything she had told him and adjusted in his seat. "Like I said in the beginning, I'm not here to question your story. It's exactly the same as you told it previously." He paused. "Let's talk about what happened at the end."

Marissa shuddered, cracking her neck and closing her eyes for a moment before she started talking. "I hadn't slept. I was so tired. But I could hear them arguing. Their voices were just noise over the music. I couldn't make out anything they were saying. They took me off the pole they had attached the zip ties to and made me kneel on the ground. I was pretty sure they were going to shoot me right there."

The memory of that moment made her feel sick to her stomach.

"That was when I got this." She gestured to the scar she had tried so hard to tear off her body a few months ago while in a delirious state thanks to her last psychologist. "He just dragged it across my body, slowly digging in. When the knife reached my hip, he pulled away and jammed it into my abdomen. He took off the headphones and I heard him laugh. The other one whispered in my ear, 'Good luck.'" She shuddered again, unable to stop the physical reaction from the memory. Ellie whined at her. "I dropped to the floor. I remember the cold floor feeling good because my skin suddenly felt really hot."

Thankfully, Sean Boswell gave her a minute. Marissa closed her eyes, petting Ellie and trying to get her breathing back to normal. She could still feel that phantom blade running through her sometimes. A familiar dull throbbing began in her abdomen, a physical reminder that flared every so often.

"I assume the chances of you recognizing that voice with everything that happened in that moment is probably slim to none?" the agent across from her asked, his expression something close to empathy. "Not a judgment. It's to be expected—lack of sleep, disorientation, physical pain, and adrenaline."

Marissa nodded. "I wish I could," she said softly.

Sean Boswell moved around in his seat again, shifting his heavy weight from one side of the chair to the other. "Now, tell me what it was like *after* the warehouse."

Marissa let out a groan. "I passed out from the pain. I was certain I was going to die. I woke up, briefly, at the hospital. They apparently had to revive me twice. I don't really remember much from the time in the hospital. It was a lot of in and out." She shook her head. "Rehab was a bitch."

"And when you got home?"

"I started receiving photographs." She sighed. "They were of mostly just me, and they came at really random intervals. I moved back out here, hoping maybe they would stop. They increased instead. And it wasn't just me anymore. The pictures included my ex-husband, who stayed by my side since the hospital." She exhaled. She was fucking tired of repeating this history. "We continued trying to live a weird sort of life after that, for a year. And then I broke up with him, hoping to keep him safe."

"Bold move," Sean Boswell muttered, taking notes. "And after that, did the photographs of your ex-husband stop coming?"

Marissa nodded. "They did."

"Okay." He looked over his two pages of notes, occasionally stopping and nodding before he looked at Marissa again. "Something I find curious." He paused, and Marissa was sure it was for dramatic effect.

"The letter that brought you out to the warehouse in the first place. It was clearly a trap. Did we ever test that letter or put it into evidence?"

Marissa blinked, letting that sink in before she shook her head. "I'm not sure. I don't remember..."

"I can look into that. With luck, it was thrown into evidence. Chances are, though, it's gone." He dropped the pen and clasped his hands together. "But it gives you another line to ask Fryer about."

"I'm not supposed to ask Fryer about my own case," she said, not bothering to hide her frustration.

Boswell frowned. "That... That seems odd. I would think that you would be gathering any information he is willing to give."

"You would think."

"Who told you not to talk about your own case?" The confusion on his face gave Marissa a sense of validation.

"ADA Gorden. SSA Walker. Agent Bennet."

He was still making a face. "Okay. I'm going to look into some things on my end. If you think of anything, or if anything happens, call me." He slid his card across the table. "And I will be in touch. I appreciate you coming in to speak with me."

Now Marissa was frowning. Her first impression might have been wrong. "Thank you," she said slowly, getting to her feet.

"Oh, and for now, let's keep this conversation between us."

Marissa turned to look at him before slowly nodding her head in agreement. As she left the room, she glanced at Jackson and waved before leaving the precinct. She had to keep the details to herself, so sticking around could not be a thing. It was going to be even harder when she got home.

Marissa really wanted a drink. She had significantly cut back on the alcohol, though not completely. But she talked herself out of stopping at Sirens. She needed to keep a clear mind and stay focused. Alcohol wouldn't help with that.

She also needed to get back home, but she just wasn't ready yet. The whole meeting with Sean Boswell had left her feeling uneasy. It had been so long now, she couldn't remember if it had ever crossed her mind that the very letter that drew them out to the warehouse could have been connected. She must have considered it. But thinking back, everything was just blurry now. Everything before the warehouse was a completely different life. The person she had been died in that warehouse. Whoever came after, whoever she was now, was very different. But the more Marissa thought about it, she realized she had only started receiving actual letters, something more than just photographs, on her birthday.

Marissa stopped along the waterway and looked out. Her head ached. She brought her hand to her neck and let her fingers trace her scar down her neck to her chest. She stopped just in the center of her chest rather than continuing. Her side ached in a way she hadn't noticed in a long while. Usually, she made the effort to just ignore it, pretending it wasn't there. That was where the alcohol used to come in. Alcohol was bad for focus but great for forgetting. Drawing a deep breath in, she looked away from the water and at the busy street.

People were walking by, going about their day like nothing bad was ever going to happen. Ignorant of the bad things that happen around them. At least most of them.

Her eyes landed on the bakery. Mel had kept everything the same when her mom had given it to her. She had fond memories of spending Sundays with her mom and her sisters in there. Madi was equally bad at cooking, so the two of them would find things to do and keep themselves occupied while their mom helped teach Melanie everything she needed to know. She really wasn't ready to go meet with her mom's doctor tomorrow. Her headspace was all wrong, not that there should have been a right headspace for hard conversations.

She thought about calling Mac, seeing where he was. Probably going over his case with Kim. Jackson had asked her to come down to the precinct by herself. She pulled her phone out of her pocket and scrolled through her contacts. She stopped at the first friendly name that popped up—someone she hadn't heard from in a while.

[Hey Jack. How are things going?]

She waited, watching the text. But it never read *seen*. A few minutes later, she shoved her phone back into her pocket. She turned from the bakery to look back out on the water, watching the waves rise and fall, and just tried to clear her mind.

Chapter 17

Marissa paced around the room, staring at the floor. Madilyn and Melanie were both seated and their mom was between them. Melanie had pitched a fit and insisted the others stay outside in the waiting room while they spoke with the doctors.

What a fucking brat.

Marissa had started biting her nails while she paced. Ellie was lying down in front of the empty chair next to Madi that had been meant for her, but Marissa couldn't sit still.

Her eyes fell on her mom. She looked tired. The color was missing from her face. She looked so fragile in a way Marissa had never seen her—a shadow of the woman she had seen in Seattle when she ran into her and Greg. She had been so happy and so full of life. Now, in this cold, empty room, she wore such a distant look on her face.

Marissa glanced over at her sisters. Melanie had always looked just like a younger version of their mom. Even her manner of speech was like their mom's. Madilyn had their mom's softer features, but she was taller with longer legs and higher cheekbones.

She had been going through test after test after the night she had collapsed. They had found a lump in her right breast that required further investigating. They had done a biopsy. When she had fallen, she had broken her arm. That had required surgery and now she wore a light blue cast that Mel's kids had decorated with doodles. Today they were supposed to discuss her biopsy results.

Marissa winced as she bit her nail too far down the nail bed, and it started bleeding, leaving a metallic taste on her tongue. The sound caught her mom's attention, who met her gaze. Mel and Madi were talking a mile a minute to each other. Since they arrived, they had done nothing but talk about how everything was going to be fine. The look Marissa was sharing with her mother said the absolute opposite.

Marissa resumed pacing, averting her eyes back to the floor. She couldn't let her mind run through any of the possibilities. She just needed the fucking doctor to come in already. She glanced up at the clock, the only thing on the off-white wall. What the fuck was it about these rooms that made someone think leaving it empty, plain, and off-white wouldn't be off-putting? It had been 28 minutes since they had been led into this stupid room. The nurse had come in, taken their mom's vitals, and then just disappeared.

Even though Mac was only just outside the door in the waiting room, she had wished that he were there to wrap his arms around her. Instead, he had been left to pass the time with Greg, Brian, and Clyde. The indignation that their mom had a secret boyfriend was still a fresh wound her sisters were more than happy to milk for all they could. Marissa found it absolutely infuriating, because the last thing they should have been doing was making their mom feel guilty about being happy.

And Greg was genuinely a nice guy. He and Marissa had spoken almost as much as she had with her mom since the night she collapsed, and they had slowly gotten to know one another. And something that Marissa could not deny was how much this man loved her mother.

"Do you ever stop moving?" Mel snapped at her as she continued to pace.

"Fuck off, Melanie," Marissa muttered, not in the mood.

"Marissa," her mom said sternly, giving Marissa a look that was less angry and more pleading. It sent a shudder of regret through her, at least until she looked at Melanie, who stuck her tongue out at her.

Finally there was a knock at the door. Marissa's eyes darted back to the clock: 43 minutes since they had been brought into the room. When the doctor walked in, she found herself immediately reading the young, lanky doctor's body language and she braced herself. She didn't bother sitting down but leaned against the wall, forcing herself to stop moving so she could focus and listen. Ellie got up from where she had been lying and sat beside Marissa, nudging her knee gently with her snout.

The doctor started off by apologizing for taking so long and then started running through everything that Marissa had dreaded hearing. His voice droned on, reminding Marissa of the teacher from the *Peanuts* cartoons. She knew he was talking, she could understand what he was saying, but the words were not coming through.

She blinked. He had said breast cancer.

Tears were already running down Mel's face freely while Madi held their mom's hand, clenching her jaw but not giving into the tears yet.

Then it got worse. He started pointing to her scan results, to where they had lit up like a Christmas tree. There was so much. It had metastasized. It was why the break in her arm had been so severe. This was stage four breast cancer.

All of the air felt like it had been sucked out of the room. The only thing Marissa could clearly hear anymore was the sound of blood pumping in her ears. For a moment, her vision seemed to blur, and she was glad she was leaning against the wall because she was sure she would have fallen over. All the wind had been knocked out of her.

The doctor spoke for what felt like forever. Her mom and Madilyn asked questions, good questions, and the doctor answered. Melanie was still crying. Marissa couldn't find her voice to speak, but she listened, grateful Madi was asking all the questions. The next step was chemotherapy. Immunotherapy and hormone therapy were also recommended. Radiation was a possibility, depending on how the chemo worked. Marissa felt overwhelmed. The life expectancy, which Madilyn had asked, was usually five years, best-case scenario. She had dragged that answer out of the doctor, who seemed reluctant to offer statistics. Because every person was different as were their responses to treatment.

When it was finally time to leave, Marissa was thoroughly numb. She was the last one to leave the room, closing the door behind her.

As they returned to the waiting room, Marissa felt a sudden irritation as she heard one of the guys ask if Melanie was okay. As if this was about her. Thankfully, Mac intercepted Marissa, wordlessly pulling her into a hug. She actually resisted at first, afraid that if she gave in, she would fall apart. But the weight of his arms around her made her breathe easier.

"Let's go outside," he said gently. Marissa only nodded against him, and he led her toward the door.

Marissa was surprised that everyone else had followed them outside. Apparently, they all needed some air.

"What can I do?" Greg asked Marilyn, who still had that distant look in her eyes.

Before her mom could respond, she heard Melanie mutter under her breath: "Maybe go and leave it to the family to figure out."

God damn, her sister was being a bitch. Based on the expressions on everyone else's faces, she hadn't been the only one to hear it either. Greg flinched but kept his eyes on Marilyn.

Marissa watched her mom shake her head, giving Greg a smile that was only meant for him, bringing her hand up to his cheek. "Can you take me home?"

Greg smiled at her, the fear that had been on his face melting away for a moment. His hazel eyes glistened. Marissa knew that man would have done anything for the woman in front of him.

"Of course." He leaned forward and kissed her forehead. "I'll get the car started."

He nodded to Marissa, an acknowledgment and goodbye that neither of her sisters got or deserved.

Once he disappeared and jogged off to his Dodge, Marilyn turned to face Melanie, her face stern. "I know you're scared, but I taught you better than that."

"Yes ma'am," Mel answered weakly.

When Marilyn seemed satisfied that she made Melanie feel maybe a little guilty, she sighed and opened her arms. Melanie fell immediately into them. Madi only hesitated for a second before she moved to her mother as well. Marilyn looked at Marissa and motioned for her to join them.

Marissa stood frozen for a second, unmoving, until Mac gave her shoulder a gentle squeeze. She walked over to her mom and sisters and got in on the hug, doing her best to hold back tears.

"I know this is scary, but it's going to be okay," their mom said softly. "We'll get through this."

She could hear the words, but Marissa didn't believe them. Marissa shook her head slightly, only for her mother's benefit, disagreeing with what appeared to be acceptance from her mom. Acceptance … that this was it?

Marilyn pulled back and gave all three of her daughters a smile. "I'm going to go home and rest for a bit. But let's do dinner, just the four of us? Tomorrow night?"

Melanie took the longest to agree, but once she did, her mom smiled at each of them, giving their hands a squeeze before heading off to the car.

Marissa watched as Greg's car left the parking lot, not hearing a word that Mel and Madi spoke beside her. Ellie pressed her cold nose into Marissa's thigh, once and then again, until Marissa looked down and pet the dog, taking a deep breath in like the shepherd was silently instructing. All the men had given the women space, lost in their own conversation several feet away.

"I hate that guy," she then heard Melanie complaining.

"You don't even know that guy," Marissa snapped before she thought better of it, turning to walk back to Mac. Mel stepped in front of her.

"I'm sorry, but I don't remember asking you." Mel had her hand on her hip, which was popped out to side, her face red with anger that Marissa knew wasn't necessarily for her. But this was the new normal. When Mel was angry about something, she hurled that emotion in Marissa's direction.

"Melanie, get out of my way." Marissa kept her voice even, but she instinctively balled up her fist.

"Hey, is this really the time?" Madi stood between them, trying to create some space.

It was strange to be on this side of her sisters. Marissa had spent her entire life playing the diplomat, always trying to make peace and keep them from murdering each other. The unofficial peacekeeper. Now she was standing in front of Melanie, imagining nothing feeling better than punching her baby sister in the face. Of course, she would never make the first move.

"What are you going to do? Hit me?" Mel was taunting her.

Marissa swallowed and let her eyes look past her sister at the three very uncomfortable men watching them closely, ready to run interference at any moment. And at Madi, who was pleading with Marissa with her big brown eyes.

"Get. Out. Of. My. Way." She emphasized every word, her hand still in a fist, narrowing her eyes at Mel.

"Come on, guys. Mom can't have us doing this," Madi pleaded.

Marissa flinched but kept her eyes focused on Melanie. Mel lifted her chin, stretching herself to reach Marissa's gaze, her tiny little frame seeming even less threatening than it did a moment ago.

But Madi was right. They couldn't do this. At least not now. They needed to get through dinner tomorrow and put together a game plan. They needed to focus on their mom.

Taking a deep breath, Marissa released her fists and straightened her back, still taller than her baby sister. She turned to Madi and let out a soft sigh. "I will see you tomorrow."

She said nothing to Melanie as she stepped around her and began walking in the direction of her car.

By the time she'd reached the driver's side door, Mac was already standing opposite of her at the passenger door. They lowered themselves into the car without a word, and Marissa began the drive home.

A few minutes into the ride, Mac broke the silence. "I thought you were gonna deck her."

Marissa glanced over at him, unable to stop herself from smiling when she saw his amused expression. "I almost did."

She had certainly wanted to. But she didn't need any more guilt concerning Melanie.

Mac nodded his head. "That was obvious." He sighed and glanced out his window before turning back to her. "Are you okay?" His voice was softer suddenly, and the weight of the situation came slamming back down on her.

Marissa swallowed, turning on her blinker and keeping her eyes on the road. She couldn't bring herself to answer, so instead she just shook her head, hair falling into eyes.

Mac reached over and took her hand, giving it a squeeze. There wasn't anything to be said. Her mom had stage four cancer. That was her new reality.

The previous twenty-four hours had been numbing. Marissa had done her best not to react to the news of her mom's diagnosis, which meant mostly just checking out. She had made a couple of phone calls trying to make sure the DNA for her cold case was being rerun. For the first time, she was really struggling to keep herself busy enough to ignore something.

Marissa knocked on the door of her mom's condo, as planned, glancing behind her at the beach view her mom had upgraded to. She hadn't made many visits to her mom's place since she had moved, despite many invites—something Marissa now greatly regretted. She heard her mom's terrier barking from the other side of the door, which caused her to glance down at Ellie, who was sitting perfectly beside her.

"Best behavior," she said softly.

At her mom's request, she had arrived almost two hours earlier than the time she had scheduled with her sisters. She had wanted to talk to Marissa. It made her dread the evening even more.

Her mom opened the door and gave Marissa a big smile that almost caused tears to return to Marissa's eyes. "Hey, sweetie. Thanks for coming early."

She stepped inside and gave her mom the biggest hug she had given her in a very long time.

Marilyn laughed when she finally pulled back. "If I had known this is what it would have taken to get you to come over and to give me a hug like that, I would have gotten sick a long time ago."

"That's not funny, Mom," Marissa all but whined at her, although the corners of her lips curled up in a small grin. Finley, her mom's rat terrier mix, was dancing at her feet for attention. Ellie had sauntered in and sat down just off to the side of Marissa, giving her space. Finley, on the other hand, did not believe in personal space.

"It's a little funny," she insisted, still amused with herself as she brushed the hair from Marissa's eyes. "Come on. We can sit out on the balcony."

She followed her mom, glancing around at the open floor plan. "This is one hell of a view, Mom."

"Yeah. I really love it." She smiled over at Marissa before looking back out over the water. "So, the reason I asked you here before your sisters come over…"

Marissa instinctively shook her head. She knew where this was going.

Her mom put her hand over Marissa's. "I know this isn't fair to put on you, but there are things I need to make sure are in place, and I just want to make sure you are prepared."

Marissa took a deep breath and nodded, sitting down on one of the chairs on the balcony. Marilyn took the seat next to her. Ellie curled up at Marissa's feet, resting her head on her feet. Marissa braced herself for the very difficult conversation she knew was coming.

And knowing how difficult it was going to be did not prepare her for everything they covered over the next hour. Her mom had been more prepared than Marissa had known; she had already made arrangements. She was leaving Marissa in charge. It was all in writing. It was not at all reassuring. But for her mom, she was able to keep her face mostly unreadable as she took in everything.

"Why didn't you say anything before?" Marissa asked shakily after her mom had gone through everything with her. She had found a lump years ago. She had known and done nothing. She made plans, made it legal and binding. But had done nothing about the cancer growing in her body. Marissa was reminded of being on a defibrillator. She remembered the forced shock waves that jolted through her when her body had tried to shut down.

Her mom brought her wineglass to her lips and took a drink before she turned to look at Marissa. "I didn't want you to worry," she said slowly. "When I found the lump, I had it checked out. I just … didn't follow through. There was so much going on."

A new lump formed in her throat as the realization sank in before her mom said the words.

"You were still in the hospital, and you were struggling so hard…"

Marissa was pretty sure she was going to vomit. She could feel her hands going numb, pins and needles beginning to rise up her arms.

This was her fault.

"I can see what you're thinking, Marissa. This is not your fault," her mom said quickly, putting her glass down on the table between them. "I was just so afraid for you, I wanted to focus on you."

"So you thought it was okay to just pretend you didn't have cancer?"

"No. I just … never followed through," her mom tried to explain. "I'm so sorry. If I could go back, I would do it differently."

Marissa didn't believe that for a second, but she held her mom's gaze and listened.

"But I can't, sweetheart. I can't change anything. All I can do is plan ahead and spend my time wisely." She put her hand to Marissa's face, giving her a weak smile. "You heard what the doctor said. Five years isn't bad, honey."

She put her hand over her mom's, but she couldn't form words. Five years wasn't enough. There would never be enough time.

"I need to go to the bathroom," she said finally, shakily getting to her feet. Marilyn also got to her feet, instinctively trying to reach for her with her broken arm, which was in a sling against her chest.

"Sweetheart…" her mom started.

Marissa stopped herself and gave her mom the best smile she could muster. "I'm fine, Mom. I just need a minute. I'll be right back."

Marilyn nodded weakly before she sat back down.

Marissa closed the door behind Ellie as she followed her into the bathroom and locked it. She leaned against the sink and stared down at the drain, feeling like her entire foundation was shaking beneath her.

She had spent so much time avoiding her mom because she hated lying to her. Because she wasn't good at it. Because she wanted to keep her mom safe, and she could only do that from a distance. And instead, she had been wasting time she didn't realize she couldn't get back. All the missed phone calls, the rain checks, and every time Marissa just made excuses not to see her mother and then justified it were all running through her head.

Slowly, she turned the cold water on and splashed her face, the cold jolting her back to the present. She jumped when she heard Finley erupt into a flurry of high-pitched barks. Marissa assumed one of her sisters had arrived. Giving herself a final look in the mirror, she wiped her eyes and sighed heavily before opening the door.

As she exited the bathroom, she saw her mom talking to Greg. He looked up and smiled at her. "Sorry to interrupt your evening. I realized I forgot my phone."

He held up his cell phone before turning his attention back to Marilyn and giving her a quick kiss before making a hasty exit.

Once the door closed behind him, Marissa couldn't help but raise an eyebrow. Her mom made a face at her. "What?"

Marissa stuck her hands in her back pockets and shrugged. "Nothing. Just observing."

"And what are you observing?" Her mom was still making that face, a small, playful smile on the corner of her lips, her eyes suddenly brighter.

"He left his phone here. Does he live here?"

"No." She shook her head, but she had a smile on her lips. "He does stay over sometimes, though."

"For what it's worth, I think he's a really nice guy." She meant it. He seemed genuinely nice and very much in love with her mom.

"I appreciate that," her mom said before sighing with some underlying frustration. "I wish your sisters would hear me out about him."

"Well, they suck, and that's why I'm your favorite."

Her mom laughed and shook her head. "I don't have favorites."

She grinned, and for a moment, Marissa forgot the reason they were having dinner in the first place. "So, can I help with dinner?"

Before she'd arrived, her mom had thrown something in the oven, and it smelled amazing and was making Marissa hungry. Her mom gave a sideways glance and opened her mouth to say something, but Marissa interrupted, "Like setting the table or something. I promise I won't touch the food."

Her mom relaxed. "That would be great, kiddo."

Chapter 18

He was going to have to call Ben. It had been an accident. He hadn't meant to kill her. But she wouldn't stop screaming. He could still hear her scream piercing his eardrum, causing his whole body to vibrate. He had just wanted her to stay quiet. Screaming took all the fun out of it. But he hadn't meant for this.

"Fuck," he said again to the empty room, running his hands through his hair as he stared at the lifeless body lying on the cold hard floor. She was right where he had left her. Lifeless. The longer he stared, the more he thought she looked like a porcelain doll whose eyes were stuck open.

She had been so beautiful. She had reminded him of Marissa. And Caroline. It was the thing that had drawn him to Marissa in the first place. She had reminded him of Caroline.

He hadn't realized when he had set his sights on Marissa that someone already had their eyes on her. Sometimes, he had to remind himself how lucky he was that Ben let him live. But keeping Ben happy was a fucking chore.

Maybe he could just leave. Disappear. Dump the phones, lose the credit cards, drop everything, and just vanish. But Ben had connections. And had already threatened to pin everything on him. He had that kind of power. Look what had happened to Daniel Fryer. They had gone their separate ways, and all had been quiet for a few years. Now, he was in prison. The likelihood that he could really disappear was essentially nonexistent, and he knew it.

"FUCK!" he yelled into the empty apartment.

He forcefully sat down on the familiar, backward wooden chair, which was situated across from the now-dead woman, and pulled out his phone. There wasn't any way around it.

The phone rang once. His eyes landed back on the dead girl in the middle of the floor. It rang a second time. He started bouncing his knee on the balls of his feet. It rang a third time. His mouth had gone completely dry. On the fourth ring, he picked up.

"I thought I told you not to call." Ben's voice was cold and impatient.

"You did. But it's an emergency." He had to focus so he wouldn't choke on his words.

"What kind of emergency?" His voice was lower than it had been previously.

"The girl. She's dead." He felt a cold chill run through him. It was bad enough he'd killed her, but giving the news to Ben was way worse.

"What girl?" Ben snapped, his voice still low.

"The girl here, in Chicago."

There was a heavy sigh on the other end of the line, followed by a long silence. For a second, he actually thought Ben had hung up the phone on him. Finally, he heard him hiss, "What happened?"

He was suddenly grateful to be two thousand miles away. Even through the phone, he felt the danger in the other man's anger. "She wouldn't stop screaming. I just needed her to stop. I had a knife and…"

"Alright. Enough," he said impatiently. "Congrats on popping that proverbial cherry," Ben said dryly on the other line.

"I really didn't mean to."

"It is what it is." Ben sighed. "We just have to deal with it now. Maybe we can use it to our advantage."

He stayed quiet on his end of the line for a long time while Ben worked out their next steps. He turned around in his chair, now facing away from the girl on the ground. The way that man's mind worked was nothing short of terrifying.

Ben relayed his instructions and said he would be in touch. A sense of relief rushed through him when he heard the click on the other line. After hanging up the phone, he dropped it on the table and laced his fingers together, resting his elbows on his knees. He sat there for a long minute before running his hands through his hair again and getting to his feet. Turning back around, he stared at the dead girl sprawled out on the floor. She could have been sleeping if it hadn't been for all the blood.

And her lifeless, icy blue eyes.

There was a lot to do. At least he could take his time. There was no rush on his end. No one knew he was there. No one knew where she was. Sure, they were searching for her, but they were looking in all the wrong places. Under Ben's tutelage, he had managed to lead the police in the direction he had wanted: away from where they actually were.

He really hadn't meant to kill her. Sure, he had done many questionable things and had some very specific urges that he had started giving into. But murder hadn't been on his bucket list.

He had no one to blame but himself. If he hadn't gotten caught sneaking around and taking some inappropriate pictures in the first place, he would have never found himself face to face with Ben. It had just been a harmless hobby. Taking photos of women in their natural habitat, comfortable, usually in their own homes, taking off clothing. Sometimes, he would go back and steal said pieces of clothing later on. Making contact, sending letters and photographs, kidnapping, torture—it was all new to him. What was the alternative, now, though? Jail? Death?

It hadn't been until Marissa had her breakdown in her bathroom that the true level of wild obsession and dangerous intent had become clear. Ben was on a whole different level. The sight of what she had done to herself had made him sick. He had wanted to stop her, tried to stop her. Ben made him step back from her, had taken his camera and snapped all those photos while she pleaded for help. He hadn't been able to handle it. He'd texted Agent Mackenzie. She couldn't be alone. This didn't follow the very strict timeline Ben had made, but his pleas for Ben to stick to the plan had worked. It had given Ben a new appreciation of him. Now, part of him wished he hadn't. Maybe she would be dead right now, and all of this would be over.

Of course, what made that hard was that he actually liked Marissa. Genuinely. She was a good person. Flawed but good. She didn't deserve this. Unfortunately, she was in Ben's sights.

Ben had tried to explain to him once. How he'd always been the good guy, always done the right thing. He followed the rules, he opened doors for women, he paid his taxes. And one day, he just didn't want to be that person anymore. He wanted more. He was sick of working every day with no recognition. He was tired of being rejected. He was tired of being passed over.

Ben had started small by breaking small rules at work. Then, he stole a few things. But all of that was easy. Too easy. No one ever suspected him of anything. He needed a bigger risk. He had attacked someone, planned the whole thing out to the very last detail. He studied them, watched their routine. And once he had gotten them down a lone alley, he had beat the shit out of them. He had done some real damage too. The man had been left with a brain injury as well as a broken ribcage and a broken arm. He'd taken his things to make it look like a robbery. The local police investigated, but there was nothing to find. Ben said that assault gave him clarity about what he had to do. He needed to direct all that pent-up rage toward someone, and he needed no witnesses. His very first murder, just like the assault, was planned down to every last detail. And taking a life? Ben said there was no other feeling in the world like it. And what was even better was getting away with it. Ben always thought of himself as the smartest man in any room, several steps in front of everyone else. So far, he had proven that to be true. It was like he was always playing a game of chess, forcing his opponent to think in the moment while he was two or three moves ahead.

He got to his feet and went over to the table where his camera lay, along with the knife he'd had slit her throat with. He took the lens cap off and played with the focus for a moment before crouching down next to the pool of blood. At the very least, he was going to get some beautiful up-close shots of those cold dead blue eyes.

A few hours later, he was in his makeshift darkroom. This warehouse space had turned out to be a real fucking find. He had been able to do everything he had needed, and there were no neighbors to hear the screaming. He watched, comforted by the dark as the image began to develop in the chemicals. She had been beautiful when she was alive, but she was absolutely stunning in death. Her ice-blue eyes, the paleness of her skin. She was as close to perfect as anyone could be.

This was a space he felt safe in. He was in control here. And it was quiet. He watched as the dozens of photos came to life and decided which he would be keeping for himself as his own souvenir. After all, he had taken his very first life. It may not have been on his to-do list, but here he was. The longer he sat with it, the more he recognized the thrill Ben spoke about.

Of course, he wasn't much of a thrill seeker. He never wanted to do this again. But he hadn't chickened out or run away like he had thought he would. He was following through.

He had thought her death had been such a waste, but in seeing the beauty developing in front of him, he realized that wasn't true at all.

Chapter 19

Marissa and Mac had made the trip to Seattle together, but he was heading into the office for a meeting with Nick Walker about god only knew what. His hearing was only a few days away.

She loved having Mac around all the time, but he was growing restless. He had rearranged her kitchen and her medicine cabinets and kept finding small projects around the house to keep him busy. She imagined that, one day, Mac would be one of those people who really sucked at retirement.

She gave him a quick kiss, and he pulled her close for a deeper one before he turned and walked off in the opposite direction. She watched him go, a smile on her lips. Shoving her hands into her pockets, she motioned for Ellie to follow as she headed toward the agreed-upon meeting place.

Detective Carmen Vega was staying at the Moxy Hotel downtown. It was easy enough to find. Once she got there, she messaged Carmen to let her know she was in the lobby.

[be right down]

Marissa glanced around. It was a nice hotel, definitely out of her price range. Ellie sat by her feet, quietly watching as people traveled by. About seven minutes passed before a woman with dark loose curls down to her shoulders came up to her.

"Marissa?" she asked slowly.

"Yes. You must be Carmen." She smiled at the woman and held out her hand.

Carmen Vega wasn't much taller than Marissa in her flats. She had a petite build with most of her height attributed to her long, lanky legs, which were on full display in her jean shorts. She wore a red shirt and a gold necklace with a beautiful stone hanging off it. She shook Marissa's hand, using the other to show her credentials. Marissa followed the gesture and did the same.

"It's so good to meet you. Why don't we go up to my room and we can look over the files?"

"Lead the way."

Carmen led her to the elevator, which had just arrived. They stepped in and she pushed the number 4.

"Your dog is beautiful, by the way," she said, her dark brown eyes smiling over at Marissa and doing their best to ignore Ellie.

"Thank you. She's a really good girl."

"How does she do with other dogs?" Carmen asked, glancing down as Ellie sat at Marissa's feet.

"She does alright. She's pretty great at ignoring others."

"Perfect. I have my search and rescue dog in the room. She does well at keeping to herself, though."

"You do search and rescue?" Marissa raised an eyebrow, surprised.

"I do! It's actually why we're in town. We're giving a presentation."

"That's so cool." Marissa meant it.

As the elevator came to a stop, Marissa followed the woman down the hall until they stopped outside room 416. She swiped her key card and opened the door, holding it for Marissa to follow her in.

It was a typical hotel room. The first thing Marissa saw was a beautiful tri-colored collie lying on the bed. She lifted her head to look at them but promptly put it back down.

"This is Foxtrot," Carmen announced with pride. "She's my best girl."

"She's gorgeous," Marissa said before glancing down at her own beautiful girl. "So are you," she said softly to the shepherd. Ellie perked up her ears and snorted as though she understood. "I love her name," Marissa commented, looking over at the collie, who remained on the bed, perfectly still.

"It's because when she's excited, she sort of does this little dance. And I'm a huge fan of ballroom dance." Carmen gave her dog some love before walking over to the table in the corner of the room.

"Okay, I've got everything already out on the table." She motioned for Marissa to follow her.

As Marissa walked over, she could see that Carmen Vega had a giant case in front of her. Several piles were assorted, filling up most of the tabletop. Marissa grabbed a chair and sat beside the Vancouver detective.

"So!" Carmen motioned to the table. "I've been compiling this case for a few years now. It started with a single missing person. Whitney Rodriguez, seventeen-year-old, assumed runaway. She had been using drugs since she was fourteen. She had called her dad, asking to come home because she was trying to get clean. He told her yes, but she never arrived. He reported her missing April 10, 2014. There was never any sign of her. But while I was looking through the database, I found fourteen similar missing persons reports of young women, ages sixteen to twenty-five. All the circumstances were close or the same. They all went missing between 2005 and 2016."

Carmen paused. Marissa nodded, taking the information in.

"Now, jump to 2016, when a body was discovered tossed off a hiking trail in a local park. We had to use dental records, but she was a match for one of my missing girls. I didn't think too much of it, except that one of them had been found. But then another body turned up. The most recent girl who had gone missing on my list. She had been missing for four and a half years. Her body was found at a different park twenty miles away but in the same circumstances. They both had opioids in their systems. Both had been stabbed and beaten, and cause of death was strangulation."

Carmen paused again, pulling out a chair for Marissa before sitting down. "Here."

Marissa smiled and sat, engrossed in the other woman's story.

"On a hunch, I started looking for Jane Does with similar deaths. From there, I found five more matches to the missing girls on my list. All close to the Washington–Oregon border."

Marissa blinked. It was more than a cold case. It was a serial killer.

"When the information came through about your case and the details of your Jane Doe's death, it was too close to ignore." Carmen grabbed a sheet of paper that had been sitting by itself and handed it to Marissa. "This is my list of missing girls."

Marissa nodded, taking the sheet of paper. "Those details are a little too close for a coincidence." She scanned it. Carmen had listed out names, ages, and the years they went missing. Along the side, clearly added at a different time, she included the ethnicity.

Whitney Rodriguez – 16 – 2014 (Hispanic)
Jackie Hernandez – 19 – 2012 (Mexican)
Leteshia Jordan – 17 – 2008 (Black)

This list went on and on. Marissa read through it twice before she stopped on a name that caught her eye. *Sarah Wickersham – 22 – 2009 (white)*. She was number 12 on the list.

Carmen nodded. "I think this might be your girl."

She reached into one of the stacks of files and, after a moment, pulled out the one she was looking for.

"Sarah Wickersham. Twenty-two years old reported missing by her sister. She is the only one on this list who wasn't a drug user, a sex worker, and who is white." Carmen looked at her piles with a frown. "But she is in the right age range, was in the right area, and went missing right between two others."

Marissa was about to ask, but before she could, Carmen handed her Sarah's missing person's report: *22 years old. Long black hair, blue eyes. 5'8", 140lbs. Last seen at Powell's Bookstore where she worked. She had been closing, seen by two other coworkers walking to her car.*

By all accounts, she should have been a low-risk victim. "Can I take a copy of this?"

Carmen smiled. "That is your copy."

"Thank you."

Her mind was racing. She needed to contact the Doe Project as soon as she left here and give them the information. Narrowing things down would at the very least give them a direction to look. But if she had been from Portland, what was her body doing in Seattle? Marissa shook her head, looking back down at Carmen's list.

"This is quite the case you've got yourself."

Carmen nodded. "And it's not necessarily an active case, so this is where my free time goes. I'm not normally a cold case detective. I work homicide down in Vancouver."

"Free time? And you do search and rescue?"

Carmen nodded. "I used to have a cadaver dog, too."

Marissa whistled, impressed. She looked over the piles that covered the table. "Just be careful." Marissa hadn't planned on saying it, but the words came out anyway. "Serial Killers are no joke." She paused. "Do you have a profile?"

Carmen nodded. "I think that while he was active, he was both a killer and rapist. There are reports of a rapist terrorizing women close to the border of Washington and Oregon. Never caught or identified."

Marissa shuddered. "I wish you luck."

She grabbed the bag off her back and put the missing person's report inside while pulling out copies of the original report and notes Tom had made.

"This is everything I have on my Jane Doe, including the autopsy report."

"Thank you so much."

They spent the next hour going over files and comparing notes. By the end of the visit, Marissa felt more than just hopeful; she felt almost confident this was her Jane Doe. She also found herself very intrigued by Carmen's case.

"If you're interested, I can always use another set of eyes."

Marissa shook her head and laughed. "It's not that I'm not interested, I'm just at my limit with serial killers right now."

Carmen nodded. "I can't even begin to imagine."

Although they hadn't specifically covered it, Carmen had made it known she knew who Marissa was. Marissa had briefly been a headline sensation, although she had no memory of it. That was during her extended hospital stay.

SOLE SURVIVOR OF
CRAZED COUPLE KILLER

"But maybe at some point, if you need to bounce ideas off someone or anything, we can get together again?"

She just couldn't fucking help herself.

Marissa had gone in not sure what to expect but came out of the Moxy Hotel feeling rejuvenated. With everything going on, this case kept falling to the bottom of the pile. Despite her best efforts, she had put an enormous amount of pressure on herself to make any kind of headway. For Tom. Because it was the least she could do.

Even the idea that she could just give this girl her name back and bring closure to a family who had been left wondering for at least ten years would be enough. At least for now.

Carmen Vega was putting pieces together that no one else was seeing. If Marissa's Jane Doe was in fact Sarah Wickersham, then Carmen was already putting in all the work trying to find her murderer. If Marissa could ever get out from beneath Ben's watchful eyes, she was more than likely to jump right in with her. It sounded like she would have been welcome to.

A quick glance to confirm she hadn't missed any messages told her that Mac was still in his own meeting. She headed toward the market, figuring since she was in town, she could at least indulge in some crab rangoons. Ellie trotted alongside her, happy to be outside. It was a warm day for June, a little bit overcast with a bit of rain but with welcome warmth.

She sat on a bench beneath the pavilion and opened her email. She scrolled down until she found her contact from the Doe Project and forwarded them the new information. Hopefully, something good would come from it.

She had been skeptical about reaching out to other departments. Most cops weren't keen on cold cases. But this had worked out better than she had ever hoped it would. She did a quick Google search for "Sarah Wickersham" just to see what would come up. She was not disappointed: several articles covering her disappearance, a Facebook page titled "Finding Sarah," and quite a few conspiracy threads on Reddit. She had just clicked on the first one when her phone rang in her hand. She smiled.

"Hey, are you done?"

"Yep. Just leaving now. Where are you?" Mac's voice made her stomach flutter.

"I'm eating some crab rangoons at the market. I saved two." She looked down at the bag. "I saved you one. Sorry."

Mac laughed. "I'll be there in ten minutes or less."

"Perfect. I'll be here." She hung up the phone and forgot about her Google search. Instead, she opened her contacts and called Kate, closing the bag of rangoons to avoid the temptation.

Kate answered on the third ring. "Hey, Marissa."

"Hey, I just wanted to see how things were going at the house."

"They're good! Ethan and I just started *The Prisoner of Azkaban.* Kim is in the kitchen on the phone with work." Kate and Ethan had started the Harry Potter series because Kate had never seen them.

Marissa nodded to no one. Having Kim and Ethan around had turned out to be lucky. The fact that Ethan and Kate got along so well was also lucky.

"Perfect. We should be back in a couple of hours. Both of our meetings are over."

"Awesome," Kate said on the other line.

Since Marissa's first meeting with Kate, the relationship had really shifted. She knew it probably wasn't the right move, but they had become more like a family with each passing day. Marissa considered calling Meredith in the moment. It was too easy to sink into the comfortable place they had built. Kate wasn't safe with her. Neither was Mac, but he wouldn't take no for an answer, and as an adult who carried a gun, he could make that choice. Kate was only fourteen. She couldn't make those decisions for herself, not legally. And she shouldn't have to.

Her thoughts wandered to Marlene. She was still refusing to give any information about Kate's father, insisting that there was no other family to take her. Rubbing her face, Marissa shook off the thoughts about Marlene. That was a headache she couldn't focus on today.

When Mac came into view, a smile spread across her face, and she wondered if she could convince him to grab some more rangoons for the road.

Chapter 20

Marissa stared at her Ring camera. An envelope lay there, having barely been thrown over the top step of the porch. She replayed the clip over and over again, only to see the envelope sliding across the step. She couldn't see where it had come from or who had tossed it. She checked the other cameras she had set up, but whoever tossed the envelope knew exactly where the line of sight ended for the cameras.

Using the kitchen counter to help her push off her stool, she got to her feet. Hesitantly, she made her way to the entry to the living room and peered in. Kate and Ethan were laughing at an episode of *Friends*. She wished Mac were there. He and Kim had left early that morning for Mac's hearing, so it was just her and the kids. Closing her Ring app, she opened her text messages. She had an existing thread with Jackson and Veronica. She opened the conversation and started typing.

[I got another letter.]

She shoved her phone into her pocket and took a deep breath. Opening her front door, she took a long look around before she moved out on the porch and stooped to grab the manila envelope.

She considered going into the kitchen, but the chance of Ethan and Kate walking in was too high, so with a groan, she started up the stairs. Marissa was going to have to get a lock for her office.

She dumped the contents of the envelope onto the desk, the familiar sensation of cold weight in the pit of her stomach bubbling up, overwhelming her. At first, it looked like just pictures. A lot of pictures. Scanning the table, she looked over the contents, touching nothing. There were definitely no flowers included this time. She did, however, find a note at the bottom of the stack. Unfolding the piece of paper, she read it several times.

WHEN WE LET OUR EMOTIONS GET THE BETTER OF US, MISTAKES HAPPEN. EVEN ME. EVEN YOU.

Frowning, Marissa put the letter to the side and focused on the photographs. There were two different sets of pictures. Some of them were up-close shots of Brenna Thompson, the lawyer from Chicago who had been kidnapped. The others were of Marissa, in moments when she was alone and looking isolated. She grouped the photos together before taking a closer look. As her eyes scanned through them, her heart caught in her throat, and she felt her knees buckle beneath her as she realized the subject of many of the photos were the lifeless eyes of Brenna Thompson. If she'd had any doubts about what she was looking at, the last picture showed Brenna Thompson on the ground, eyes wide open and empty, blood spilling from her neck and down her chest. Grabbing the table for support, she forced her eyes to find to the other pile of photos and began flipping through.

These were just photos of her, standing off to herself, alone. Marissa stared, running back through her memory to remember when the events in those photos took place. The first one was taken weeks ago, maybe nearly a month ago. Right around the time Marissa received the pictures of Brenna Thompson after she had been taken. But she couldn't identify the timeline of the pictures that focused on her. There was no way to tell when these photos of Brenna had been taken either.

Grabbing her phone, she scrolled down to Mac's name. He was likely still in his hearing since she hadn't heard from him, so she decided to just send him a text.

[Brenna Thompson is dead.]

After she hit send, she groaned and scrolled to find Nick Walker's phone number. Chances were he was at that hearing, too. But she sent him the message as well.

She all but jumped when her Ring alarm went off before she could shove her phone back into her pocket. Opening the app, her body relaxed when she saw Veronica standing at her door. She shut the office door behind her and hurried down the stairs to let her in.

"Hey," Marissa said before Ronnie pulled her in for a hug. Ellie nudged her way through, tail wagging and whining softly in greeting.

"You okay?" Ronnie frowned, looking over Marissa's face before peering into the living room. Kate glanced and waved at Ronnie before turning back to the TV.

Marissa just shrugged. "I guess. You got here fast."

"I'm not working today. I was just at the sandwich shop for lunch." She lowered her voice when she said, "You want to show it to me?"

She nodded and motioned for Ronnie to follow her back up the stairs. Once they were in her office, Ellie trailing in behind them, she shut the door.

"It's all right there." She motioned to the photographs strewn across her desk. She glanced down at the photos warily, the images already burned into her mind. At least the ones of Brenna Thompson. She stepped over the piles all over her floor to make her way to the window, plopping down in the chair that was homed there.

Veronica was quiet, sitting in Marissa's office chair, studying each photo with the same intensity until she came upon the first one of Brenna. She gasped softly, doing a double take before she scanned the rest of the images. Finally, she turned back to Marissa.

"Did you call the FBI?"

She shook her head. "I sent them all messages. They're at Mac's hearing today."

"Likely whoever left this for you knew that. I assume you didn't see anyone?" Her work tone had turned on.

Again, Marissa shook her head.

"Jackson is working. We should call it in. This should be the escalation Nick Walker was talking about."

Marissa hadn't even thought about it. This entire thing had left her feeling numb now that the shock had worn off. Again, she found herself feeling disconnected. But she needed to. She had to compartmentalize. It was the only way to keep functioning.

"Marissa?" Ronnie's voice broke through Marissa's thoughts.

"Sorry." Marissa swallowed, shaking her head.

"What are you even apologizing for?" Veronica didn't hide her surprise.

"I don't know," Marissa mumbled, running her hand over the back of her neck. "I'm just... I don't know. I'm tired."

"I'm not surprised." Ronnie stood, pulled her in for another hug, and led her to the office chair. "Sit for a minute."

She grabbed her phone, punched in a number, and pressed it to her ear, giving Marissa a small smile.

"Hey," Veronica said into the phone, turning away from Marissa.

She knew it was Jackson on the other line. She turned her eyes from Veronica, giving her as much privacy as someone could when both occupying a small room. Her gaze fell on the photographs.

This was her fault. There wasn't any way around it. She closed her eyes when she felt tears threatening to escape.

"Okay, perfect." Ronnie turned back to Marissa. "We'll see you soon." She shoved her phone back into her pocket and gave Marissa a small smile. "Jackson should be here in about ten minutes."

Marissa huffed. "I hate being a burden."

"You're not a burden." Ronnie shook her head. "Come on. We're gonna go downstairs, maybe get some fresh air, and wait for Jackson. I'm gonna take all of this with us, though." She gathered the pictures up and shoved them back into the envelope and then shoved the envelope into her pocket. "Come on."

Marissa nodded and got back to her feet, following Veronica down the stairs. As they reached the bottom, Kate walked past, a tall glass of water in her hand. She smiled at Veronica and then Marissa before heading back into the living room to with on the couch beside Ethan, who was holding popcorn. They were on *The Goblet of Fire* today.

Marissa followed Ronnie out to the front porch, Ellie tailing right behind her. They plopped on the bench, and Marissa noted that the weather had turned gray, like any normal day in June. Rainy but comfortable.

Marissa couldn't help trying to work it all out for the millionth time. The envelope had to have come from somewhere. She couldn't understand why they couldn't get this guy on any surveillance. Usually, sitting on her porch made her feel like she was making some kind of statement. One that said, *Fuck you.* But right now, she just wanted to run back inside and lock her doors.

"I just want this to be over," Marissa said, letting her head fall to the back of the bench.

"I know. We'll get it figured out." Ronnie was trying to be reassuring, but it was falling flat on her ears.

"Will we though?" Marissa groaned. "Because it's been years since I've been receiving the photographs and letters and flowers, always being watched. We have made literally zero progress on figuring anything out." Marissa straightened and met Ronnie's gaze. "I can't live the rest of my life like this."

"I know, hon," Ronnie said gently.

Marissa knew she meant well, but her frustration was toppling over. The FBI was supposed to be in Chicago, finding Brenna. They had discovered who she was, where she was last seen, but then the trail had gone cold, and there hadn't been any updates since.

And there wouldn't be. Because she was dead.

By the time Jackson arrived, Marissa's anger was boiling.

"So what do we have?" Jackson glanced at Marissa, sitting curled up on her corner of the bench, her arms folded across her chest, and then turned his attention to Ronnie. Clearly the better choice.

Veronica handed over the photographs out of the envelope and sighed. She sat back down beside Marissa while Jackson flipped through them. Marissa knew the moment he flipped across the photograph of Brenna Thompson and her lifeless, strikingly blue eyes.

"We alerted the FBI?"

"We tried to. All of the contacts we have at the FBI are currently in Mac's hearing."

Jackson paused, watching her for a minute. "I'm surprised you stayed home."

Marissa shrugged. "Nick Walker thought it would be better if I weren't present." It hadn't really been a suggestion.

Jackson bristled, not bothering to hide his own frustration. "I don't like that man," he muttered, flipping through the photos. "What about that guy you met with the other day?"

Marissa met Jackson's eyes and took a deep breath. "I actually forgot."

She grabbed his card out of her phone case and started typing a message.

[I received another batch of photos. The girl in Chicago is dead.]

She sighed and put her phone back down.
"Same as usual? You didn't see anything?"
Marissa just shook her head.
"I went across the street and spoke to the PT officers who are supposed to be on watch. Stalinski and Colbert. They said they didn't see anything out of the ordinary, and after looking at the cameras, they didn't find anything."

"How?" Marissa snapped, not really directed at anyone. "How could no one see *anything?* Is it a ghost? Magic? I don't fucking understand."

Jackson sighed before he nodded. "What if we put a patrol car out front?"

"Because we have the resources for that?" Marissa knew the answer, and Jackson's expression showed that he did as well. "I'm so fucking tired."

She shook her head, the feeling of defeat just washing over her.

"I know," Jackson said gently, giving her a sympathetic look. "Look. I don't know what the answer is." It was the softest she had ever heard Jackson speak. "But we will figure it out. With or without the FBI, we will figure it out."

He paused and looked over at Veronica before meeting Marissa's eyes again.

"Have you thought about a safehouse or Witness Protect—"

"Nope. Not happening." She shook her head. "Especially with how things are right now. I can't just leave my mom."

"Alright, kid." He gave her shoulder a squeeze and sat down in the empty chair.

"Don't you have to get back to work?"

Jackson shrugged. "It's a slow day." He sat back and let out a heavy breath. "I want to at least wait until the feds get back to town. I got nothing else going on that requires my immediate attention."

"And it's my day off, so it looks like you're stuck with us for now."

Marissa forced a smile. They were only trying to help. "I guess it could be worse," she said finally.

The stress had actually caused Marissa to fall asleep. Not a fitful sleep by any means but more of a coping mechanism. When she opened her eyes, she was still on the bench, but Mac was sitting beside her. Someone had brought more chairs out to the porch.

Marissa had never considered her porch small—it was wide and wrapped around the house—but with everyone currently congregating on it, she felt closed in. She glanced around, looking at who had shown up.

Mac was right beside her, and Ronnie sat on the other side of him. Nick Walker was leaning against the banister in front of them, and Herbert Jackson was still sitting in the chair next to the bench. Clyde Bennet was sitting on a backward chair beside Walker.

It was a whole party, and they had arrived while she was sleeping. She rubbed her face and leaned into Mac, who opened his arms and wrapped them around her. Despite the comfort his arms offered, she felt uncomfortable and out of place on her own porch.

"Why don't we get out of your hair for the evening?" Jackson said.

Marissa blinked, glancing around. It hadn't gotten too dark, but evening was in the air. She meant to sit up but instead found herself getting more comfortable.

"Let's meet up tomorrow. Your local precinct?" Nick Walker looked to Jackson for permission, and though Jackson made a face, he nodded. "Perfect. I'll see you tomorrow."

Marissa watched as everyone sort of filed off her front porch, saying their quick goodbyes until she and Mac were alone on the bench.

"What the hell just happened?" she asked without moving from where she was resting.

"I didn't want to wake you." Mac kissed the top of her head. "We were just discussing surveillance and photographs." He paused. "Jackson said you had a few choice words about it."

Marissa nodded against his chest. "I'm tired of being hunted by a ghost," she said, the anger boiling back up.

"I won't let anything happen to you," Mac whispered in her ear.

Suddenly, Marissa remembered why he hadn't been there when she received the new photos. She sat up and turned to face him. "How did the hearing go?"

Mac smiled at her. "Cleared. Officially reinstated. And now, our relationship is now officially above board."

The anger she was feeling momentarily subsided and she leaned forward to kiss him.

"I wish I had been here instead, though."

Marissa shook her head. "No. It's fine. We needed you not to be fired."

"That's fair." He sighed and pulled her in to lean against him once again. She didn't fight it. "I feel like we're in for a long meeting tomorrow."

Marissa nodded. "Probably." She closed her eyes. "Can we just stay here for a while longer?"

"Of course," he said gently.

Chapter 21

Marissa sat at the table, her agitation slowly increasing as time passed. She drummed the fingers of one hand on the top of the table, picking her cuticles on the other hand. They had been waiting for Nick Walker to make his appearance. So far, they hadn't seen anyone since they had been escorted in. It was the first time Marissa felt this uncomfortable in her own precinct. At home. In Port Townsend. Mac was sitting beside her, his hands folded over the table, his eyes on the table. He hadn't said a word since they sat down. It made the whole thing even more unsettling.

This was about Brenna Thompson.

Marissa hadn't slept well since the arrival of that letter the day before. She glanced down at Ellie lying at her feet, sleeping soundly. It wasn't usually like her to sleep on the job, but Marissa had kept both of them up the night before.

Her blood was still running cold. Whether it made sense or not, no one could tell Marissa that this girl's death wasn't on her hands. Her hand wasn't on the knife, but the words from that first letter when her first photo appeared ran through her mind.

UNTIL THEN, I WILL KEEP LOOKING FOR SOMEONE TO FILL THE HOLE YOU'VE LEFT ME WITH.
BUT THERE IS NO SUBSTITUTE FOR YOU.

No one could convince her this wasn't her fault. Brenna Thompson's death was the direct consequence of not pleasing Ben or whoever the letter may have been from.

"You're bleeding."

Mac's voice broke through her thoughts. He spoke softly, his eyes full of concern, but he didn't move.

"What?"

Marissa had to pull herself out of whatever trance she was under. Looking down at the finger she had been digging at, she saw he wasn't wrong. The corner of her thumb was bleeding.

"It's fine," she said, clamping the rest of her fingers over the bleeding thumb, folding her finger into her palm.

"Marissa, this isn't your fault." His voice was still soft, watching her as though he could hear her thoughts.

"Isn't it though?" Her voice strained. "If those letters are to be believed, and at this point, I think they probably should be, the only reason she was taken in the first place is because she looked like me."

Mac opened his mouth to say something, but the door opened. Nick Walker stepped into the room, holding a folder in his arms, a deep frown across his face.

He stepped around them and stood behind the table. When placing the folder on the table between them, he let out a heavy sigh.

Marissa didn't bother to wait. "Does this count as escalation, *Supervisory Special Agent Walker*?" She did not hold back, adding emphasis to his title.

Walker didn't seem surprised by her attitude. He looked between Marissa and Mac and nodded his head. "As a matter of fact, Ms. Ambrose, it does."

"*Detective*," she corrected.

"Brenna Thompson's body was recovered in Lincoln Park earlier this morning in Chicago."

Mac seemed to snap to attention. "Do we have—"

Walker held his hand up. "I've already got Clyde on the way out there to help local police and the Chicago branch. With luck, we will be able to find her crime scene. It's clear the body was dumped after death, especially considering the photographs."

"Oh, are we taking those seriously again?" Marissa leaned back in the chair, wrapping her arms around herself.

"Now that isn't—"

"What? Fair? Uncalled for?" she snapped. "I *told* you she was in trouble. I told you you needed to fucking do more." Marissa glared at him, barely acknowledging Mac's hand on her arm.

Nick Walker stared back at her, not exactly glaring but meeting her gaze. Finally, he blinked and dropped his head.

"And you were right. Is that what you want to hear?" He met her gaze again, this time fully glaring back. "We could go back and forth and play the blame game, or we could talk about what comes next."

Mac gave Marissa's arm a gentle squeeze before getting to his feet. "Alright. What's next then?"

"Well, we will be working on what's going on in Chicago. Meanwhile, we will get surveillance back on you, double what we had before." He paused. "Honestly, I would much rather put you in WITSEC."

"No." Marissa shook her head.

"Maybe we could have a conversation—" Mac started but Marissa shook her head.

"No. It's not an option."

"Riss."

If they had asked her eight or nine months ago, her answer may have been different. But now? There was too much to walk away from. Mac included. And then there was her mom.

"I'm not going to run."

"Why not, detective?" Nick Walker leaned against the back wall beside the window looking out into the precinct and crossed his arms. "It's not running. It's protective custody. And it not only removes you from danger but your loved ones as well."

Marissa huffed in frustration. He was hitting all of her points, and he knew it.

Nick Walker held the pause before he continued, "Please correct me if I'm wrong, but you left your ex-husband to keep him safe after you received pictures that included him, right?" He looked down at the desk and opened the file he had walked in with. He pushed some of the contents around until he stopped on the photo he was looking for. Keeping a finger on the photo, he slid it in her direction.

Marissa let her arms go and leaned forward, her frown deepening at the photograph. It was one of the photographs of Mac.

"Nick—" Mac started, but his superior put his hand up, his eyes lingering on Marissa's for a moment before he looked at Mac.

"Agent Mackenzie, I'm going to ask you to step outside for a moment so Marissa and I can talk."

Mac made a face and shook his head, but Walker continued, "Please, Mac. Just give us a minute."

Marissa could see the shift in superior officer to friend. Mac was still making the face, but his shoulders dropped. He looked down at Marissa and leaned close to her ear. "I'll be right outside the door." He kissed her cheek before he gave Nick Walker one more look of disapproval and left the room.

Once the door was closed, Nick Walker pushed himself up from the wall and sat down in the chair, twirling his chair ever so slowly from side to side, all while watching her with an unreadable expression that made Marissa uncomfortable. Ellie sat up, letting out a big yawn before nudging Marissa's leg, sensing the tension in the room.

Finally, Nick Walker let out a slow sigh. "If whoever is leaving these photographs on your doorstep *is* in fact the other half of the Couple Killer Team, then you know exactly what this means."

Marissa studied his unmoving expression, trying to determine if it was Supervisory Special Agent Nick Walker or James Mackenzie's friend talking to her now. Either way, the knots in the pit of her stomach were growing and contracting.

"Of course I know what it means. There is already another girl dead. A girl that you should have found. And now he has maybe another? Or at least, he's watching her."

Something was starting to snap in Marissa and her cheeks were beginning to feel hot.

"I don't mean to make light of any aspect of this case—"

"Then why don't you do your job? You're the one who walked away when you thought some rules were broken. Put a man back out on the street while you had a man you supposedly trust and admire investigated when you know he did nothing wrong. I told you that you needed to find her, and now she's dead. You're the one who's fucked up here. You're the one wasting your time and dragging your heels, waiting for fucking Daniel Fryer to give you answers he's never going to give. Why? So you can have something noteworthy on your record? You're no better than that piece of shit Gorden."

Nick Walker's face remained still, although she could see him grit his teeth at Fryer's name. She held back a smile of satisfaction and continued, "When you arrived, you told me I was well within my rights to sue this department for their negligence regarding my case. What about you? You told me you didn't want to let me slip through the cracks like they did. But that's exactly what you've done—to me, to Brenna Thompson."

She saw a look of surprise flash across his expression, although it was only for a moment. She straightened in her chair, leaning slightly forward. "Tell me I'm wrong."

Nick Walker wasn't a large man by any means, but he usually found a way to look imposing. At this moment, he looked his age, older and tired. His shoulders dropped and he ran his hand through his salt and pepper hair, letting out a heavy sigh.

"You're not wrong," he said finally, though hearing him admit his defeat did not bring Marissa any joy. "Let me fix what I can." He paused. "If you won't consider WITSEC, what about a safe house..."

Marissa was already shaking her head.

"Explain it to me."

Without hesitation, she nodded. "For starters, my mother is dying." Marissa choked on that last word. She had to force herself to swallow the heaviness of that truth down. "I can't leave her now. Especially if I couldn't explain why." She shook her head, letting her eyes fall to Ellie, who stared back up at her adoringly. "I need to be here to help my sisters take care of her."

She paused.

"Then there's Kate. I need to make sure she lands somewhere safe. She deserves that much. And—"

Nick Walker held his hand up again, but this time, his posture was different.

"You had me convinced with your mom. I lost my father two years ago, unexpectedly to an aneurism." He sighed before continuing. "Although, keeping a teenage girl under your roof with everything going on is..." He shook his head. "Is a discussion for another time."

He pushed the photographs around on the table before piling them back into the folder and closing it. He hit the buzzer on the corner of his desk and spoke to the receptionist outside: "You can send him back in."

He didn't bother waiting for Mac to close the door behind him to start again. "I want cameras inside and outside, front yard and back yard, side yard. On the street. I want the FBI back across the street and local PD in front of your house."

He pushed himself out of the chair and straightened his tie.

"We'll wait 'til Clyde gets back to go over the Thompson case. Meanwhile, I will get the team on trying to narrow down the identity of this other woman." He looked from Marissa to Mac.

"I want you to limit where you go. If you do go somewhere, I want an agent with you. Aside from Mac." He picked up the folder and made his way back around the table toward the door. "I will let you know as soon as Clyde gets back, and we can go over their findings together."

He didn't bother waiting for an answer from either of them before exiting the room.

Mac didn't say a word the whole walk back to the car. As they got in the SUV, Marissa buckled in, expecting a lecture or words about her behavior to his superior officer. Instead, he turned himself as best he could to face her.

"I meant what I said there. This is not your fault. This is the result of a lunatic who has no care or regard for human life. That is not your fault and not your responsibility. You need to stop taking it all on your shoulders, or it is going to crush you." He brought a hand up to her cheek and searched her eyes. "Please. Hear me. You are not responsible for the actions of others."

Marissa put her hand over his, holding it close to her cheek, and closed her eyes. She could hear his words. They made sense. But that didn't mean she believed them.

"I guess we'll just have to see."

Chapter 22

Marissa inhaled a deep breath, her eyes on the fish tank in the waiting room of Dr. Bailey's office. This appointment was long overdue. Dr. Bailey had been gone on vacation for over a month. Although she had picked up the phone many times and almost called the emergency number she had been given, Marissa never bothered to use it. It didn't feel right to impose on someone else's vacation.

She had to admit, though, that the last several weeks had been a lot.

When she was finally called into the office, she got to her feet, Ellie standing up right next to her, and took a deep breath. She didn't even know where she would start.

Dr. Bailey looked refreshed and relaxed, a natural smile on her face. "Good afternoon, Marissa. How are you?"

Marissa took another deep breath and sat down in the big blue high-back chair beside the couch.

"I've been better." It was an honest answer. "Did you have a good vacation?"

Dr. Bailey nodded, adjusting in her chair and grabbing her pen. "It was wonderful. Got lots of sun, did a lot of swimming. My husband and I had a great time."

It was good to hear her voice. Maybe Marissa should have called while she had been gone.

"Why don't you tell me what's been going on? I didn't hear from you, so I was hoping that meant things were okay. I take it that wasn't the case."

Still, Marissa didn't know where to start, so she just shook her head. Thankfully, Dr. Bailey could see she needed some leading.

"Did Mac make it back from D.C.?"

"He did." She nodded, scratching Ellie's ear as the dog plopped her head into Marissa's lap. "He got back maybe, four or five weeks ago? Just after our last session. He had his hearing and was cleared and has been reinstated." She glanced down at Ellie and brushed the hair from her own eyes as she looked back up at Dr. Bailey. "His ex-wife followed him back and helped him with his case. She's a prosecutor."

"Oh, I'm so glad to hear he's been reinstated." She gave Marissa a big smile. "What is his ex-wife like?"

"She's really nice. I like her a lot. And their son. They've been staying in town." She shrugged. "It's been good, but a little weird."

"Like the situation is weird, or it feels weird, or..." She left the statement open for Marissa to answer.

"The situation. Like she's actually really nice. We've had a couple of one-on-one conversations now, and she's just a really nice person. They're still good friends, and it's easy to see why."

"Okay, good."

Marissa nodded in agreement. "Kate is also back with me again. She ran away from her last foster home."

Dr. Bailey started writing on her legal pad. "After having an empty house for a few weeks, how does it feel to have a full one at times?"

Marissa shrugged. "I don't hate it," she admitted. "Kim and I have been getting to know each other. Kate and Ethan get along great, and she's settling back into the house, which I know probably isn't the best. But it feels good to make someone feel safe, even if it isn't true."

"Why do you say it isn't true?"

Marissa made a face. "Still being stalked. The woman who was taken in Chicago is dead."

"That's awful." Dr. Bailey couldn't hide her horrified expression but smoothed it out quickly.

"It is. And it's my fault."

"How so?" Dr. Bailey adjusted, waiting patiently for Marissa to continue.

"She was taken because she looked like me. The first letter with her first photo said as much. Now she's dead." It was that simple.

"You did not pull the trigger or hold the knife. If you had, then it would be your fault and we would be having a different conversation. But these are the actions of someone who is out of their mind. And you cannot take responsibility for someone else's actions."

"Mac said the same thing."

"He is a smart man." Dr. Bailey smiled and made the decision to change the topic for the moment. "How is it having him back?"

Now it was Marissa's turn to smile. She couldn't help it. "It's been really nice having him home. Back! Having him back." She tried to correct herself, but the words were already out there.

Dr. Bailey didn't miss a beat. "I assume he is happy to be home, as well?"

Marissa smiled and nodded. "It's so effortless with him," she added after a moment. "I don't feel like it's work with him, if that makes sense."

Dr. Bailey nodded and waited for her to continue.

"Even with everything going on right now, I feel safe while he's around. I don't feel like I have to be on guard all the time. I don't have to be anything I'm not. I don't have to keep my feelings in check. I don't have to lie to him. And he accepts me despite all of it."

Marissa sighed, looking down.

"Not that Jared *didn't* accept me in all my craziness. But with everything going on, since the warehouse..." She paused and gave an involuntary shudder. "I've been on guard ever since. I've had to be. It's not his fault," she said sadly, picking at her thumb's cuticles.

"Have you spoken with him at all?"

"No." She shook her head, meeting Dr. Bailey's brown eyes. "I saw him a few weeks ago. He couldn't even look at me."

"I can't imagine that felt good. "

"No. It's ... hard. I understand. I made the situation what it is. But I just thought my friend would still be there," Marissa huffed, slowly building frustration. "Sorry. I always seem to come back to him."

Jared definitely had a starring role in her sessions. It was just unavoidable.

"Don't apologize. These sessions are for you to talk about whatever you feel you need to talk about."

Marissa nodded, letting out a sigh. "I did talk to Brian, though."

Dr. Bailey nodded, jotting down more notes on her pad. "And how did that go?"

"A little awkward with us both apologizing. We talked about my first nephew, who I still haven't officially met, but I did see him. He's absolutely beautiful. Did a little catching up."

She left off the part of the conversation with Brian about Jared. She wanted to talk about almost anything else.

Dr. Bailey finished writing whatever notes she was taking and looked up to meet Marissa's eyes. "Alright, what else has been going on? I can tell there's something that's weighing on you."

Marissa swallowed and looked back down at Ellie. "My mom collapsed and ended up in the ER a few weeks ago. It's where I saw Jared and Brian. After a lot of tests, it turns out my mom has stage four breast cancer." Marissa forced her eyes up from the dog to Dr. Bailey, whose look of sympathy made her want to crawl away.

"I'm so sorry to hear that," Dr. Bailey offered.

Tears were already interfering with her vision. "She's already made all these plans. She got things in writing, had a lawyer look it over and sign it. She put me in charge."

"Sounds like she is a practical thinker." Dr. Bailey paused. "We haven't really discussed your mom very much."

Marissa shook her head, leaning into the high back chair. "No. There isn't much to say. She was a great mom. A little strict. She went easier on my sisters than she did me. She raised us on her own. My dad had a second family. Out on the east coast. He left before Mel turned two."

Marissa sighed. Thinking about it, it was strange that for as much time as she had spent in therapy, this was the first time she found herself really talking about her mom.

"My mom was a rock. I couldn't have asked for a better one." She shook her head. "I've been trying so hard to keep a distance from her, and everyone, because of everything. I didn't think I would run out of time."

She took in a deep breath, sniffling every few moments.

"She had a secret boyfriend. For the last nine years. I'm pretty sure he lives with her." Marissa brushed a chunk of her hair from her eyes and pushed it behind her ear. "He's a really nice guy. I found out by accident. My sisters found out at the hospital."

"I imagine that went over well?"

"Not even a little bit."

Marissa suppressed a laugh, shaking her head. But the humor only hung in the air for a moment before all the heaviness dropped back down.

"The doctor said maybe five years. Maybe less with how much it's spreading." Just letting the words leave her lips made her ache all over. "My mom is dying," she said, a lot softer than she had meant to.

"I'm so sorry." Dr. Bailey watched Marissa for a moment and put her legal pad and pen down on the table. "Unfortunately, everyone dies. And I am so sorry that you and your family are going through this. But it is hard enough all on its own without you blaming yourself for something you had no control over."

"I have spent the better part of the last two and a half years pushing her as far away from me as I could. My mom, my sisters, my ex, my friends. I have shut everyone out and been so focused on my own shit, I haven't noticed the things around me. And now that's time I can never get back."

"You've had some pretty big things, Marissa. And all of them have been outside your control."

"Everything is out of my control," Marissa mumbled, burying her face into her hands.

"Now that isn't true," Dr. Bailey said gently. "Let's talk this through."

Marissa straightened in her chair.

"It may not feel like much, but you can control how you respond to everything happening around you. You can only control you."

"It's not enough." She could feel defeat rising within her.

"Why is it not enough?" Dr. Bailey asked gently. "Not everything is your fault."

Marissa met her gaze but said nothing.

"It's not, Marissa. I know it must feel like a lot. But not everything bad that is happening is *because of you*."

Marissa blinked but didn't agree. Dr. Bailey continued, "Did you know your mom was sick?"

Marissa shook her head.

"Is there anything you could have done to keep her from getting sick?"

Marissa felt the tears well up in her eyes, but again, she shook her head.

Dr. Bailey nodded. "You made the choice to keep your distance because someone dangerous is stalking you. Is that something you have any control over?"

With a heavy sigh, Marissa reluctantly shook her head.

"Do you have the ability to explain the situation to them without putting them in any kind of danger?"

Marissa paused. She *had* told Brian. And Brian had told Jared. And so far, the only consequence was their personal anger directed at her.

"Maybe. If I had told Jared in the beginning, he would have stayed. He would've been dead. He knows now, though. And Brian knows, and besides his wife's rage... I don't know."

"Okay, let's reword the question a bit: What would happen if you told your sisters and your mom what was going on?"

"My mom would panic. She would want to be with me all the time. My sisters—none of them should have to live in that kind of fear." She shook her head firmly. She couldn't tell them.

"Right now, we need to be focusing on my mom. Getting her to her appointments and trying to keep things positive."

Dr. Bailey nodded her head, clearly expecting that answer. "So again, what in this situation do you have control over?"

"Nothing." Marissa shook her shoulders out, the tension at the base of her neck growing since her arrival.

"And I think that's something we should talk about next."

Marissa blinked.

"About how to deal and function when things are out of your control."

Marissa huffed but sat attentively listening.

The rest of the session was spent talking about coping mechanisms and how and when to utilize them. The session seemed to come to an abrupt end. Marissa had so much more she'd wanted to say.

Chapter 23

Marissa stepped outside and sighed heavily, pulling back and leaning against the wall. Talking about her mom had sent her into a spiral, and while she had managed to gather herself up inside the office, Dr. Bailey had been sitting right there. Now that she was outside and alone, the swirling of panic was rising in her chest again. Ellie nudged her gently and whined, stressing to Marissa that she needed to take it easy.

Marissa rubbed the back of her ear and took in a deep breath before slowly letting it out. She was supposed to meet Mac back at the precinct, but he wouldn't be out of his meeting for another few hours, maybe more. Walking to the other side of town wasn't going to be a thing. Putting her hand over her chest, she tried to focus on breathing, but it felt like a twenty-pound weight was bearing down on her. She looked to the busy street and gathered her bearings, trying to figure out where she could go.

She considered going back into the office until she could calm down.

She wished her condo wasn't currently occupied.

She could think of only one other place to go.

Adjusting Ellie's leash, she straightened and started walking. She forced herself to move quickly because she could feel her whole body freezing in the tense position it was forming.

Ten minutes later, Marissa stood in front of Jared's house, wetter than when she had started walking as the simply overcast weather had become a drizzle. It felt like the clouds were spitting on her. She looked down the street and already regret was washing over her. She was too far down into Queen Anne to go anywhere else now.

Choking back sobs, she forced herself to get it together. If she was going to knock on the fucking door, she wasn't going to do it falling apart. At least she was going to try. She just hoped Kristie wasn't there.

She opened the little gate into the front yard and walked up to the door. It was a newer home, skinny but tall with many windows. Glancing down at Ellie, she swallowed and knocked.

While waiting, she noticed the Ring doorbell and let out an audible sigh. If he was home, Jared could see it was her. The chances of him answering the door just went down. Bouncing her knees, she scratched anxiously at the side of her arm, and Ellie nudged her repeatedly.

Several minutes went by without a sound. Marissa turned around with a heavy sigh, certain he wouldn't answer the door.

"Fuck," she muttered under her breath, stepping off the front step. The light drizzle had turned into a steadier rain in the few minutes she had stood there.

Behind her, she heard the door click as it unlocked and opened.

"What?" Jared's voice was already full of disdain.

Marissa closed her eyes and stopped, breathing in through her nose before she turned around. The moment her eyes landed on him, hot tears came pouring out of her eyes, and instead of words, an unwanted sob escaped. Ellie whined toward Jared before she hurried back over to Marissa, gently jumping up on her side to tell her to get off her feet.

Jared didn't move for almost a minute, standing awkwardly in his own doorway. Despite what she was sure were his better efforts, his expression noticeably softened as he stared at her.

"Come inside." He didn't move, but his tone had softened with his expression.

Marissa waited for a beat before she nodded, rain now dripping down her face, mixing with her tears as she walked slowly back to the house. As she reached him, she stumbled, and he caught her by the arm. If he hadn't been aware of the panic attack she was trying to keep at bay, he was now.

Keeping hold of her arm, he gently led her inside the house, through an entryway, and into a big living room. He helped her get on the couch and didn't grumble when Ellie jumped right up next to her, laying across Marissa's lap. He sat beside her, still holding her arm, and put his other arm around her shoulders. He took steady, purposeful breaths for her to follow, pulling her into him and resting his forehead on hers.

Marissa closed her eyes and let him wrap his arms around her, holding her just tight enough. She listened to him breathe, felt him inhale and exhale against her before trying to match her own breath to his. It didn't take long for her breathing to ease up. Her body was still trying to curl into itself, but Jared's weight holding her kept her from completely doubling over. He must have felt her body unclench, so he relaxed his grip on her. With one hand, he stroked her hair, which was matted to the side of her face thanks to the rain. He turned his body slightly, so he could comfortably rest his forehead against hers, keeping her still.

Swallowing, she pulled back just slightly, meeting his hazel eyes, which opened to look back at her. Her breathing slowed even more.

"What level are we at?"

He was referencing the level of her panic attack. They had done this countless times, and just like riding a bike, there was muscle memory.

She shook her head. She couldn't form the words, let alone get them out of her mouth. Her chest convulsed from a suppressed sob, but her breathing continued to grow steady.

"Okay," he said softly, leaning forward to rest his head on her forehead again.

She exhaled and closed her eyes again, resting against him and following his breathing pattern.

They sat there for a long while until Marissa's breathing had returned almost to normal. Her hands and arms still felt heavy with pins and needles shooting throughout her body. Jared pulled back when she'd calmed down a bit more and got to his feet.

"I'll be right back."

Wiping her eyes, she glanced around his living room. The couch she was sitting on was a large L-shaped charcoal couch that was both comfortable and comforting. His living room looked the same as the last time she saw it, industrial and modern with metal and wood finishes. High ceilings, hardwood floors. But behind her in the corner of the couch, Marissa's eyes were drawn to the bright pink blanket that screamed Kirstie.

Jared reappeared. "If you want to dry off, there are some towels in the bathroom. And you can use the shower if you want to."

Marissa nodded, looking down at her soaked clothes. She hadn't even noticed that her clothes were plastered to her skin, soaking wet and freezing.

"Okay. I might do that."

But she didn't move.

She stared at the floor for a long moment before she raised her eyes to meet Jared's. "My mom is dying," she managed.

"I know," Jared said gently, sitting himself on the ottoman portion of the couch across from her. "Is there anything I can do?"

Marissa gripped her arms, trying to literally hold herself together. She couldn't have another episode. All she could do was shake her head, words escaping her again.

"She knew," she said finally, out loud for the first time.

She probably should have said so back in Dr. Bailey's office. Or to Mac after she had gotten home that night. Instead, the words just began falling out of her mouth as she stared at a single spot on Jared's couch beside him.

She couldn't meet his gaze. "She found the lump. Two and a half years ago. When I was still in the hospital. She didn't want to add to everyone's worry."

Slowly, she raised her eyes to meet Jared's, who wore the same shock she had experienced as he processed her words.

They were both silent for a long time before Jared shook his head. "You know that doesn't make it your fault, right?"

Before she could stop herself, tears began streaming down her cheeks again as a sob lodged itself in her throat. Jared leaned forward and took her hands in his.

"Marissa. That is not your fault."

He was shaking his head. She tried but couldn't stop the sobs from escaping. A moment went by, and then another, before Jared moved beside her and pulled her close again, wrapping his arms around her. Neither of them said anything, Marissa because she was crying hard enough again not to be able to form words and Jared because there was nothing else to say. He just held her close and let her cry.

Once she had gotten herself under some control, Jared straightened, letting his arms drop from around her.

"Here."

He got back on his feet and took her arm, helping her stand. She sniffled and nodded her head before she rocked herself forward to pick up the momentum to get on her feet. A tingling in her feet shot through her legs as she stood, causing her to wobble in place. Jared steadied her, his free hand coming along her hip. As she straightened, he let go.

"You remember where the bathroom is?"

Marissa nodded her head weakly, and he started to walk into his kitchen.

"I have to call Mac."

He stopped and slowly turned back around, clenching his jaw.

"I was supposed to meet him back at the precinct after my appointment. Can I have him pick me up here when he's done?"

She noticed him clench his fist, but as he let go, he nodded. "Okay."

Marissa swallowed. "Thank you." Her voice was still shaky, and it was softer than she had meant it to be.

He gave her another half nod before disappearing into the kitchen. Turning, she made her way down the hall and to the giant bathroom.

He might not have known exactly what she was feeling right now, but she knew he could sympathize. And even relate. Something many people didn't know about Jared was just how much money he had inherited from his mother, who had died before he reached double digits. He hadn't been able to access any of that money until he turned twenty-five, but he was making good use of it now.

The bathroom, like the rest of the house, sported high ceilings with steel and wooden finishings. There was a giant standing shower with gorgeous tile and a double vanity with a mirror that was too well lit. Marissa stared at her reflection in the harsh bright light, squinting for her eyes to adjust.

She looked like a drowned rat. Her hair was matted on her pale face, and her clothes clung to her skin. In the corner on the counter, she noticed a small pile of neatly folded clothes, and they looked … familiar.

These were her clothes. Clothes she hadn't seen in a long while. Clothes she had obviously left here at some point.

Beside the clothes were the towels Jared had mentioned. Glancing behind her, she looked at the shower and then down at Ellie, who sat at her feet watching Marissa closely. She was cold; she could see the goosebumps on her arms in her reflection.

She retrieved her phone from her pocket, hoping it hadn't gotten too wet. Thankfully, the OtterBox case had done its job. She hit Mac's number and waited, but it went straight to voicemail. Rather than leave a message, she hung up and started typing a message.

Hey. I had a panic attack after my session with Dr. Bailey. I came to Jared's because it was the closest. Can you pick me up here?

She typed in the address and hoped he wouldn't be upset. Or at least that he would understand.

She stepped into the giant walk-in shower, turned it on, and stepped to the side while the water came up to temperature. Carefully, she peeled off her soaked clothes. It shouldn't have taken much effort to remove them, but the searing pain against her skin as the fabric came off changed things. Throwing the clothes into the corner, she got into the hot water and immediately felt relief through her body.

Marissa had completely fogged up the entire giant bathroom by the time she had turned the water off. She felt significantly better than before she had stepped in. She also felt foolish for falling apart so completely. Despite the relief she felt now, she knew later, possibly even tomorrow, her body was going to feel the consequences of falling to pieces. Everywhere that had tensed, everywhere that frozen in place, that had strained, was going to feel it tenfold. For the moment, though, she felt relief.

Once she was content with the dryness of her hair, she tossed the towels in the hamper and exited the bathroom, Ellie on her heels. She walked back into the living room to see Jared sitting on the couch, staring at his phone.

"Hey." She stood there awkwardly, shoving her hands into the pockets of her reclaimed jeans. They were a lot looser around her waist than she remembered.

Jared looked up from his phone and almost smiled. "Hey. You feeling better?"

Marissa nodded. "I am. Thank you." She swayed slightly on her feet. "I didn't know what you wanted me to do with the wet clothes, but they're still in the shower."

"That's fine. I'll get them back to you."

"Thanks."

"Did you get a hold of Mac?" She noticed Jared clench his jaw, but his expression remained calm.

"No. I sent him a text though." She shifted and stood there in an uncomfortable silence that stretched on way too long. "I'm really sorry. I just didn't know where else to go."

"Don't." Jared sighed. His tone was even and almost soft. "You don't have to apologize." He motioned to the couch beside him. "Just sit."

Marissa sat, feeling momentarily relieved. She noticed the Tylenol and a glass of water on the end table, and she couldn't stop the weak smile. This was the way Jared had always taken care of her. On the coffee table in front of her was a bowl of popcorn she was certain hadn't been there before she had gone to take a shower. This was how their relationship used to be. He wouldn't tell her what to do, but he always made what she needed available. She regarded the bowl of popcorn but instead grabbed the Tylenol and water.

Chapter 24

Marissa adjusted, craning her neck in a failed attempt to relieve some pressure, and winced. Ellie, who was already sprawled over Marissa's lap, looked up at Marissa before deciding she was fine and laying her head back down. Jared reappeared from the kitchen, a new bowl of popcorn in his hands.

"Here," he said, sitting back down on the couch beside her. He put it back on the table, where she had been nibbling from it every so often—often enough in the last hour to go through a whole bowl.

"No, I'm good. Honest."

But they both knew her hand would more than likely end up back in the bowl.

He made a face at her before shaking his head.

"Don't give me that look." She made a face back at him.

Jared shook his head but reached out and gave Ellie scratches behind the ears.

"Well, you look like you haven't eaten in months," he said flatly, grabbing a handful of popcorn.

Marissa started to protest but then just shrugged a shoulder. He knew her too well. It was a pretty normal pattern. In times of extreme stress, her appetite was nonexistent. Partner that with that fact that even though she was thirty-seven years old, she couldn't cook worth a damn and lived on junk and fast food? It was not a great mix.

"I'm fine," she finally said weakly.

Jared raised an eyebrow at her. "Bullshit."

She grumbled at him but winced, closing her eyes and clenching and unclenching her fists, trying to relieve the tension. Everything hurt. Every breath felt like a stab between her rib cage, her chest feeling the weight and consequences of her panic. She felt Jared's hands on hers, and she opened her eyes. He had turned himself to face her as he ran his hands over hers, trying to work some warmth into them.

"You are anything but fine," he said plainly.

She met his eyes and let out a sigh. "I'm doing my best."

"Are you though?"

He let her hands go but didn't turn away, holding her gaze.

"Because it looks like you're taking everything on your own shoulders and hiding behind walls in the name of the least amount of collateral damage."

Marissa stared at him, unable to pull away from his eyes. "I'm not hiding behind walls." It came out more like a mumble than she had meant it to.

"I hope you're at least able to share some of it." He paused. "With someone."

Marissa couldn't hide her surprise at his words. He raised his chin slightly and continued to hold her gaze. Something familiar fluttered in the pit of her stomach.

There was a sudden notification sound that made them both jump. Marissa swallowed and shook off whatever was just happening.

Jared looked at his phone and she saw his jaw clench. "Your boyfriend is here."

Marissa made a face at him, and he got to his feet as there was a knock at the door. She struggled to get to her own feet with Ellie was planted firmly in her lap, so she watched as Jared got to the door and opened it wide enough for her to see Mac just past him.

"Can I come in?" she heard him ask.

Jared shook his head. "Nah. I don't think so. She's coming," he said casually, shoving one hand in his pocket and leaning up against his door frame.

Marissa rolled her eyes and shoved herself off the couch. With a heavy sigh, she grabbed her phone off the coffee table and patted her side for

Ellie to follow. Making her way to the door, she ducked under Jared's arm and gave both men a look of exasperation.

Then she gave Jared a weak smile. "Thank you."

Jared pulled his eyes away from Mac and nodded at her, leaning down to talk in her ear softly. "Always."

A sense of relief rushed through her as, for a second, she saw the friend she had lost all those months ago. Marissa nodded before stepping past him and walked over to Mac, lacing her hand in his. Mac gave her hand a squeeze and glanced down at her.

"You okay?"

Marissa nodded her head. There was an awkward pause before Mac raised his chin, looking at Jared. "Thank you."

Marissa saw Jared's jaw tense again, but he nodded at Mac. It was polite. It was more than Marissa could have asked for.

But then, Marissa heard Kirstie's nasally voice behind her. "What's going on here?"

"We're leaving," Marissa answered, glancing at Jared before she turned and forced a smile for Kirstie.

The blonde's belly was huge, her hands resting on top of it. She looked from Marissa to Jared, her expression one of annoyance. The annoyance grew when Ellie stretched out her nose to sniff the newcomer.

Marissa waved to Jared and headed for the black SUV parked right in front of the yard. Once they were in car, Marissa turned to Mac, a feeling of anxiety pushing against her.

"I'm sorry. I just didn't know where else to go. You were still in your meeting—"

"Marissa," Mac said gently, turning his head to face her, "you have nothing to apologize for. I'm glad you went somewhere you knew you would be safe." He gave her a small smile. "Besides, if anyone should be apologizing for an ex, it's probably me."

"No. I like Kim. It's been nice getting to know her."

The look of relief that briefly flashed over the man's face almost made her laugh.

"Seriously though." His face grew worried again. "Are you okay?"

"No," Marissa said flatly, looking down at her hands. "But I'll be fine," she said finally, meeting his eyes again. "Right now, I'm just tired."

"Well, close your eyes for the ride. We can get home and settle in and then I'll tell you everything I can about the meeting with Walker."

He took her hand in his and kissed the back of it before starting the SUV.

Marissa turned to look out the window. Jared was still standing in the doorway, Kristie standing in front of him, her hand on her popped out hip. It was possible they were arguing.

He must have known she was looking at them because she saw his eyes flash over to her before rubbing his face and turning around. Kirstie whirled around to glare as they drove off before she started followed him inside.

With her eyes closed, Marissa leaned back into the seat and let herself drift off to sleep.

Marissa opened her eyes again as Mac pulled into the driveway. He put the car in park and turned to face her, putting his hand on her knee. "You ready to go inside?"

Marissa looked at the house. A heavy fatigue keep her in the seat. With a sigh, she turned back to him. "Not really."

Mac adjusted and took her hand in his. "We can sit here for a while." He studied her, clearly concerned. "Do you want to talk about it?"

Marissa could only shake her head. She couldn't find the words, let alone say them.

"Then we'll just sit here." He gave her hand a squeeze.

After several minutes passed, Marissa finally nodded. "Alright. Let's go."

Those minutes hadn't changed anything. What she really wanted to do was just drive. Run away from her problems. But it wouldn't solve anything.

And something told her that she couldn't drive far enough away to actually escape.

Kim had ordered pizza for dinner. Ethan and Kate were chilling on the couch, watching TV, eating, and talking. Something about the ease of how quickly they got along made her smile slightly. Once again, she felt a strange appreciation for the new normal she was experiencing within the chaos that was currently her life.

Marissa found herself in a weird state through the evening, smiling and nodding, but she wasn't really there. It was almost like an out of body experience, except every single inch of her body ached. The panic attack lingered, the tightness, the aches. It was still there. The fatigue never eased.

Once she and Mac were upstairs, he gently put a hand on her shoulder.

"Hey." His voice was soft as he sat next to her on the bed. "What can I do?"

"I don't know. Nothing?" She shook her head, looking at the floor. "I don't even know where to start with everything I'm feeling. It's too much."

She stopped and looked at him, tears now falling down her cheeks. "My mom might be dying."

"I know," he whispered.

Marissa shook, trying to shake off the weight that was pushing down on her chest, and wiped the tears from her face.

"I'll be fine."

Chapter 24

She had to be fine. She couldn't afford to fall apart. She already knew that, depending on how things went, her sisters weren't going to be in any shape to handle anything. And they shouldn't have to. She was the oldest.

She also couldn't let her guard down. She needed to stay focused, vigilant. There was a crazy stalker out there. She couldn't allow herself to be distracted—by anything. She needed the breakdown today so that she could feel it and then put it in a box and compartmentalize.

"I have to be fine. I just needed to feel it, I guess. I'll be okay."

Mac didn't necessarily look convinced, but he nodded his head, rubbing her back gently. She rested her head on his shoulder, leaning into him and closing her eyes. Mac pulled her close, wrapping his arms around her and kissing the top of her head.

"I want you to know you don't have be fine with me. You don't have to put on a brave face with me. I promise I will keep you safe."

His words had weight to them. She felt herself relax into him, her shoulders dropping further. He must have felt her relax because his grip around her also loosened a little.

"I love you."

His words were enough to break the dam that had been holding back her tears, and rather than speaking, she sobbed.

"Well, you really know how to give a guy a complex." He laughed a little. "First, you cry when I lie down next to you, then you cry when I tell you I love you."

He was trying to lighten the mood, but the emotional weight of those words had just tipped her over the edge.

"This is when you decide to say it?" She managed a shaky laugh. "When I'm all snotty and blubbery?"

"You're perfect," he assured her.

She shook her head but smiled at him.

"I love you, too."

The words felt strange. The truth was she hadn't ever said those words to anyone but Jared. Not in a romantic way.

He smiled down at her, brushed the hair back from her tear-stained face, kissed her forehead gently. She stretched her neck slightly to lean up for a kiss, which he seemed to welcome. She stretched her arms around his neck and turned her body to face him, deepening the kiss. He laced his fingers in her hair, and that was enough of a signal for her to throw her leg over his lap so she was straddling him.

He pulled back just enough to murmur in her ear. "Are you sure?"

She didn't even bother to answer, nodding her head briefly and pulling him back into a kiss.

Marissa lay staring at the ceiling. Everything about the day dictated she should have been fast asleep. It wasn't for lack of exhaustion. Physically, she felt like she was sinking deeper into the bed with each passing minute. The only thing keeping her afloat was Mac, who was sleeping soundly beside her. He had started with his arm around her as she curled into his chest. But the room was warm, and over time, they had shifted in different directions. She closed her eyes, once again trying to give in to the sleep she so desperately needed. But her mind was racing too fast for sleep to take over.

Rolling on her side, she grabbed her phone from her nightstand and punched in the pin. Once her phone was unlocked, she opened her messages and scrolled down until she found Jared's name.

[I just wanted to say thank you again for today.]

She was sure he wouldn't see the message, let alone answer it. It was 3:20 a.m. She couldn't get him out of her mind. After not speaking to her for months, he had been there for her. A selfish part of her was happy she hadn't damaged their relationship so much that he wouldn't be there for her. It was a relief.

To her surprise, the word *seen* appeared on the bottom of the message. And then little dots started bouncing, telling her he was typing back.

[You okay?]

[Not really. I don't even know.]

Marissa watched the dots dance, stop, and start again. She didn't expect him to carry on a conversation with her, but here he was, responding. Or at least he was thinking about it. The dots were still moving. But before he could finish, she typed a question that had been in the back of her mind since that afternoon.

[Why do you still have my clothes? I'm surprised you didn't burn them]

This time, the response was instant.

[Why do you think?]

She started to type that she didn't know but deleted it. It would've been a lie. She knew why.

It was the same reason she had his things in a box in her office closet. She didn't look at them, but knowing they were there was important to her. It was comforting. They may have been over, but he had been such a big part of her life, and he always would be.

It was for reasons she would never voice out loud.

[I'm sorry for showing up today. I know it isn't fair to you]

[stop fucking apologizing.]

Marissa winced and took a deep breath. She should have just put the phone down. The urge to apologize again and again was always there.

[Do you think maybe we can occasionally talk? Like, would it be okay if I reached out sometimes?]

She hated herself for pushing send. While the sentence conveyed the thought, the words came out wrong. And really, she had no right. No dots followed. Marissa felt like that was her sign to put the phone down and did just that, turning on her back and staring at the ceiling. After spending her evening disassociating, she couldn't make her mind stop racing. It was everything. Her mom. Ben. Daniel Fryer. Jared. Kate. Brenna Thompson.

It was all just too much.

And then she heard her phone buzz. Rolling back over onto her side, she picked it up and brought it close to her face without sitting up. Jared had texted her back.

[Always]

Chapter 25

"**F**ucking child," he hissed between his teeth, irritated that he was being forced to clean up someone else's mess. Again.

There had been so many struggles and issues working with Daniel Fryer, but at least he was a fucking professional. He knew what he was doing. He had been doing it for years, decades. Of course, that asshole was still proving to be problematic, even behind bars. There had been a moment, back at the beginning of summer, where he had been put on suicide watch. It would have been convenient had he just taken himself out.

This kid, though. He had been given one job. He was supposed to divert attention away from Ben. Have some fun with the girl, take pictures, mail them. That was it. It was simple.

Instead, he had killed her. And not just killed her but made a bloody fucking mess of that, too.

Ben often thought he should have just stuck to being on his own. Fryer had been a mere accident, but it was an opportunity too good to pass up. There was something to be said about mutual destruction. It had been so easy to set him up in Ohio. The fucker never saw it coming.

Not that he had needed the ego boost, but he was still riding that high. He had outsmarted everyone. The police, the FBI, even a serial killer with decades of murders under his belt. He had masterminded not only the perfect ending to the story but all the acts in between. What was unfortunate was that it took so many moving parts to keep things going.

He had this idiot in Chicago whom he'd brought into the fold. He was young, had potential. He should have been malleable. All the right urges, all the potential to be just as dangerous as Ben was. Mostly, he was just an idiot and a disappointment. Then there was the man on his personal payroll delivering all the letters. It was becoming more of a production than he had wanted it to be, but so far, at least, it was working.

Of course, the police were no closer to answers. The FBI were no closer to answers. And Marissa was still completely in the dark. None of them had a fucking clue.

It was a waiting game now. His end game was coming together; he just needed to wait a little longer. He had been tempted to move things up, but the timing was crucial. Marissa was not an easy target, and she was going to be even harder to keep. And that was the whole point, wasn't it?

So many moving parts. He poured himself another glass of whiskey, swirling the liquid around the glass in and out of the ice. He inhaled the sweet smell and closed his eyes before shooting it to the back of his throat. The fiery liquid flowed over his tongue before he swallowed it. He set the glass back down and got to his feet.

When he had started all of this, he never could have imagined ending up where he was now. He had explained it to the kid once. He had always been the good guy. Always following the rules, didn't color outside the lines. And one day, he woke up and just didn't want to be that person anymore. He was sick of it. There was no reward for being the good guy. No perks. No promotions. He certainly never got the girl. It was all just bullshit.

He started out small. He broke some rules, took some things he shouldn't have. The first time he attacked a man, it had been exhilarating. The first time he had killed someone, there was no going back. He understood now why killers did what they did. Most just weren't smart enough to get away with it. That was why it was so important to pay attention to the details. To plan ahead and make contingency plans.

Things had escalated quickly from there. The day he had been discovered by Daniel Fryer and their unstable partnership was born was the one and only time there hadn't been a backup plan. It had changed the entire trajectory of Ben's life. It had given him purpose.

He stepped outside and cupped his lighter as he brought it to his cigarette. It was dark out, and for the moment, it was quiet. He took a drag off the cigarette and watched the smoke as he blew it out. He hated the quiet.

Just a few more months, and he would be at his end game.

Chapter 26

Marissa felt more exhausted than she had in a long while—and that was saying a lot. The emotional rollercoaster of the past couple months was taking a toll on her. The flare-up started small, inflammation causing her body to ache, but soon simply breathing made her chest hurt. She was lying in bed, soft blanket beneath her and wearing as little clothing as she could get away with. A heating blanket lay on top of her while Ellie sprawled out alongside of her. A fan blew directly onto her face and an ice pack was tucked beneath the base of her head.

She had absolutely zero desire to move from this position. The blinds were shut and the door was closed, the only light in the room from her phone and a candle that sat beneath the TV atop her dresser.

It was still pretty early in the day. Mac had already been out and back for his run and had made breakfast. He was currently downstairs, hanging out with Kate and Ethan. She tried to force her eyes closed again, but her discomfort currently outweighed her exhaustion.

Her phone buzzed and lit up the room with a flash. Reluctantly, she grabbed the phone from its resting place on top of Mac's pillow and used her fingerprint to unlock it.

Marissa stared at her notification, frowning before she sat up, opening the email. It was from the Doe Project. Marissa read the email multiple times before throwing her legs over the edge of the bed. There was a rush of blood to her head, but she shook it off and moved on to her contacts.

The phone only rang twice on the other end before Carmen picked up. "Hey Marissa, what's up?"

She didn't even bother with a hello. "She's a match. My Jane Doe is Sarah Wickersham."

It was a quick phone call. They made arrangements to head to Portland the next day to meet with Sarah's mom and give her the news in person. Carmen was going to reach out and make sure she was home and that they were good to go. Marissa would see if Mac wanted to go with her. If she was still in her current physical state, she was going to need him to drive.

She was sitting on the edge of the bed when Mac came in a few moments later.

"You okay?" he asked, his expression full of concern.

Marissa nodded, considering stepping off the bed but also considering just lying back down. "Yeah. I just heard from the Doe Project. She's a match for the missing girl Carmen thought she was."

"Well that's great!" he said, keeping his voice low for the sake of her headache.

"It is. We're going to meet with her mom tomorrow. Carmen is arranging all the details." She paused. "Would you be willing to drive me down to Portland tomorrow? Just if I still feel like shit…"

"Of course." He smiled and sat down next to her. "Ethan and Kim booked their flight home for the end of the week."

"I bet they're ready to be home." Marissa had enjoyed having them visit so often, but she was also ready to have the house a little emptier during the day.

"They are. And Ethan is going back to school already." He sighed. "It was really nice having him around, though."

"It was nice having *both* of them here," she added and bumped his shoulder, but the movement was more than her head was prepared for.

"Okay. I was going to get up, but I think I'm going to lay here a little bit longer." She groaned but didn't move. "My head feels like it's going to crack open."

"Then here, lay down." He got back on his feet and pulled the covers over her before sitting beside her again. He stroked her hair as she adjusted her head on the pillow. "You need to rest. You're no good to anyone if you aren't taking care of yourself."

"I take perfectly good care of myself," she lied before closing her eyes.

"Sure you do." His tone was amused, and she felt the smile on his lips when he leaned down to kiss her forehead.

"Hey, you ready?"

Marissa nodded, glancing over at the woman beside her. They had met up at Carmen's place, and Mac had parked the car and was doing a little exploring in the city while Marissa and Carmen met with Sarah's mom.

"As ready as I ever am for these."

Giving families news was usually the worst part of this job. But after ten years, answers would hopefully be welcome. Even if they weren't complete answers.

Carmen took a deep breath and straightened herself before knocking on the door. They heard a dog barking inside and a woman's voice hushing it. A moment later, an older woman with shoulder-length blonde hair opened the door. "Can I help you?"

"Hello, ma'am. We are looking for Shelly Wickersham?"

"That's me," she said, a hesitation in her expression.

"I'm Detective Marissa Ambrose, and this is Detective Carmen Vega." She saw the woman watching the shepherd sitting at her feet. "And this is Ellie."

"You're here about Sarah?" Her voice had a smooth calmness to it, but when she lifted her eyes to meet theirs, Marissa could see the tears welling up.

"Yes ma'am, we are," Carmen said, stealing a look at Marissa. She gave Carmen a nod, letting her take the lead. "Could we maybe go inside and sit down?"

"Just tell me." She had a grip on the door.

"Ma'am, we..." Carmen stumbled.

Taking a breath, Marissa spoke the words Carmen momentarily couldn't. "We've identified your daughter's body," she said gently.

Shelly inhaled, tears falling down her cheeks. She loosened her hold on the door and stepped back, letting them step inside the home. She led them through the entryway and into the living room.

Marissa let Carmen enter the house first. She took a moment to look around, pictures of Sarah lining the entryway. She had been so young and truly beautiful.

She took a seat next to Carmen on the couch and felt her heart ache for the broken woman who sat across from them.

"Where was she?" she asked softly, making eye contact with Carmen.

"Her body was found in Schmitz Preserve Park in Seattle on August 8, 2010. She was reported as a Jane Doe. Detective Ambrose was looking into the Jane Doe case, and I've been investigating a series of murders with victims who had been found in a similar way..."

"August 8, 2010?" Shelly looked past them, lost among her thoughts. "That was just two weeks after she had gone missing," she said softly. "Where is she now?"

Carmen nodded, ready with the answers. "Her remains were cremated, but they still have her ashes if you would like them. I actually brought the paperwork you would need, if you want."

Marissa was glad this was something they had asked before making the trip because before the case, she hadn't known what happened to unclaimed bodies.

Shelly nodded before she gave both of them a small, sad smile. "I would like that very much, thank you." Her voice was soft but steady. "I can't tell you how much this means to me... My husband, Sarah's father, died two years ago of cancer without any answers. It was his biggest regret. He had never given up hope that she would come home one day."

She glanced over to the fireplace, which had a collection of photographs that Marissa assumed were of her late husband. Shelly sighed sadly. "I always knew she was gone, that she wasn't coming back. A mother knows." She shook her head. "But the not knowing always left space for some hope, even when I was certain there was none. It left us frozen in time." She wiped the tears from her eyes.

"I'm so sorry for your losses," Marissa said with sincerity. She couldn't imagine what this poor woman was going through.

"Would you like something to drink? Or to eat?"

Both Marissa and Carmen shook their heads. "Thank you but no."

She straightened, wiping the last of her tears away, and with them the heavy sadness that had been there moments before. She turned to Carmen, now curious. "You said you have been investigating murders? Plural?"

Carmen nodded. "The girls were all found in a similar fashion after being reported missing in the same general area. Sarah is the only one who has been found this far north and away from home." She paused, clearly uncertain how much detail to go into.

"How many girls?" Shelly folded her hands into her lap, sitting straight in her blue chair across from them.

"Fourteen missing girls, seven girls found, now including Sarah."

"That's so many girls," she said softly before nodding. "And that's the case you're working on?"

"Yes, ma'am." Carmen nodded.

"And you were looking into my daughter as a Jane Doe?"

Now it was Marissa's turn to nod. "I was. My late partner had been working her case from the very beginning. He actually brought her case files home years ago. He just wanted to give her her name back." Marissa let out a sigh. "He wasn't able to, but I wanted to see it through."

As she said the words out loud, her heart ached, this time for Tom.

They had spent a good chunk of the afternoon in Shelly Wickersham's living room, answering the questions they could and just listening to Shelly tell stories about Sarah, and what a beautiful and unique woman she had been growing into. By the time they got back in the car, the state of devastation was heavy in the air.

"She took that better than I anticipated," Carmen said, putting the key in the ignition.

"That poor woman has been through so much," Marissa said, shaking her head, which felt heavy.

Her head still hurt and her body ached, but Marissa was sure it was nothing compared to the pain that Shelly Wickersham was feeling—and had been feeling for a decade now. She clicked her seat belt and rolled the window down, the warm breeze feeling good against her face. Ellie stretched out in the back seat, instantly relaxing.

Carmen started the car and made her way out of the neighborhood, heading back toward the freeway. "Seven out of fourteen missing girls." She shook her head and muttered under her breath. "I always feel a sense of accomplishment for like, a minute, and then realize it means another girl is never really coming home."

Marissa sighed. "I don't know how anyone works in cold cases." She meant it. Years without answers, trying to follow cold leads, she couldn't imagine the level of disappointment.

She looked over to Carmen, who had one hand on the wheel and one hand resting on her forehead, lost in her thoughts. Before she could stop herself, the words just came out.

"If you ever need someone to brainstorm with or an extra pair of eyes, you can always give me a call."

Carmen smiled at her. "I would like that."

The rest of the ride passed in silence, windows down with the warm air flowing through the Kia Soul. Mac was already waiting by the Mini when they pulled up. Marissa gave Carmen a heartfelt hug, much like the one they had both received from Shelly Wickersham, and wished her luck.

Lowering herself into the passenger seat of her own car, Marissa sighed. She would need to call Lydia and give her the update. And check in. They hadn't spoken since Lydia had brought her the case files. She turned as Mac got into the driver's seat and gave him a smile.

"So how did it go?" He clicked the seat buckle.

Marissa shrugged her shoulder. "Okay, I guess." She sighed. "She was grateful for answers, but it was still rough. Her husband died a few years ago of cancer."

Mac winced. "That's hard. I can't even begin to imagine."

"No," she agreed. "And they were only partial answers. Carmen has the really hard job now. I don't know how someone can work on cold cases."

She reiterated her thoughts from earlier. Working homicide was hard enough, but cases that had grown cold or only had dead ends? That was a different level of hard.

"You ready to go home?" Mac reached over and gave her hand a squeeze.

Marissa smiled and nodded. "Yeah."

Once they were home, Marissa got comfortable before heading to the back porch and resting on the bench swing. Pulling out her phone, she scrolled to Lydia's name and tapped. It only rang twice before Lydia's sweet voice came on the line.

"Hey, Marissa."

"Hey, Lydia. Is this a good time to talk?"

"Oh, yeah." Marissa heard Evelyn giggling in the background. "Is everything okay?"

"Yeah. Everything is great. I just wanted to give you an update on the case you gave me."

Ellie trotted over to check in, resting her head in Marissa's lap momentarily to receive a few absentminded pets before running back off into the yard.

"Oh! Wonderful! Let me get to the kitchen—" Lydia must have pulled the phone from her ear because she momentarily sounded muffled. "Ev, I'll be right back. *Little Einsteins*?"

A few moments later, she came back on the line clearly. "Okay. She's all situated. Sorry about that."

"No worries," Marissa assured her. "We've identified her."

"You have?" Lydia sounded stunned. And relieved.

"We have. Her name was Sarah Wickersham." Marissa dove into what she could tell Lydia about Sarah, leaving out the part about the serial killer.

Lydia was quiet for a long moment, but when she came back, her voice was soft and shaky. "Marissa, I can't tell you what this means to me. To know that you were able to close something that Tom felt was important enough to bring home... It means the world to me."

"He wanted to give her her name back. I just wish he had been here to see it happen."

"He knows." Her soft voice on the end of the phone brought a dampness to Marissa's eyes. "God, I miss him."

"I'm sorry, Lyd—" Marissa started, but Lydia cut her off.

"We both lost him, Marissa. We both lost him."

Chapter 27

"Agent Mackenzie. Welcome back," Daniel Fryer said, his tone flat. He appeared less than excited to have someone else sit in on their conversation, but Marissa didn't care.

"This was the last batch of photographs I received. Along with the letter. It took some doing for them to let me show these to you," Marissa said grimly, shoving the folder forward.

They were only copies, but she wanted him to see everything. Because if he could give her any hints or clues as to what Ben's next move was, it was worth it. Nick Walker and ADA Gorden were not sold on the idea, but they agreed regardless.

Daniel Fryer took the file and started flipping through the photographs. He looked at the letter and raised an eyebrow, glancing over at Marissa before putting that to the side. He then grouped the photos together. One pile for Marissa's photos and another for Ms. Thompson. In total there were thirteen photos: six of Marissa, seven of Brenna. As he looked through Brenna's photographs, his expression changed multiple times. From surprise to amusement to an expression she couldn't find the name for. Carefully, he put those photos down and looked through the ones of Marissa. This time his expression remained neutral. Putting the pictures back down, he folded his hands on the table, his eyes still looking at the two piles he had made.

"Now this is interesting." He lifted his cold, gray eyes to look at Marissa.

"Interesting is a word for it," Marissa grumbled, folding her arms across her chest.

"I'm going to assume the dead girl is his mistake. It's kind of a given." He shrugged. "Does that mean he didn't mean to kill her yet? Kill her in that way? That she was the wrong victim?" Marissa tried to hide the shudder that ran through her. "But what mistake have you made?"

"I couldn't tell you," she said plainly.

"Alright, let's look at this from another angle," he said slowly, pointing to the letter. "What kind of emotions are getting the better of you?"

Marissa's eyes dropped to the table. "That's really no one's business."

"I can't offer you any insight without information, Marissa."

She hated the way her name sounded coming off his lips. Tightening her already folded arms and adjusting herself anxiously, she lifted her eyes to meet his. "My mom has cancer," she said softly.

Daniel Fryer surprised her with a look of understanding. Not sympathy or empathy but recognition. It almost looked like he was going to say something else before he finally spoke.

"Have you made any kind of decisions since you received that news? Because I'm assuming this is new?"

"We're still in the diagnosis phase." She swallowed, trying to run through her mind if any kind of decisions had been made in the last two weeks. Shaking her head, she furrowed her brow. "No. No decisions..."

"Personal decisions? Nothing since the last batch of photographs? Has anything of note happened?"

Marissa started tapping her foot anxiously, looking at Mac beside her.

"Mac—Agent Mackenzie came back. I told him about the letter that arrived the night he was suspended. We got the news about my mom. I've been struggling with it." Marissa stopped herself from going into detail about ending up at Jared's. That was irrelevant. Shaking her head, she shrugged one shoulder.

Fryer stared at her for a long time, his eyes causing her to shift again. Finally, he let out a sigh and looked over at Mac before looking back down at the piles in front of him.

"Alright. Let's talk about the dead girl." He picked up the pile of pictures of Brenna and inspected each one, stopping on the third. It was the photo of her lifeless body on the floor, blood spilling out of her neck. He narrowed his eyes as though to focus on something before putting the pictures back down.

"This is your new guy," he said confidently. "This is sloppy. Even if this had been Ben losing his cool and letting emotions get in his way, this is too much blood. He's not a fan. Too much DNA. Too much mess to clean up. This is definitely your new guy." He raised an eyebrow. "From the looks of things, this is probably the first person he's ever killed. If I had to guess, killing her was the mistake. If I had to put money on it, I would bet Ben is less than pleased by this development."

Marissa nodded, glancing over at Mac, who was taking notes. She frowned, about to comment on what Ben's reaction might be, but then she stopped. Instead, she thought about her meeting with Sean Boswell. "Whose idea was it? To send the letter that lured us to the warehouse?"

Daniel Fryer and Mac both looked equally surprised. Fryer straightened his shoulders, sitting taller in the chair than Marissa had seen since that first visit. He grinned, making her skin crawl.

"It was Ben's idea," he said finally. "You had been on the news since Christine Cochren had been threatened. He found you fascinating. So, he cooked up that letter, trying to bypass the tip line. I didn't think you would fall for it, and even if you did, I certainly didn't think that they would have approved just the two of you to come out and walk right into it." He laughed. "I actually lost twenty dollars to him for that one. I had expected my lure to Amy Teagen to work first. We placed bets."

"So everything at the warehouse. It was planned."

Daniel Fryer nodded his head. "Everything at the warehouse was planned. Down to your partner, changing locations, the headphones. What was not planned..." he held out a finger, still wearing an amused expression on his face, "was leaving you alive. The cops were closing in on our location, and Ben wanted to take you with us, and I told him absolutely not. We argued over it. I stabbed you, assuming I would just take you out of the picture." He leaned forward and lowered his voice. "I didn't expect you to pull through. Luck was really on your side that day."

He wasn't wrong. She had technically died on the table twice, spent over a week in the ICU. Marissa shuddered. Mac placed a hand on her arm. She felt like she was underwater, the sounds in her ears suddenly muffled. She glanced at the door, considering taking a minute. But if she stepped out there, Gorden, Walker, and Bennet would be there to scold her for the detour in conversation. She needed to keep going.

"What if Amy Teagan had ended up there instead?"

"Then we would have followed a different plan."

"Who did the planning?"

Fryer shrugged. "Mostly him. I've never been much of a planner." He drummed his fingers on the table again. "I prepare. I'm always prepared. But planning every single detail takes the fun out of the hunt, out of the kill."

"But Ben is a planner?"

"Oh yeah. Real type-A kind of asshole." Fryer shook his head. "I'm more of a 'go with the flow type.'"

"So." Marissa had to let her brain catch up. Her thoughts were whirling around a mile a minute. "Was there a plan after the warehouse, or did things change when I didn't die?"

"Absolutely. The plan was to keep going, keep doing the same thing. When you didn't die, we both agreed it would be best to suspend all activities and go separate ways." He paused, giving her an unsettling smirk. "He didn't keep up his end of the bargain, though. He stuck around. He kept taking pictures, kept threatening you." He shook his head. "Fucking obsessed, I tell you."

Marissa couldn't stop herself from visibly shuddering.

"Are you afraid, Marissa?" He lowered his voice and leaned forward slightly. "I mean, you're under surveillance, right? And he keeps getting by? Why do you think that is?"

Marissa blinked and her nose involuntarily twitched. It was a question she had been asking herself for well over a year.

"He's more like a ghost than a person. Operating around all the things that *should* keep you safe. It's interesting, isn't it?" She could feel the taunt in his voice, but his expression was unamused.

Just then, the door opened, Nick Walker on the other side of it. "Can I speak with you for a moment, detective?"

Mac went to stand up beside her, but Walker shook his head, motioning him to stay where he was.

Marissa made a face but got to her feet and followed Nick Walker out of the interview room.

He folded his arms across his chest and frowned at her. A whole minute must have gone by before he spoke. "Wasn't I clear about what you could ask?"

Marissa couldn't stop himself from glaring at him, tapping her foot anxiously. "He can answer so much more, though."

"Detective..."

Marissa threw her hand up. He may have been in charge, but he wasn't *her* superior. "I understand the goal is to find as many victims as we can. But I was a victim, too. And that fucking monster in there? He has all the answers."

He let out a heavy sigh and rubbed his face, not bothering to hide his own annoyance. "I understand, but Marissa—you have to know he is taunting you in there. He wants a rise out of you."

"Obviously. But he's talking."

"But it's the new information we need. We want to get victims' families the answers they deserve." He shook his head. "I gave you the okay to show him the newest letter, and you just ran with it. If you want to continue to be a part of this case, you need to listen to direct orders."

Marissa glared at him. On one hand, what he was asking made sense. On the other, Marissa knew that Daniel Fryer wasn't talking to anyone except for her and that gave her the advantage. They needed her.

"And if I don't?" She held his gaze, raising her chin stubbornly. "I just want answers. I want to find this asshole, and so far everything you have tried hasn't worked."

Nick let out a sigh and turned to look at the one-way window where Mac and Daniel Fryer sat before turning back to her, shifting from side to side on his feet. "Take everything he says with a grain of salt. Remember, he wants to get a rise out of you. It's likely the only thing he can get off on anymore. Please. Try and get more confessions out of him. Get us names."

Marissa didn't feel victorious, but it hadn't been a total loss. She nodded and patted her side for Ellie to follow, walking past him and back into the interview room. Once inside again, she took a seat, Ellie sitting down beside her, and watched the man across the table.

"Sorry about that," Marissa said, looking at Daniel Fryer before glancing over at Mac, who had a grim expression on his face.

Fryer was leaning back, a half-smile on his lips, looking as though he had won something. It had seemed to her that the two men had gotten into a bit of a deep conversation that no one else had heard because Nick Walker had been too busy lecturing her.

"No worries, Marissa." Fryer's smug expression made her uneasy. "Where were we?"

"We were discussing Ben," she said plainly. "Can you give me anything that will help me either apprehend him or stop him?" She was trying to work out how to word things in her head. "It's not like you owe him anything. He's the reason you're in here."

The serial killer across the table stared at her for a long time, perhaps actually considering her words. She felt a shred of hope. But after a moment, he shrugged his shoulder.

"I wish I could, detective." He was formal again, and Marissa knew the opportunity was gone.

"Then let's circle back to our original deal." Marissa tried to keep the disappointment out of her voice. "You give me a name. I answer your questions."

Daniel Fryer nodded his head. "I'll go first." His eyes flickered to Mac, who just barely flinched beside Marissa before his eyes landed on hers. "How much control does the FBI have over you and your life?" Marissa was surprised by the question, and it must have showed on her face because he clarified. "Are you two allowed to be together? Do they give you an approved list of questions you are allowed to ask in here? Are they *actually* watching your every move?"

Marissa huffed and looked over to the mirrored side of the one-way window. "More than I would like."

"That's a little vague." Amusement had returned to his tone.

"Yes, we are together. No, there is no list, but there are topics we are supposed to stay on. And who the fuck knows?" Marissa folded her arms across her chest, feeling thoroughly irritated.

"Alright." Fryer nodded before folding his hands together on the table. "Gerry Goldblight, 2004." He paused, glancing at the window before continuing. "Picked him up in Centralia, Washington. Left him in Forks, Washington. That time was a gunshot to the head."

Marissa blinked. She wasn't used to him being so forthcoming. Mac was already jotting down notes beside her. "Just because?" she finally asked after a long moment of silence.

"I needed some money. Wanted to upgrade the car I was driving." He shrugged like he was talking about something as mundane as grocery shopping.

"You gave me three straight answers. I gave you three facts." He paused. "My turn."

He leaned forward on the table, causing Marissa to flinch and lean back. "What are you going to do now?"

Marissa stared at him quietly for a long moment. The truth was she didn't have an answer. She didn't know what to do that would bring in different results. She didn't know how to make it stop. "If you don't give me any answers, I don't know," she finally replied honestly.

Daniel Fryer gave her a thoughtful look that made her skin crawl. "Come on. You're more resourceful than that. You've got to have some ideas."

Now he was outright taunting her.

"Maybe I'll have an answer for you next time." She got to her feet. She couldn't do this now.

Mac stood beside her, gathering his notes and the files they had sprawled over the table. She quickly turned and headed for the door. Once again, whatever form of a roll she had been on had died during Nick Walker's interruption.

Once they were on the other side of the door and it was closed, Marissa took a deep breath. Mac used his free hand to rub her back and gave her a look that said they would talk about it later.

Chapter 28

arissa sat in her office, leaning against the back of her chair, her knees brought up to her chest. She was staring at her whiteboard, something she had found herself doing a lot recently. Mac was downstairs in the kitchen with Kate getting ready to make dinner. They had invited Ethan and Kim over since they would be heading back to D.C. in a couple days.

She knew she was hiding. After the interview with Daniel Fryer, she just wanted to be alone. The tightness in her chest hadn't eased, and the fatigue washed over her. She couldn't shake any of it.

She leaned her head back and rubbed her eyes, wanting nothing more than to just curl up in the darkness of her room and sleep. But she knew if she did that, she might just sleep through dinner or even the rest of the week. Swallowing the lump in her throat that kept coming back, she stared at the board again. The pictures, all of her notes. The urge to set it on fire was real.

Her thoughts wandered back to what Daniel Fryer had said: *"You had been on the news since Christine Cochren had been threatened. He found you fascinating."* She couldn't remember doing anything noteworthy that should have caught anyone's attention. It felt like it had been a lifetime ago.

One couple was already dead: Miranda Harris, the defense lawyer, and her boyfriend, Keith Jacobson. Jacobson had been found in a back alley two blocks from his apartment. Miranda Harris was killed in her own home. She had been receiving harassing letters and photographs for a couple of weeks. Her reports hadn't been taken seriously as far as Marissa was concerned. She had taken Ms. Harris's last police report herself. The woman was a wreck; she was afraid to leave her home. Her boyfriend had come along with her, and while he wasn't necessarily scared, he was also taking the threat seriously.

"I will do everything I can," Marissa had said, knowing that it likely would not be enough to make this woman feel safe.

"This is the fourth report I've made. Nothing has changed. I've had a patrol come by the house twice a day, conveniently not when these are being left."

She dropped the envelope full of photographs on Marissa's desk.

Once they left, she had gone to her lieutenant. He promised he would talk with the captain about getting surveillance out for them. The next day, Keith Jacobson was dead. A week later, so was Miranda Harris. Marissa hadn't been able to sleep since.

"I could have done more."

"What more could you have done?" Tom had asked.

So when Christine Cochren came in to file a report because someone was leaving photographs on her doorstep, Marissa wasted no time. It had only been about three weeks since Ms. Harris's body had been found.

"You can't tell me this is a coincidence," she had said to their captain directly, determined not to let this woman fall through the cracks.

"What do you suggest we do? We can't do much about stalking..."

"But this is the exact same pattern as the homicide. This is exactly how it started. We can't just pretend that there isn't something there."

"Not every sicko out there is a serial killer, detective. We will keep an eye on the situation. It's the best we can do until there is escalation."

"This is bullshit," she had told Tom, who nodded in agreement.

"It is bullshit. Unfortunately, there isn't a lot we can do about it."

"What is the point if people come to us for help and we can't do anything about it?" She shook her head. "I don't understand."

Lieutenant Cooper asked to speak with her later that day. "I hear you're making waves, detective. I feel like this is going to be a pattern with you." He raised an eyebrow and shook his head at her. "Captain said you two can go set up a surveillance team."

So they built a surveillance team and got to work. Marissa had even gotten to hold a press conference, urging people to be cautious. She hadn't felt great about putting the spotlight on the situation, but Christine, who was a journalist, insisted that she would not hide. Unfortunately, two days later, Russell Cochren was found dead at his office after he didn't come home one night. Christine was killed a day later in her own home—with patrol officers sitting right outside her house. Had it been the press conference?

After Christine's murder, Marissa stood off to the side as her captain held another press conference, commenting on the fourth homicide inside a month. He didn't use the word "serial killer," but he didn't need to. The city was up in arms and panicked.

She had gone home that night and sobbed. "I don't know if I want to do this anymore," she had told Jared. "What is the point if we aren't making a difference?"

It was the very first time she had felt helpless. If only she had known it wasn't going to end anytime soon.

Jared called Tom, who came over. He had disappeared to give them space to talk, messing around in the kitchen.

"How long have we been partners?" he asked her, sitting beside her on the couch.

Marissa had to actually think about it. It had been a minute. He had been her partner since she had been promoted to homicide. "Six years?"

Tom nodded. "That sounds about right." He smiled at her. "So it's taken you six years to let a case get to you. It happens to everyone. There is no shame in this. It means you aren't a robot." He shook his head. "So, take tonight and maybe tomorrow and then shake it off so we can get back to work. Because at the very least, now the connection has been made. So we can work with that."

Marissa nodded her head, but she didn't necessarily feel better.

"We have a stellar record, Riss. We've got this. So take a minute, do what you need to do, and then get your head back in the game."

Marissa jumped as her phone buzzed on the desk beside her, her loud ringtone slicing through the silence she had gotten lost in. She made a face when she saw the caller's name and picked up the phone.

"Dr. Bailey?" She glanced at the clock on her computer to check the time: 5:44 p.m.

"Hello, Marissa." The woman's soothing voice came over the line, and Marissa felt the smallest piece of the tightness in her chest loosen. "I wanted to call and check in with you, see how you were doing. Agent Mackenzie said you had a difficult day. Do you want to tell me about it?"

A sigh escaped her lips before she could stop herself. She had considered calling Dr. Bailey herself. She and Mac had talked about it during their ferry ride back to Port Townsend. But she had decided against it. She couldn't even remember the excuse she had made.

"I had another interview with Daniel Fryer today," she started, letting her legs drop to the floor, pins and needles rising up both limbs as her feet hit the ground. "We talked about the warehouse today—"

She had intended to say more, but she choked back a sob that had snuck up on her.

"Okay," Dr. Bailey said softly. "Why don't you try the 5-4-3-2-1 method we've talked about? And then you can tell me about it? Or not, if you don't want to."

Marissa let out a hard breath, the phone shaking in her hand. "Okay."

It was as though, from the moment she had spoken, the dam had broken, and she couldn't hold back anything she was feeling.

"Since I'm not there, can you tell me five things that you can see?"

Marissa eyes obediently looked around, trying to find something to land on. "My whiteboard." Literally the largest thing in the room. "My computer. The cat tree in the corner." She took a deep, shaky breath. "My boots. A red marker."

"Good," Dr. Bailey praised before jumping to the next step. "Now, four things you can feel."

Marissa let out another long, heavy breath. "The rough rubber arm of the office chair." She blinked and ran her hand through her hair. "My hair. The cold wood floor under my feet. The softness of my pajama pants." She ran her hand over her thigh to feel the soft cotton.

"Very good. Almost halfway through it. Tell me what you can hear other than me on the phone with you."

Marissa closed her eyes. "I can hear Ellie's steady breathing while she sleeps." She opened her eyes to glance down at the dog who slept soundly beside her before closing her eyes again. "I can hear the whirring of the heat running through the house. I can hear the clock on my wall ticking."

"Perfect. Now two things you can smell."

"I can smell the remnants of the vanilla candle that I've burned in here previously." She breathed in and tightened her already closed eyes, adjusting the phone from one ear to the other. "And whatever delicious thing they are cooking downstairs. It smells amazing."

"There we go," Dr. Bailey said gently, her voice still soothing. "Finally, what do you taste?"

"Does my dry mouth count?" she asked, half as a joke but also a little serious. She was likely dehydrated, and there was no liquid in sight.

"It does count," Dr. Bailey agreed, laughing gently before her tone got serious again. "Now, do you want to tell me about how that went today? Or how it made you feel?"

Marissa considered the question for a minute before letting out a long sigh.

"It made me feel afraid. Panicked. Powerless." Her already dry mouth felt as though any moisture that had been present had evaporated. "Like being there all over again." Her voice had dropped to almost a whisper.

"I can't imagine what it must feel like to look the person who did those horrible things to you in the eye, to sit across from him and entertain conversations," Dr. Bailey started. "But you know, despite all of that, *he* can't hurt you anymore. He is in handcuffs, chained to the table. The warehouse is behind you. Years behind you."

Marissa nodded into her phone, her free hand holding her forehead as though to keep everything from spilling out. "I know," she finally managed.

"You need to keep reminding yourself of this. He can't hurt you anymore. Don't give him that power," Dr. Bailey said with a level of certainty that made Marissa sit up in her chair, though her shoulders were still slumped down and forward. "Did you learn anything new?"

Again, Marissa nodded to no one. "I did actually." Her voice was still shaky and quiet but was above a whisper now. "We fell for a trap that had been set for us. For me."

And Tom was just collateral damage.

Chapter 29

It was overcast and a little chilly for a Sunday morning in July. Taking a deep breath, Marissa had stopped on the corner across the street from For Goodness Bakes and planted herself along the waterway.

She would have been on time if she had walked straight in, but she had been standing at the water's edge for almost fifteen minutes, trying to find the will to go in there. She didn't want to. She wished Mac could have come with her. Melanie had insisted they meet with just the three of them because it was no one else's business, as she put it. She had seen Madi arrive, Clyde walking up with her and giving her a kiss before opening the door for her to go inside. He lingered in the doorway for a moment before he stuffed his hands in his pockets and walked back in the direction from which he'd come. He noticed Marissa and nodded to her before continuing. She nodded back and looked to the sky, trying to soothe her nerves.

Clyde had gotten back from Chicago only a few days before her interview with Fryer. He hadn't come back with very much at all. No evidence left at the crime scene. No leads on where the body had been moved from. She had been dead only a week before her body was found.

It was really a toss-up as to what was keeping her from just going into the bakery. The idea that they needed to discuss their mom's health and how to proceed forward was surreal. The fact that they had to have an adult conversation together was daunting. The last time they had tried to have a conversation, it had not gone well. Dinner at Mom's had been a colossal failure.

Ellie, who was sitting alongside Marissa, looked up at her and whined loudly. Marissa glanced down and nodded at the shepherd before looking back at the turbulent waters.

"Yeah. Okay," she said to really no one, but Ellie got to her feet. Marissa turned and walked to the corner before running across the street. Forcing herself to keep up the momentum, she pushed the door open and walked into the bakery, which was always closed on Sundays.

Madi was sitting at the counter, twirling her stool around to look at Marissa as she made her entrance. Mel was behind the counter, leaning forward on her elbows, already glaring. Her auburn hair was thrown up in a perfect messy bun on the top of her head with a couple of loose strands hanging in front of her big brown eyes. The way she looked in that moment made Marissa pause. She could have been looking at her mother.

"Nice of you to join us." Mel already had a bite to her tone.

Marissa shook off whatever she had been feeling and walked up to the counter, sitting beside Madi. Ellie huffed audibly, sharing her discontentment over having her vest on and not being allowed to say hello before she lay down.

"Sorry I'm late," Marissa muttered, frustrated that she could have arrived before Madi if she had just forced herself to walk in.

Madilyn gave Mel a look before leaning over and giving Marissa a hug. "Glad you made it, even if the context of this get-together sucks." It was still weird that Madi was trying to play the peacemaker between them. It had always been Marissa's role. Melanie had always been the center of the drama.

Pulling back from the hug, she looked between her sisters. "Sucks is an understatement." Marissa sighed. "So. Where do you guys want to start?"

There was no way to start with small talk. She wanted a drink.

"We're just going to jump right into this?" Mel seemed surprised with Marissa's forwardness.

"Yes, we are." She had no intention of putting up with Mel's aggressive bullshit today. She was already too tired. "We need to figure things out. We can't even talk about treatment until we finish with the tests. Greg offered to take her—"

"No. It's none of his business," Melanie snapped.

"Mel, they've been together on and off for nine years. It's absolutely his business."

"No. If he was that important in her life, Mom would have told us."

"Like she would have told us when she found a lump a few years ago?"

"Marissa!"

"What?" Marissa snapped. "Stop being so fucking self-centered. We need to do what's best for Mom and get her through tests so we can move on to treatments."

Melanie looked like someone slapped her in the face. "No. It's—"

"For fuck's sake, Mel. Why does everything have to be about you?"

Madi threw her hand up. "Riss."

"No. What we should be talking about is who is taking Mom to what appointments. Not whether or not her boyfriend just shy of a decade gets to be involved."

Melanie whirled around on her heels and disappeared into the back.

"I'm not sure this was the best way to have this conversation," Madilyn said gently.

"No." Marissa shook her head. "But this isn't about her. It's about Mom. And if I have to be the one to remind her of that, fine. I'm already her punching bag."

"You're not my punching bag." Her little sister reappeared, leaning against the door frame that separated the kitchen from the space behind the counter.

"No?" Marissa raised an eyebrow. "Because every time we've been in the same space, you have done nothing but lash out at me."

Mel opened her mouth to respond, but Marissa threw up her hand, stopping her. "I understand where some of it came from. Secrets are fucking hard, but you never stopped to consider maybe there was reason I had to keep them." She had to pause to catch her breath, to steady herself before continuing. "But everything that was going wrong became my fault."

Ellie nudged her side, and Marissa stopped to scratch behind the shepherd's ear, taking the extra breath she clearly needed. "But this is not my fault. Mom being sick isn't my fault. It's not my fault she never told *any of us* that there was a lump. It's not my fault she felt like she had to keep her dating life private from us. Those were her choices. Not mine. And if you want to spend your time being angry, I won't stop you. But I will not be the reason for everything wrong in your life."

She let out a long, unsteady breath, only momentarily feeling relief for all the words she had needed to get out.

And then she looked back at her baby sister. Melanie stood there, leaning against the door frame, her arms folded in front her chest, shaking, tears rolling down her cheeks. Immediately Marissa was hit with guilt followed by the frustration that she felt guilty at all.

"Mel..." she started, but Melanie shook her head.

"No. You're right," she said between sobs, holding herself steady in the doorway. "I've been awful. I'm so sorry. I just... I don't— I couldn't—" The words wouldn't come out.

It had felt too good to get all of that off her chest, but Marissa hated it when Melanie cried. Especially when it was her fault. And this *was* her fault.

"I'm sorry, Mel. I just can't do it anymore," she admitted. "I love you, and I miss the fuck out of you. Everything has been so hard, and no, I can't tell you why, but you being angry at me has just made it that much harder."

Mel continued to stand in the doorway, crying but nodding her head in acknowledgment of what Marissa was saying. Marissa took a deep breath and rubbed her eyes, wiping away her own tears, which were threatening to escape.

Madilyn moved first, jumping off the stool she had been sitting on and walking over to where the counter opened. She held it open while motioning for Melanie to walk through. Their baby sister came into the dining space, and Marissa got off her stool and pulled Melanie into a big hug.

"Fucking finally," Madilyn said in loud exasperation, throwing her hands up.

"Shut up," Marissa said, pulling her into the hug.

Once the hugging and crying had come to an end, they all sat down at a table with cookies and sodas that Mel brought out for them. Fuck, she had missed those cookies. They spent the next thirty minutes working out their mom's schedule, full of appointments. They also called Greg and put him on speaker phone to finalize details, during which Melanie did her best to apologize.

"So, now that we're all back on speaking terms, I do have something to tell you both," Madilyn said, taking a bite of her fourth or fifth chocolate chip cookie.

"Oh?" Marissa raised an eyebrow. Mel looked just as curious.

"I've decided to stay in town."

Marissa had been pretty sure that was a given, considering their mom's health, so this wasn't shocking.

"I mean, I've found a place to stay!"

"Oh. You mean, you're not staying at my house anymore?" Mel looked horrified.

"I'll be close. Tyler Drake is going to rent me his Airbnb."

"You mean Allison's house?" It was Marissa's turn to be surprised.

"I do," Madi said, nodding her head.

"Oh." Marissa blinked. She knew it was inevitable that the house would be used, but she had been caught off guard.

"That's okay, right?" Madilyn looked worried.

"Of course." She didn't have any say one way or the other but knowing that someone would be occupying the house sent an ache through her. "When?"

"Tyler is coming up next week for the tour and key."

Marissa nodded, holding back a sigh. It made sense—the house couldn't stay empty forever—but it was a harsh reminder that Allison was gone and not coming back. As though she needed another one.

The conversation continued, but Marissa's mind drifted.

The girls left at the same time about an hour later. Madi and Mel hopped into Mel's car to go for lunch. They invited Marissa but she declined. They each seemed relieved that the air appeared to have cleared despite the fact that Marissa was still keeping secrets.

Marissa leaned against the wall of the building and looked out onto the street. It was predictably bare for a Sunday morning. At the end of the block, she spotted a familiar face exiting the coffee shop. Frowning, she focused her eyes and realized who she was looking at.

"Hey, stranger," she said as he got closer.

Jack looked up from his coffee, and a huge grin flashed across his face. "Hey, beautiful! What's new?"

Marissa shook her head, trying to remember the last time they spoke. "Not much. When did you get back in town?"

"A few days ago."

"You've been here a few days, and you didn't call me?" She made a face at him. "I'm kind of insulted."

He laughed and nodded his head. "I may have been waiting. I'm going to be heading to my sister's for a couple of days for her birthday before I settle back in here." He paused. "And I'm sorry I never texted you back. Things have been a little crazy."

"How long will you be around for?"

He shrugged his shoulder. "Not sure yet. Kind of feeling over the whole fishing thing for a minute."

"I can't even pretend to imagine that it is an enjoyable profession." She smiled at him, squinting in the sun. "The flexibility of being able to do what you want when you want still seems appealing, though."

Jack smiled. "It pays the bills. It's hard to complain. But it's also exhausting." He looked her over, his blue eyes landing on hers. They were still striking as ever. "You always look so sad."

Marissa sighed and shrugged her shoulder. "Maybe."

"You've got a beautiful smile. You should go easy on yourself. It can't always be that bad."

Marissa gave him a small but genuine smile. "You'll have to give me a call when you get back to town. We can have lunch, catch up. As friends." She added that last part a little quickly.

"So the boyfriend is still in the picture." He raised an eyebrow, sipping his coffee.

Marissa nodded, her smile growing just a little bigger. "He is."

"He would have been an idiot to walk away." The last time they had spoken had been after Mac left— by choice because of Jared. He nudged her with his elbow. "I've got to go, but I'll be in touch."

Marissa nodded. "See you around. Welcome back to town."

She watched him disappear down the street, her smile slowly fading. His name was on the board, like everyone else's that had made recent appearances in her life. Everything he had told her had checked out. He did have a sister out of state. He did work on a fishing boat in Alaska. And yet...

Maybe it was just paranoia. Shaking her head, she silently swore at herself. The looming threat made everyone look like a suspect. And it was making her crazy.

Chapter 30

Marissa looked out into the yard from her kitchen table. She had really grown to enjoy her table talks with Kim. She was going to miss having Kim and Ethan around. She almost regretted not going with Mac to take them to the airport, but she figured they deserved that time together since Mac wasn't sure when he would be back in D.C.

When Kim was just someone that Marissa knew about but had never met, she had felt threatened. Like Kim was someone Marissa could never amount to. Despite the fact that they had been divorced for almost decade now, Mac thought very highly of her. Now that they had met, Kim was someone who deserved to be on the pedestal that Mac held her on, but Marissa no longer felt threatened.

She was snapped out of her thoughts when her phone rang. She frowned at the private number and hesitated but ultimately answered. An automated voice on the other end of the line asked if she would like to accept a call from the Washington State Corrections Center. Marissa sighed.

"Yes, I'll accept," she grumbled into the phone and leaned back into the chair.

"Marissa?" Marlene's voice came on the other line. She sounded tired.

"Hey, Marlene, what can I do for you?"

They had exchanged a lot of phone calls when she was trying to help her through the early process of her arrest. Despite everything, she felt bad for the woman. But Marissa was sure this was about Kate.

"I spoke to that Ms. Parker earlier. She said Kate is back with you?" The woman's voice held a familiar desperation.

Sighing, she nodded to no one. "Yeah, but it's just temporary."

"Oh," she said and paused on the other end. Marissa already knew what was coming, and she got to her feet. "Do you think maybe I could talk to her?"

"I will see if she's available," Marissa said into the phone as she walked into the living room, getting Kate's attention.

Kate glanced over from the couch, focused on the sketchpad in front of her. Her face grew pale as she shook her head. Marissa wasn't shocked.

"Marlene, she's sleeping right now."

"She still doesn't want to talk to me, does she?" Marlene's disappointment echoed through the phone.

"I'm sorry, Marlene. I will let her know you called."

"Yeah, okay," she said softly. "Can we talk a little?"

Marissa sighed. All the fight was gone from her. It was hard to believe this had been the same woman who had been screaming on her front lawn months ago.

"Sure, Marlene." Marissa headed into the kitchen and let Marlene fill the next thirty minutes.

She waited for the opening, but when it was apparent Marlene wouldn't give one to her, she jumped in.

"Speaking of Kate's placement, I know we've talked about it before, but is there any relative you can think of? Maybe her father?"

She heard Marlene sigh on the other end of the line. "No, Marissa. We've been over this. She would be better off literally anywhere else." She paused on the other end of the line. "Maybe if you bring Kate up here for a visit, I can tell you the story."

Marissa closed her eyes, shaking her head as she leaned against the doorway, giving Kate a small smile. "Sounds good. I'll talk to you soon."

She kept her eyes on Kate as Marlene gave her a weak goodbye. Marissa made her way into the living room and sat on the arm of the couch, shoving her phone in her back pocket.

"I'm not ready to talk to her," Kate said softly, looking apologetic.

"There is no pressure here, hon." Marissa shook her head. "If you don't want to talk to her, you don't have to."

"But I feel bad. And then I hate that I feel bad!" She put her sketchpad down on the coffee table. "She doesn't just get to make me a priority now that she's in jail."

"Maybe now she just has the time to straighten out her priorities," Marissa offered.

"Well, she killed her husband, so she has no one else to focus on," Kate mumbled.

Marissa sighed. She didn't know how to make it better, but she really wanted to. She couldn't say she blamed Kate. She couldn't imagine what it was like having a mom like that.

Marissa rested her head on Mac's shoulder, adjusting how she was sitting on the couch. Kate was already up in bed, and the house was quiet. Marissa wasn't disappointed. It had been an experience having Kim and Ethan around often, not nearly as uncomfortable as Marissa had expected, but they had added to the noise of the house. Ellie was curled up and sleeping on the other end of the couch. TMC was playing on the TV, although Marissa had no idea what movie it was. A western of some kind. It was exactly how the end of the day should be. And then Mac's phone rang.

Marissa begrudgingly straightened and let him answer the phone, letting out a heavy sigh. She glanced at her own phone, seeing it was already 10:30 in the evening. Who the hell would call this late?

"Hey Nick, what's up?"

Mac glanced at her, frowning. His expression grew grim as the silence stretched on his end of the phone call. His gaze drifted back toward the TV before he got to his feet.

"Okay. Thanks for letting me know." He nodded as he began pacing. "What do we need to do?"

He was nodding his head again before his eyes landed back on Marissa.

"Yeah. I'll let her know. Thanks."

He pulled the phone away from his ear and put it down.

Marissa waited and braced herself, knowing she was probably going to hate whatever he was going to say.

"So that was Nick. Apparently, sometime between 7 p.m. and now, during the shift change, Johnny O'Rourke jumped house arrest."

They knew there had been a delay in his appeal hearing, but it had been denied. He was set to go back to jail earlier that day.

"They found his ankle tracker in his bathroom and no sign of him anywhere in the house or in the surrounding areas. They've already got people out on the road and in the airports and on state lines. He shouldn't get far."

Marissa nodded slowly, taking that information in. The last time she had seen Johnny O'Rourke, he was promising to make their lives a living hell. To say that the man held a grudge was an understatement. It had been five years, but the likelihood that he had forgotten that promise was slim. It was because of them, specifically, that he had been arrested, convicted, and sentenced to life in prison.

"Okay." She was still nodding her head. "So… are we in danger?"

It felt like a stupid question. They were *already* in danger. Being stalked and harassed by a murderer was nothing to laugh at. But the added danger of a mob boss convicted of murder, violent crimes, and human trafficking was no joke either.

"It'll be fine. He won't get far." He gave her the first fake smile she had ever seen him direct her way. "Besides, he has no idea where either of us are."

She wasn't convinced but nodded her head regardless. "Okay…"

Mac knelt down in front of her and took her hands in his. "Hey. Seriously. It's going to be fine."

She studied his eyes as he searched hers, and she could see the worry he was trying to hide.

"Besides," he tried to sound upbeat, "that just means more surveillance."

Marissa bit her tongue to keep from mentioning how much good surveillance had been so far.

"You trust me?"

Marissa was thrown by the question but nodded. "Of course I do."

He pulled her as he stood and wrapped his arms around her, kissing the top of her head. "It's going to be fine."

Mac had been called into the city to discuss the O'Rourke situation early the next morning. O'Rourke was still out there somewhere. Clyde had gone with him. Jackson had come by to check on her just after Mac left, and Meredith Parker had come to pick up Kate for counseling evaluations and to discuss the next steps in finding a foster home. Marissa had forced herself to stay home, to stay out of it. She was on her second cup of tea when Ellie barked at the door. Marissa hadn't heard anything. Her Ring camera hadn't gone off and neither had her alarm. But when she opened the door, there was a large manila envelope on her porch. A jolt of anxiety ran through her, and she immediately felt the tension in her neck.

Marissa opened the envelope and dumped the contents onto her desk. So many photos. The first one was of Marissa alone in Seattle, a cup of coffee in her hand, walking into what looked to be Dr. Bailey's office. Sunglasses covered her eyes, and Ellie was right by her side. She wasn't sure exactly when this one was taken, but the fact that she was essentially alone stood out.

The next picture was Marissa sitting in the cemetery at Allie's grave. Again, alone.

Next was a photograph of Mac, standing beside the black SUV at the airport, bag over his shoulder and his jaw set in a deep frown. It was probably when he was flying back from D.C. Then another of Mac standing on Marissa's porch, coffee cup in hand. It could have been taken at any point since he had come home.

Next, a photo of Mac kneeling down beside Marissa in the driver's seat of her Mini Cooper in the hospital parking lot. It was her breakdown, just before they left the hospital after her mom had collapsed.

Then there was Marissa breaking down in Jared's front yard with Jared standing in his doorway. The following photo was only taken a few moments later as he helped Marissa into the house. Then there was one of Jared, frowning with his hands stuffed in his pockets, probably walking into work. She couldn't tell where in the city he was, but chances were he was heading to the radio station.

She kept flipping through the photographs, horrified at the mix between photos of herself, of her ex-husband, and of Mac. Each one was careful to only highlight the single focus of the photo. If there should have been someone else with them, they were carefully not visible. The very last photo was of that same brunette woman from the batch of photos before Brenna Thompson's death.

The man behind the camera had been very specific about the subjects of his photographs. She was sure it wasn't an accident. Was this his next victim? Why was he still tormenting her while he was actively preying on someone else? There were a couple of possible answers.

One was that Brenna Thompson and this new victim were fulfilling whatever need he wasn't able to reach with Marissa. Maybe the surveillance and FBI shadows were working.

Two was that Marissa was the target of the original Couple Killer, as he'd been stalking her for years now, and Brenna Thompson, as well as this new brunette, were targets of the new partner.

There was a chance that it was a combination of both.

Rolling her desk chair over to her whiteboard, she wrote down both theories along the side. She also attached the new picture of the brunette and added a question mark below it. The FBI had the first picture that they were using to hopefully identify her. Rolling back to the desk, she stared at the new photos, unease growing in the pit of her stomach.

The first photograph she had gotten of Jared had been it. She broke it off with him and sent him away. It had seemingly worked. But he was back in the mix. And the photographs of Mac hadn't slowed down. If Marissa was working off of the original Couple Killer case, she would have said with one hundred percent certainty that both men were the next targets.

She looked at the newer additions to her board: Jared, Mac, and the mysterious brunette. She grabbed a photograph of herself and tried attaching it to the top, but it dropped to the floor. When she leaned down to pick it up, what she spotted made her blood run cold.

On the back of the picture of her was one word: *Soon.*

"Fuck," she whispered softly, a tightness growing in her chest.

Book Club Question

1. How did you feel about the pacing of this book?

2. Do you think there was enough tension built up? Do you think that it has built well throughout the series so far?

3. How do you feel about serial killer Daniel Fryer? Has your opinion of him changed?

4. What more do you think the FBI, Seattle PD or Port Townsend PD could be doing about Marissa's stalker(s).

5. How did you feel about Kim and Ethan? Would you want to see more of them?

6. Were you happy to see Kate return? Why or Why not?

7. Did you see the difference between how both Jared and Mac handled Marissa's panic attack? Which was more helpful?

8. Were you satisfied with the cold case outcome?

9. What do you think of Carmen and the case she's working on?

10. Who do you think the other half of the Couple Killer team is? Who do you think was in Chicago?

Author Bio

A.K. Ramirez is a mystery writer tucked in a corner of the Pacific Northwest. She likes to weave mystery and family drama with a little bit of romance all in one. She has participated in NaNoWriMo on and off for years, reaching her goal three times with three different novels, in both the mystery and fantasy genres. When she isn't writing, she runs a dog training, boarding, and daycare facility or spends time with her husband, kids, and pack of dogs. You can find her and all her socials at www.akramirezwrites.com

Discover more at
4HorsemenPublications.com

10% off using HORSEMEN10